THIS TIME LOVE

Also by Elizabeth Lowell

THIS TIME LOVE

ELIZABETH LOWELL

HarperLargePrint

An Imprint of HarperCollins*Publishers*

HarperCollins books may be purchased for educational,
business, or sales promotional use. For information please write:
Special Markets Department, HarperCollins Publishers Inc.,
10 East 53rd Street, New York, NY 10022.

FIRST HARPER LARGE PRINT EDITION

Printed on acid-free paper

Library of Congress Cataloging-in-Publication Data has been
applied for.

ISBN 0-06-053329-3

02 03 04 05 06 WB/RRD 10 9 8 7 6 5 4 3 2 1

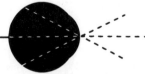

**This Large Print Book carries the
Seal of Approval of N.A.V.H.**

To everyone who got it right
the second time

PROLOGUE

Gabriel Venture slumped on the floor of the crowded airport and wondered how long it had been since he'd had more than three hours of sleep at a time. If someone had asked where he was, he couldn't have told them. After the first fifty or sixty airports, they all looked alike. To someone as worn out with travel as he was, they sounded alike too—a babble of strangers.

That was why he had a finger stuck in one ear and a cell phone pressed to the other, making contact with the only people in the world who gave a damn whether he lived or died. Whenever he'd needed them, his family had been there. He tried to be there for them too.

"Sorry if I woke you or whatever," Gabe said to his brother. "I don't even know what time it is where I am."

"You sound beat." Dan's voice was sympathetic. "Hard assignment?"

Since Peru they all had been hard, but Gabe

didn't think his family needed to hear about that. Even more than the money he sent them when the family company was having a tough time, Dan and their mother got a real kick out of following Gabe's global travels. There was no reason to spoil their pleasure.

"Just squeezed for time," Gabe said, yawning.

"Maybe you should take a vacation. How many countries have you been in during the last year?"

Gabe tried to count. His brain fuzzed. "I'd have to check my logbook, and it's packed. How's Mother doing?"

"Much better. The dental implants have her chewing steak with the best of us, and the knee surgery really helped her too. She should be playing tennis again soon."

Gabe smiled. One good thing had come of his packed assignment list—enough money to pay for family medical needs that weren't covered by cost-conscious insurers. "Just what the world needs—a carnivorous geriatric terror on the courts."

Dan laughed. "Hey, get used to the idea. Our parents were in their forties when they had us. At the rate you're going, you will be too. You should quit trotting over the world and find a good woman."

"That's not what you told me seven years ago," Gabe said before he could stop himself.

"Seven years ago I was picking up the pieces of

my pride after I fell for the wrong woman. Times change. You should change with them. Suzy is a good woman and I know it."

"You getting any closer to marrying her?"

"The church she wanted is booked for the next twenty months."

"Man." Gabe yawned again. "No wonder people live in sin."

"That's why we did the justice-of-the-peace thing. As of yesterday, we're officially married. We'll throw a big party later."

"Hey, that's great! Congratulations! Give her a kiss and a hug from me."

"I tried to reach you but—"

"No worries," Gabe said quickly. "Only God could have gotten through to me where I was. And at your advanced age, you can't afford to lose a second."

"Yeah, yeah. I'm a whole three years older than your thirty."

Gabe didn't say anything. He felt a hell of a lot older than thirty. He felt older than the mountains that had nearly killed him.

"We're going to wait a few years to have kids," Dan added. "But not too long. I don't want to be like Dad. He used to get so pissed when someone thought he was our grandfather."

Gabe made a few sounds that said he was listening. He wasn't. He was thinking of seven years ago, when the woman he might have loved had casually aborted his child. He'd thought about it a lot while he dangled head-down over a cliff and saw his climbing rope coming apart strand by strand. He'd come very close to dying with nothing more to show for his life than a few books, a trunk full of articles, and a fistful of book offers he never had time to take on.

Life coming apart strand by strand by strand.

The rope and his life had unraveled while years raced through his mind, his life for better and for worse. The biggest emptiness, the deepest regret, the greatest hurt all came from the same source . . . a slim girl-woman called Joy Smith-Anderson. She hadn't been his first lover, but she'd been the only one that mattered.

And she had betrayed him.

"You still there?" Dan asked.

"Yeah. Can barely hear you. The noise in this place could drown out a Brazilian soccer game."

"I asked when you're coming home."

"Not right away. I'm headed for New Mexico."

"Stateside? That's a first."

"Second, actually." Gabe swallowed a yawn. "I'm going to do a follow on my first big article."

"Lost River Cave?"

"Yeah."

"Why? After all the places you've been, that one is pretty small beer."

Gabe tried to find a glib answer but was too tired for anything but blunt honesty. "Because of all the places I've ever been, it's the only one that still haunts me."

"It's that girl, isn't it?"

"That would be pretty stupid. It's been seven years, she isn't there anymore, and we didn't have anything worth being haunted about in the first place."

"I hear you. But you've never come close to loving another girl and I feel like I had something to do with—"

"Leave it," Gabe cut savagely. "Just fucking leave it alone." Then he reeled in his temper. "Sorry. I'm real ragged at the moment. How's the company doing? You need any more cash?"

Dan's sigh was long and unhappy, but when he talked again, it was about the ups and downs of the family business, Venture Construction. "It's doing a lot better now than it was seven years ago, and the stock market has crawled out of the toilet. We have 'play or pay' contracts stretching over the next five years. From now on, we'll all be looking for ways to **spend** money rather than save it. Jesus, what a difference a few years makes."

Gabe listened and tried not to see Joy's face, hear her laughter, taste peppermint on her tongue, on his own.

The taste of betrayal.

ONE

I couldn't have heard right.

Joy Anderson closed her gray eyes and fought to breathe. Hand clenched on the radiophone, she prayed that she hadn't heard her boss say Gabriel Venture's name. This was just a nightmare and all she had to do was wake up.

Warily her eyes opened.

Nothing changed.

She was still sitting in a patch of pure yellow sunlight pouring through the cottage's four-paned kitchen window. The phone was hot to her touch, all but burning her ear.

She couldn't see the man she was talking to. She didn't have to. The memory of Harry Larkin's broad, professionally amiable face was imprinted in her mind. He was the one who had managed to land the two-year grant that was running out while she sat in the New Mexico desert and listened to the name of her nightmare.

Gabriel Venture rising out of the past, haunting her in daylight as he had in dreams.

"Yeah, it's quite a shock, isn't it? The great Gabriel Venture is coming to your very own boondocks to do a major article." Satisfaction rang in Harry's voice. "But then, he makes a specialty of places that are so remote they don't even have cell phone coverage. He was even here some time ago, back when nobody but dedicated amateur cavers knew much about Lost River Cave."

Some time ago?

Joy started to close her eyes, then forced them to stay open. No place to hide. No way out. Just herself and the past crashing down around her, bruising and cutting and battering.

Oh yeah, Gabe was here. Six years, eleven months and twenty-nine days ago, give or take a few hours. But who's counting?

The bitter words went no farther than Joy's mind. She was too shaken to speak and much too careful of her own and her daughter's privacy to reveal that she knew the time of Gabe's departure to the day and hour.

It was hard to forget. Kati had been born nine months after Gabe drove out of New Mexico's pale, searing deserts in pursuit of the Orinoco River's steamy green mysteries. Joy had loved Gabe then, and had envied him the freedom of the world waiting at his feet.

When he left, she'd hated him.

And resented his freedom even more.

Joy slammed the door on that line of thought.

No matter how difficult it had been to watch while Gabe explored the world the way she had always wanted to, she wouldn't have traded Kati for all the freedom on earth. Not then. Not now.

Resenting what couldn't be changed was a game for spoiled children. She was no longer either spoiled or childish. A mother couldn't afford to be. Especially a single mother.

"I told Gabe's editor that we would be only too happy to help him," Harry continued, unaware that he had lost his distant audience. "It's about the only way the Lost River grant might be renewed."

Realizing that it had been too long since she had put air in her lungs, Joy took a quick, shallow breath, then another.

"I don't have to tell you what a grant renewal would mean," Harry said. "Not only your own job, but those of the people who work for you. The National Park Service has been very pleased with your groundbreaking exploration and academic papers on Lost River Cave. So has the university. The whole thing has been quite a feather in our cap, publicity-wise." He paused, waiting for her response.

Silence.

"Dr. Anderson?"

With an effort Joy pulled her shattered thoughts together. From her subconscious she called up the last few moments of Harry's speech.

Only too happy to help him.

She shuddered as she felt the full force of feelings she thought she'd buried so deep she would never have to face them again. Or face herself . . . the child she had been, certain that all she had to do was ask, believe, love, and what she wanted would come to her wrapped in a shiny big bow.

She had been wrong.

When she realized how wrong, she'd wanted to bury her foolishness in the past along with Gabe, bury it beyond recovery. But it was all coming back now, knives of rage twisting through her.

All I want to do with the great Gabriel Venture is never to see him or hear his name again.

Ever.

Barring that piece of good fortune, I'd like to drop him down Lost River Cave's deepest, blackest hole and throw the damned rope in after him.

The savagery of her own bleak emotions shocked Joy even more than hearing Gabe's name had. Until this instant, she believed that she'd forgotten—if not forgiven—Gabe's sweet smile and sweeter touch, and the terrible bitterness of his betrayal.

Betrayal? No. Stop right there. That's the

spoiled child whining about life being unfair. That child grew up.

She had to.

Unconsciously Joy squared her shoulders.

The adult knows that Gabe didn't betray me. He never promised me one single thing. He just took what I offered, thanked me kindly, and left me holding the bag. Quite literally.

But Kati was inside that bag.

Hating her father won't do me any good, won't do Kati any good, and it sure as hell won't bother Gabe. Hating him almost destroyed me once. I won't let it touch me now. I won't let him touch me.

Ruthlessly Joy shoved her emotions into the dark pit she called the past. After Gabe had left her, she'd raged in silence against him, cried out her loneliness in her parents' arms until her throat was raw, and kept on raging inside herself until she was emotionally exhausted.

Then her parents had stepped on the wrong helicopter and died in the kind of crash that left little to be buried except her own childhood. At twenty, she was on her own.

A few weeks later she learned she was pregnant.

It had been very easy to hate Gabe then. Very easy to blame him. It brought a kind of acid satisfaction that had almost destroyed her.

"Dr. Anderson?"

Harry's words came like a voice through a deep cavern, distant, echoing. The sound quality had nothing to do with the radiophone's reception and everything to do with Joy's state of mind.

"I'm thinking," she said, her voice thin.

Harry chuckled and said in a soothing tone, "Don't you worry about a thing. We know how busy you are wrapping up the Lost River explorations before the grant runs out. The magazine editor who made the arrangements assures us that Mr. Venture can handle himself in any kind of country, is an expert technical climber, and in general won't get in your way."

This time Harry didn't wait for Joy to make polite noises to show she was following him. He simply marched ahead like a man with two days of work and an hour to do it in, which was a fair description of his job as a fund-raiser, grant-finder, and general rainmaker for the university.

"I've sent all the information about Mr. Venture's schedule that you'll need. It should be at the Carlsbad post office, along with a package of his most recent articles and a summary of his needs while he's staying at Cottonwood Wells with your team."

Dazed, her normally quick mind floundering, Joy let Harry's words pour over her in a numbing waterfall. His enthusiasm should have been contagious. Normally it would have been. Harry had been her angel on more than one occasion. Without him she would never have gotten the original federal grant that had made exploration of Lost River Cave possible. Now he was talking about the kind of publicity that could ensure eventual funding for further explorations.

Yet all she could do was stare through the window across a desert basin hazed with sunlight and heat and distance.

Not that what she was seeing made a difference to her right now. She wasn't really looking at the desert any more than she had really understood anything Harry said beyond one fact.

Gabe here, with me, in Lost River Cave.
Again.

The thought was like a climbing rope whipping out of control through her hands, burning her until she bled.

Harry cleared his throat and asked a bit impatiently, "Dr. Anderson, is there something wrong with the connection on your end?"

"No." Her voice was barely above a whisper. With the gritty determination that had brought her through the shattering year after Gabe had left her, Joy cleared her throat and gathered her thoughts. "If I sound a little dazed, chalk it up to hard work. We've all been going at top speed, trying to cram everything in so that the long-term experiments won't be lost."

It was the truth. Just today they had gathered the last samples of cave water at various levels. They would send the samples to the team of chemists that had left a month ago when their own money ran out.

A dazzling thought came to Joy. She grabbed it and hung on to it like a lifeline. "There's so much for me still to do. Someone else can show Gabe—Mr. Venture—around. Jim Fisher would be perfect. He's the best amateur caver west of the Mississippi. He's been working with us on and off for years and—"

"No, not Fisher," Harry cut in, his voice both calm and certain. "This was bucked all the way up to the president and the Board of Regents. It came back down with your name on it."

She swallowed against the sudden tightness of her throat. "Why me?"

Harry laughed and said dryly, "You've been down in the dark too long, Dr. Anderson. Take a look in a mirror."

Joy grimaced. She didn't need a mirror to know that she was small, slender, and appealing if you liked pixies. With her pale blond hair and rain-water eyes, she made great photo material, as Harry had pointed out more than once in the past. Add to that her relative youth and expertise in an unusual area of academia and you had a publicist's dream.

And the answer to a fund-raiser's prayer.

"The president and I agreed that you're our best hope of keeping the Lost River grant alive," Harry said.

"The article won't be finished or published in time to do us any good."

"Not this year, or maybe even the next. But the cave has been there a long time. It'll be there a lot longer. Sooner or later the money will come in again. I'm betting it will come within months of the date Venture's article is published."

Joy didn't say a word. She already had her résumé out to the few other employers in the world who might need someone who had both a thorough knowledge of how water of varying chemistry shaped caves and the expertise to explore even the most treacherous underground passages in search of new knowledge. Unfortunately, the demand for hydrospeleologists wasn't great. Add to that the fact that she was a woman and the answer was simple.

No.

She had been offered other kinds of jobs, but the prospect of teaching geology or hydrology to bored freshmen in well-scrubbed classrooms made her extremely restless. She would do it in order to support Kati, but she would look at every other job possibility first.

If she couldn't have the velvet darkness and unearthly beauty of Lost River Cave, then she hoped for work in some other remote and unusual place. There were so many incredible landscapes on earth, so many of the planet's secrets that had barely been glimpsed, much less researched. She wanted more than a classroom, more than the security and closed horizons of tenure.

If helping a nightmare called Gabriel Venture would make it possible for her to get out of the classroom and go back to unraveling the mysteries of Lost River Cave or some other equally unique place, then she would be the most helpful cave guide ever born.

"You're right." Joy's voice was normal again, crisp and no nonsense. Her eyes focused on the sunny vastness of New Mexico's Delaware Basin spreading out at the foot of the Guadalupe Mountains. "I'll do whatever I can to help research on Lost River Cave get the recognition and funding it deserves."

"Excellent. We're counting on you, Dr. Anderson. Mr. Venture's itinerary puts him in El Paso six days from now, and at Carlsbad in a week. He'll call and tell you where to pick him up. You be sure and let me know if Mr. Venture needs anything at all for his article."

The sound of Harry's voice became muffled. Obviously he had put his hand over the receiver and was talking to someone.

"Sorry, but I've got to run," Harry said into the receiver again. "I've got a rich estate waiting on line three. You should have all the Venture background material in two days. Three at the worst."

The rush of words stopped, leaving nothing but static to listen to.

Slowly Joy replaced the radiophone on its hook and looked past the black shortwave set to the hot serenity of the late-afternoon desert. After long minutes she came to her feet with the grace of a dancer or a gymnast or a caver, someone who was accustomed to testing the physical limits of her body on a regular basis.

With her short hair, casual clothes, and barely five foot two inches of height, she appeared more like an undergraduate than a Ph.D. The impression faded when she was close enough for people to look into her eyes. There was a measured quality in her glance that came only from hard experience.

Watching dust devils rise out over the basin, Joy thought and thought hard. It was a long dusty drive from Cottonwood Wells to the nearest post office. The closest city of any size at all was Carlsbad. Undoubtedly Gabe would be flying in there, unless he landed in El Paso and rented a car. That would be a lovely solution to part of the problem. Let the great explorer rent a four-wheel drive vehicle and find his own way to Lost River Cave.

Even as the thought came, Joy was shaking her head, knowing it wouldn't work. The braided dirt tracks leading up a dry wash to the exploration headquarters were carefully **un**marked, as was the path to the locked entrance of the cave itself. No one wanted crowds of self-important visitors demanding to be shown around, or amateur cavers determined to leave their mark on a virgin cave.

Joy had been coming out to Lost River Cave since she was seventeen. Even now, at twenty-seven, she sometimes had a hard time finding the way home after seasonal cloudbursts washed out the tracks of previous vehicles.

Someone would have to pick up the great adventurer and lead him by the hand to Cotton-wood Wells.

For a moment Joy thought about letting Davy Graham fetch the visitor. The Ph.D. candidate was photogenic, intelligent, and probably in awe of a well-known world-traveled explorer like Gabe. Assigning Davy taxi duty would save her the trouble of thinking up polite things to say during the long drive in from Carlsbad.

Tempted, she enjoyed the idea before she rejected it. No one alive knew that she had fallen in love with Gabe when she was twenty, had had his daughter when she was twenty-one and hadn't trusted herself with a man since Gabe left her crying. Only Fish even knew that she had worked with Gabe years ago in Lost River Cave's seamless darkness.

She couldn't hope to keep their old professional tie a secret, but the old personal tie was no one's business except hers. And, eventually, Kati's. As for Gabe, he hadn't cared enough even to write and ask if the baby had been born.

And that, too, was another thought she would shove back into the deep well of the past, when she had been a child. Right now the present was all that mattered, because that was where she and Kati lived.

So the decision was easy after all. If she hoped to keep her past affair with Gabe a secret—and she must—she'd have to be the one to pick him up. Too bad just the thought of dealing with Gabe again made her tight, brittle, teetering on the raw edge of fury. She'd have to put a lid on her emotions and screw that lid down real tight.

The famous Gabriel Venture couldn't affect her unless she let him.

She'd had nearly seven years to forget many things and learn some others. She wasn't worried about succumbing to him sexually again. She knew now what she hadn't known at twenty: Gabriel Venture was a man who put his career first and love second. She'd given him her love and physical innocence. He'd given her physical passion and a child he didn't want.

No, I'm not worried about loving Gabe again. I'm only worried that he'll discover how much I hate him.

The bitterness of own thoughts startled Joy. Then it gnawed at her. For years she'd turned aside all thoughts of Kati's father, pushing them away, ignoring them, refusing to admit they even existed. She didn't want to feel anything for Gabe at all, love **or** hate. What he had once meant to her was fixed in her past, unchanging, like the dry upper reaches of Lost River Cave where water no longer came to dissolve and re-form the very stone itself.

Dead.

It had to be that way. There was no other choice. She couldn't let her emotions eat into her until she was so raw that she wanted to scream with pain. She owed Kati more than that. She owed herself more than that.

She hadn't hated Gabe in years. She wouldn't hate him now. She couldn't. He meant nothing to her. He no longer had the power to make love or hate run hotly through her.

Her emotions were her own and they were calm.

With a long sigh Joy let out the breath she'd

been holding. There was a lot to be done in the present. She'd wasted too much time exploring the dangerous, brutal landscape of her past. What she'd felt for Gabe was buried now, like Lost River itself, consumed by darkness.

Let it stay that way.

TWO

Gabe shifted against the weight of his carry-on baggage. With each movement, the muscles of his left leg and hip ached, protesting a year-old injury and more recent confinement in airline seats designed for short, skinny teenagers. At least it shouldn't be long before he was out of the cramped plane. There were only seven passengers on the little feeder flight. Six of them were tourists from Germany who had chatted in their native language the whole trip.

The young flight attendant and Gabe were the only English speakers in the cabin. The woman found Gabe a lot more fascinating than he found her. He'd been hoping to catch a nap during the ride from El Paso, but short of being a lot ruder than he wanted to be, he hadn't been able to escape the friendly attendant.

He walked a bit stiffly down the plane's narrow aisle toward the exit. Although he wasn't due in Cottonwood Wells for another week, he'd worked overtime wrapping up his Asian story. Then he'd gained another day by trading in his first-class ticket. Despite the fact that it meant a long, uncomfortable flight in tourist class, he'd leaped at the ticket with an eagerness that he didn't understand.

Or didn't want to.

The flight he took out of the Philippines had given him just enough time in Los Angeles to clear customs and get on another plane bound for El Paso. Once on the ground in Texas, he didn't do the sensible thing and hole up in a motel to sleep the clock around. Instead he boarded a plane to Carlsbad, New Mexico. The little plane was even more uncomfortable than the transpacific flight had been, but was mercifully brief.

While Gabe waited for the flight protocol to finish so that the exit door would open, he wished he had a free hand to rub over his face. Three days of stubble—or was it four?—itched. He scratched his chin against his shoulder and wondered if he'd packed a razor. He couldn't remember. He had lived on the road for so long that time, like place, no longer held a lot of meaning for him. Everything he'd done in the past seven years ran together in his mind.

Except Lost River Cave.

Joy had been an innocent twenty to his experienced twenty-three. At least he'd thought he was experienced. Then she had taught him just how little he knew about passion. But he'd been too young to know how rare she was. And she'd been too young, period.

Though he'd done everything he could for her short of canceling out on his Orinoco contract, she hadn't been willing to wait even a few months for him to come back.

Yet she haunted him.

When he'd hung head-down over a chasm, looking at his own grave two thousand feet below, it had been Joy's face that came to him, her voice that he heard. He regretted losing her more than he'd ever admitted to himself until that moment, when it was too late.

In the end, the rope had held.

So had his regret.

You're riding for a fall, fool, he told himself bluntly. **Nothing is as good as time and distance make it seem. Especially a woman.**

The weary words echoed in his head without rebuttal. He was too tired to hold up both ends of an inner argument that had no resolution and no end.

Besides, she's long gone from New Mexico and Lost River Cave. With her brains and looks she probably married a Greek shipper or a Microsoft millionaire. She sure as hell didn't hang around a small town like White City waiting for her first lover to come back.

That Gabe was certain of. There was no listing

for a Mr., Mrs., or Ms. Smith-Anderson in Carlsbad or White City. There hadn't been for at least
six years.

**So why am I here? Why did I break my neck
to cram in an assignment to a place I've already been? I've never done that.**

"Have a nice trip, Gabe," the flight attendant
said. She smiled with unusual warmth as her
glance roamed over his finger-combed dark hair
and wide shoulders. "If you ever get to Dallas,
remember to call me, hear?"

Automatically he responded with a polite
smile. "Thank you . . ." **What the hell is her
name? Cindi? Sandi? Mandi? Mindi? They all
run together after a while, times and faces and
places. Except one. She's in my blood like
malaria.** He focused on the attendant's name
plaque. "Cindi," he said. "You'll be at the top of
my Dallas list."

He heard his own words and winced.

The attendant didn't seem to mind being one
of a list of things to do. She simply smiled more
warmly and touched his arm with searching fingertips, tracing the hard line of muscle beneath.

It was all Gabe could do not to draw back. He
managed to smile at her while he wondered if he
was going crazy. The woman was pretty, bright,
experienced, and likely came with a USDA
stamp of approval on her shapely ass. There was

no reason for him to act like a kid getting his first proposition in a back alley.

"Sorry. Jet lag," he said as he stepped out of the plane into Carlsbad's hot, slanting sunlight. "It's tomorrow where I came from."

"Where's that?" she asked, holding him with her words and fingertips on his sleeve.

"I don't remember."

She laughed. "So, where are you going?"

"I don't know."

"Then why are you going there?"

"Don't know that either."

She laughed again, then realized he wasn't quite joking. Reluctantly she let him go. "Be safe, hear?"

"Thanks. You too."

Gabe started down the steep metal steps. Though it was late afternoon, the intense heat of the day radiated back from the cement in waves. He broke into a sweat immediately. His body had spent the last nineteen hours in a temperature that was at least twenty-five degrees cooler than the Carlsbad afternoon. His heartbeat increased as the dry hot air wrapped around him.

Even while he blamed his accelerating pulse on the heat, part of his mind jeered silently. It was heat all right, but its source wasn't the sun. It was memories brought on by the unique feel of summer in southern New Mexico, and the first vague smell of the desert seeping through the machine odors of the airport.

Dryness.

Sharp scent of creosote.

The taste of Joy sweeping through him as he kissed her beneath a noon sun that wasn't nearly as hot as the first touch of her tongue against his.

A passenger bumped against Gabe. He realized that he was standing at the bottom of the plane's metal stairway, lost in memory, blocking other people from whatever awaited them inside the artificially cool terminal.

"Sorry," he said, stepping aside.

The man said something in German as he and his five friends hurried off toward the terminal. The eagerness on their faces as they looked at the magnificent desert mountains rising into the late afternoon needed no translation.

Gabe wished he could feel that way again, a kid at Christmas, the whole world waiting to be explored. But he didn't feel that way anymore. He didn't know what he'd been looking for all over the face of the earth. He only knew that he hadn't found it.

He followed the group with long strides that helped stretch the kinks out of his body. No one was waiting for him inside the building. He hadn't expected anyone, because he hadn't notified the cavers that he was on his way. He didn't even know who to call. He had left the Philippines before the packet with all the pertinent information about Lost River Cave and its recent explorations and explorers reached him.

Not that it mattered. He preferred to make up his own mind about the qualifications and personalities of the people he would be writing about. When he read the background information—if he ever did—it would be at the end rather than at the beginning of the assignment.

He went to the car rental desk, smiled wearily at the bored young woman behind the counter, and found himself being offered the only four-wheel drive she had left. The vehicle had been promised to someone coming in tomorrow, but Gabe was here now, and he had a natural male charm that had melted much colder, harder material than the car rental girl. He paid the extra insurance, thanked the clerk, and headed back into the desert sun.

A rather shopworn Explorer waited outside, baking in the heat. Gabe started the engine, cranked the air conditioner up to max, and drove into town. Although it had been almost seven years since he had left Carlsbad, he found the post office on the first try.

That didn't surprise him. He remembered everything about his time in New Mexico with unnatural clarity, a vividness that tantalized, infuriated, and confused him. He had been so many places. Why should this one be burned into his memory beyond forgetting? There was no reason. No reason at all.

But there it was just the same. He could see everything in his mind as though it had just happened—the long drives into Carlsbad to pick up the mail, Joy sitting close, watching him with eyes as clear and inviting as spring water welling up from the desert. Joy smiling, Joy touching his hand, Joy, always Joy.

Cursing silently, Gabe dragged his thoughts away from the past and into the present. Carlsbad, the post office, and all the stuff waiting for him. At least he hoped it was. He had traveled enough to know that anything he didn't carry on himself couldn't be counted on to be there at the other end.

A few minutes later he found out that, as usual, Dan had come through. A package of mail and two trunks were there for him to pick up. Mentally Gabe thanked the older brother who was also his mail drop, business manager, and financial consultant. Without Dan to forward clothes and equipment around the world and keep track of the day-to-day details of the life that Gabe had left behind, it would have been much more difficult for his career to flourish. Thanks to Dan, Gabe could vanish into the unlikely places of earth and return to a clean apartment, paid bills, and mail neatly weeded out to the essential business communications.

Sometimes Gabe thought that Dan must have been born to organize everyone's lives. Though Dan had been only twenty, he had taken over the family finances after their father died of a heart attack. He had found the millions of dollars were down to a few threadbare investments. Dan had comforted their mother, and then gone to work with a shrewdness about money and people that had baffled Gabe even as he admired it. When Gabe offered to stay home and work rather than go off to college, neither his mother nor Dan would hear of it. They insisted that he go and have the full college experience.

But Gabe hadn't wanted the closed ivy walls of a university. Restless, relentlessly curious about the world, he shipped out with the merchant marines. In the next few years, he discovered a gift for telling the people back home about very different lives abroad. It was the beginning of a hand-to-mouth career as a freelance journalist.

The Orinoco River assignment had been just what Dan said it would be—the turning point of his career. **You can't flush that for an affair! Shit, brother, if the babe is really in love, she'll wait a few months. If she isn't . . . well, better to find out now.**

Dan had been right again.

The only thing the two brothers had ever seriously argued about was Gabe's refusal to finish college and then his desire to put off the Orinoco assignment until he could find out if Joy was pregnant. Dan said he would handle that problem just like he handled all Gabe's other bills.

Gabe had exploded. **Joy's not a bill, she's a woman who loves me!**

Dan wasn't buying it. **That's what you said about Whatshername, the cutie from Christchurch, New Zealand. Once she learned that the Venture wealth didn't exist, she took off.**

Joy is different, Gabe had insisted.

I'll tell you what's different, little brother. You broke Mother's heart when you left school. She got over it, finally, when you started making a living writing articles. Now you stand to make more than a living—you could have enough left over to help support her if the construction market hits the toilet again. Don't fuck up your career just when it's getting launched.

Gabe had wanted to argue that Dan was just bitter because his own fiancée had dropped him a year ago when she found out she would be marrying into the hard-working middle class rather than the leisured wealthy class. But yelling about women who wanted money more than love was useless. Dan believed what he believed, and had the scars to prove it. Making Dan bleed all over again wouldn't help.

So Gabe emptied out every bank account he had and borrowed money against his Orinoco job. Finally he had $3,744 to leave with Dan for Joy if she was pregnant.

Few people outside the family knew that Gabe worked for every penny he spent—and he spent as little as possible. Invariably the personality magazines and columnists referred to him as a "scion of the wealthy Venture family" first and a journalist second.

It was the lure of easy money that had put him in the center of two paternity suits before he came to Cottonwood Wells the first time. The fact that he hadn't even slept with one of the women and positively hadn't impregnated the other was proved only after long, very public wrangles that had taught Gabe more about yellow journalism, easy women, and greed than he'd ever wanted to know. Since then he'd become very adept at spotting women who wanted more from him than a mutually pleasurable time.

Joy had been different. He'd trusted her not to be after his supposed wealth.

He'd been wrong.

When Dan told her that $3,744 was all the money Gabe had in the world, she took it and had an abortion. So much for her protestations of love.

Then why are memories of Joy an obsession? Gabe asked himself for the hundredth time. **Why do I keep circling around them like a vulture around carrion?**

"Mr. Venture?" The postal employee's voice was gentle and patient, like her eyes watching the weary man in front of her. He looked dead on his feet, pale beneath his tan, his green eyes the only thing alive in a face lined with something deeper and more painful than physical exhaustion. "Will you be able to take the other mail?"

Gabe yanked his mind back from the questions that had been haunting him more and more since the accident in the Andes. He'd come to New Mexico to find answers, not to repeat the same old middle-of-the-night questions until he wanted to scream or curse or cry like a child.

"Excuse me?" Gabe said, his voice ragged.

She smiled encouragingly. "I noticed that we were supposed to forward that package and the trunks to Cottonwood Wells if you didn't pick them up in ten days. Are you going out there right away?"

He nodded as he picked up his package. He was too tired for casual conversation with strangers.

"There is other mail for the Wells," the woman

said hurriedly. "Fish has been out at the cave for three days, so no one has picked it up, and he won't be back here for three more. Would you mind taking the mail with you? One of the packages is express. Must be important."

"Sure." Gabe smiled and shook his head, ashamed. "I should have thought of that myself. It's really remote."

Unless Cottonwood Wells had changed, it was as isolated as any place he had visited anywhere on earth. No electricity except by a portable generator that rarely worked, water pumped by windmill into a tall tank and delivered by gravity to the cottages, communications dependent on mail, rare visitors, or a temperamental shortwave radio.

As for Lost River Cave itself, it was like another universe. There had been nothing to equal it in all Gabe's years as a roamer.

Or maybe it was that nothing else had equaled Joy.

"Thanks," the employee said, smiling and handing Gabe a pile of mail for Cottonwood Wells.

"You're welcome." **For almost taking my mind off an obsession,** he added silently.

He carried the small trunks one at a time to the car. The pavement sent transparent, shimmering waves of heat up to meet him. It was hard to believe that in a few hours the air would be chilly and the sun's searing embrace just a memory. The wide temperature swings were one of the stark contrasts of desert lands that always surprised and fascinated Gabe. Australia's Outback, Africa's Sahara, the Atacama of Chile, the Great Sonoran Desert of America, Mexico's Chihuahuan desert, the Empty Quarter—location didn't matter. The underlying realty of a desert was the same everywhere in the world. Drought. Heat. Unveiled sun. A clarity of life and death that knew no equal in any other landscape on earth.

Except one—the dark mysteries and startling beauties of a cave carved by water deep within the very bones that supported the desert itself. Water glistening on impossible stone sculptures, air saturated with moisture, coolness that varied only a few degrees from season to season. In all ways, the caves of the Guadalupe Mountains were the opposite of the arid, light-drenched land above them.

Like the desert itself, life and death were intensely focused in caves. The margin was very fine. A frayed rope, a body too tired and chilled to revive, rocks kicked loose to strike a caver far below. The rewards, too, were very fine. Virgin landscapes of a beauty seen only in dreams. A sense of being in the presence of something far greater and more enduring than a single human life. The feeling of having touched eternity.

That's why I came back, Gabe assured himself. **That will all be here long after the woman and the I-love-you lies are gone. The fantastic stones and the silence and the darkness pierced by a single cone of light. It's all still here, waiting for me. It will answer some of my questions and make me forget the rest.**

It will give me peace.

It will be enough.

The other half of his mind pointed out coolly, **It better be. The cave is all there is. Joy is gone as surely as the baby she got rid of.**

He had no answer for the caustic voice within him. When he'd left Cottonwood Wells and Joy, he'd planned to be in South America only for a few months, four or five at worst. Jungle fevers, politics, and wretched weather had stretched the assignment into a year. The resulting articles had been gathered into a book that made his career. For the first time since his father died, Gabe could help his family out financially.

Six years ago he'd come out of the Orinoco Basin flushed with fever and so tired he staggered . . . and he'd read Dan's old, brief message. **The New Mexican cutie was satisfied with $3,744 and an abortion.**

Reading those words had brought a fury that

was still with Gabe. His rational mind said that of course a twenty-year-old wouldn't want to be tied down with a kid and no husband and no money to help her out. The rest of his mind said that lots of younger women got pregnant and kept the baby and worked their asses off, especially the women who truly loved the baby's father.

It wasn't like Joy had been totally on her own. She was very close to her parents. They'd been a long way from rich, but they would have helped their daughter until Gabe was back in civilization and able to help her himself.

Joy hadn't wanted to wait around.

At the time, Gabe had wanted to track her down and tell her what he thought of her. Instead of giving in to his fury, he took a long assignment on the Indian Ocean. Again, a series of articles became a best-selling book. He didn't stop to enjoy not having to worry about every dollar. He took another assignment in the Sahal. Then another in Tierra del Fuego, and another and another and another, world without end.

None of it was enough.

Although he had gotten over the sting of being taken in by sexual experts, he had never gotten over the rage of being taken in by innocence.

THREE

Sun poured over the converted resort cottage where Joy lived. The resort had failed years ago, leaving behind ten weathered, sand-roughened cottages and a "lodge" that had burned down before Joy was born. An old ranch house was similarly ruined. The desert had little wealth and it gave what little it had grudgingly.

Even if the land wasn't a gold mine in terms of making money, it was beautiful to Joy. The cottonwood trees spread huge branches and blessed shade over the cottages and the seeps that made the difference between life and death in the desert. Water lay just beneath the dry surface of the earth. There wasn't enough water to make a cattle ranch profitable, much less the irrigated fields of a farm. There wasn't even enough for a decent resort. The man who had last owned Cottonwood Wells had gone broke. When he died, he willed the weathered remains of his dream to the university. Then Joy's parents had discovered a new passage below a cave known only for a failed guano mine, and the university permitted them to explore farther. Joy was thirteen.

A year ago, even a few months ago, all the cottages would have been alive with activity as teams of cavers and scientists explored Lost River Cave. But not now. There simply wasn't enough money to support that level of exploration any longer. Her team was down to herself, four grad students—two of them would soon leave—and an amateur caver called Fish.

Frowning, Joy looked up from the computer that kept track of the finances for Lost River Cave. A quick glance at her watch told her that she still had plenty of time to pick up Kati at the Childer ranch, which served as a school bus stop. Then she remembered that Kati was spending the week with her closest friend, Laura Childer.

A feeling of hollowness settled in Joy. Without Kati, there wasn't much reason to go back to the cottage at the end of the day. She wished she hadn't let Kati spend the week at the Childer ranch.

Instantly Joy scolded herself for being selfish. It would be cruel to keep Kati from sharing a large family's warmth just because Joy missed having her nearby. Susan Childer was a wise, laughing ranch wife who had eight children and would have loved eight more.

Between the comings and goings of all the Childers and their friends, it sometimes seemed that half the kids along New Mexico's southern border lived at the Rocking Bar D. Joy had even lived there herself, earning room and board and pocket money while she worked her way through the university, thanks to a generous scholarship. When she received her master's degree, she was invited to complete a Ph.D. while living at Cottonwood Wells and exploring Lost River Cave.

It was a wonderful opportunity, but it had been wrenching for Kati to leave the Childer family. Even now she spent as much time at the ranch as she did in the cottage at Cottonwood Wells. Joy simply didn't have the heart to deny her daughter the chaos and companionship of a big, loving family.

Unconsciously Joy sighed, remembering her own childish dreams. She'd been her parents' sole child, a "lonely-only," as she called herself. She'd promised herself that she wouldn't do that to her own child. She'd have a houseful of kids, and they would all grow up laughing and fighting and sharing and exploring caves and everything else the world had to offer.

It hadn't turned out that way.

The older Joy got, the more she realized that life offered everything and promised nothing.

Deliberately she turned her thoughts to something else. Wailing over the past didn't do any good and could do a lot of damage in the present. The plain fact was that Kati would have no sisters or brothers. After Gabe's betrayal and her parents' sudden death, Joy simply didn't trust life enough to love.

She'd tried dating a few years ago. Bad idea. Being abandoned by the man she loved had killed the passion that sent a woman willy-nilly into a man's arms. It wasn't that Joy didn't hunger for sensual satisfaction. She did. But she'd learned that it came only in her memories and dreams. Having Gabe walk away had cut her too deeply, too completely, for her to risk passion again. Being touched by other men made her very uneasy . . . and at the same time, being touched brought a longing for Gabe so vivid that it terrified her.

She'd stopped dating and started looking at sperm banks. In the end, she just couldn't do it. She wanted to know what the father of her child looked like, to hear his laughter, to see his eyes darken with passion as he—

"Dr. Anderson?"

The deep-voiced call came from the front porch of the little cottage. Joy took a fast breath and dragged her mind out of the past.

"Come in, Davy."

Moments later the screen door snapped shut behind Davy Graham. The grad student filled the doorway with equal parts of muscle and eagerness. Both were very helpful to Joy in her job as leader of Lost River Cave expeditions. His size was also a problem. His broad shoulders had become a joke around camp because some cave passages were very tight. In order to get through the various limestone squeezes, Davy had to strip down to his shorts, put one arm over his head and the other along his side, and wiggle on his stomach through the fine silt that cavers called cave mud.

Gotcha Passage, one of the main thoroughfares on the way to the cave's lower levels, was Davy's daily challenge. There had been talk of renaming Gotcha everything from Bloody Shoulders to Naked Squeeze in Davy's honor, but Joy had stood firm. Gotcha it was and Gotcha it would remain.

"Did you get the message to call Harry?" Davy asked, curiosity in his blue eyes.

"Yes." Knowing what he really wanted to ask, she said briskly, "It wasn't a reprieve. The grant still runs out in six weeks."

For a moment Davy looked away. At twenty-three he hadn't had enough harsh experiences to teach him how to hide his feelings. His disappointment was as clear as his hope had been.

"I'm sorry," Joy said. "I know how much you want to finish mapping what we've discovered. I wish you could too. Your maps are incredibly good. Someday they'll save cavers months of time, and the techniques you've worked out in your computer programs will revolutionize underground mapping. No matter what happens, you should be very proud of what you've accomplished."

Her words were not only comforting, they were true. Despite his size, Davy was one of the best cave mappers she'd ever seen. His large, blunt hands had miraculous patience with muddy clinometers and Brunton compasses, as well as much more high-tech surveying equipment. Laser, sonar, or anything else they could beg, borrow, or charm from the military surplus store—no matter what, if it was electronic and could survey a cave, Davy made it work.

"As for your three-dimensional computer model," she added, patting his arm briefly, "it's simply the best I've ever seen. Somehow I'll find a way for you to complete the work and get your doctorate."

Davy's smile was fast and crooked, but real.

"In fact," she said, "I've been talking with Dr. Weatherby of Subsurface Minerals, Inc. I asked him to consider funding your research when the grant runs out. He seemed interested, so I sent copies of your maps. If that doesn't work out, there are other things we can try. USGS, for one. It will get done, Davy. Your work deserves it."

"Thanks," he said simply. "Your support has meant a lot to me. Most faculty I've worked with only want to take credit, not give it."

She didn't argue. She knew better than Davy how fiercely competitive the supposed ivory tower was. "How could I possibly take credit?" she asked with a sly smile. "Everyone knows that I couldn't have hauled all that stuff through the cave without you."

He made a comic, pained face. "That's all you see in me—a strong back and a weak mind."

"But of course," Joy said, wide-eyed, teasing him as she always had, keeping him at a distance while reassuring him that she valued him as an assistant and a person, but **not** as a potential lover. It wasn't personal. She treated all men the same. "Why else would anyone put up with a moose like you?"

He snickered. "Last time I was a walrus."

"Yeah. Wonder what you'll be next time."

Smiling, shaking his head, he looked at his watch. Two o'clock. "Is the other team out yet?"

Automatically Joy checked her own watch. Like Davy's, it was a hardy stainless-steel model that could take water, cave mud, and scraping against rocks. "They haven't checked in. Give them twenty more minutes, and then we'll start for the cave."

"Okay." He turned away. "I'll go see if my

computer has finished running the modeling program I just modified. Meet you at the washing machine in five."

The screen door snapped shut loudly behind him.

The wind blew with a dry sound, then faded, leaving only stillness beneath the sun. Joy listened for a long moment, savoring the peace even as she thought about what lay ahead.

Today she would be helping Davy survey one of the many intriguing leads that radiated out from the Voices. The big chamber on the second level of the cave was alive with liquid sounds that came from groundwater squeezing through limestone until it reached a cavern filled with darkness and air. Pulled by gravity and pushed by the weight of more water above, the groundwater fell through air and sank liquidly into the unearthly beauty of pools that had never known the sun.

The huge cavern called the Voices fascinated Joy not only for its eerie, murmuring beauty, but because she was certain that somewhere within the echoing room there had to be at least one passage that would lead to unexplored portions of Lost River Cave. There was simply too little water falling into the Voices to account for all the ghostly voices she heard in the big room itself.

Despite repeated attempts, she'd never been able to find a single passage out of the Voices. Yet the sounds remained, tantalizing, promising new worlds to explore.

Maybe this time she would get lucky.

Maybe this time she would see a shadowy corridor or a dark opening that would ultimately lead her to the possibilities that had haunted her since the day after her parents died, when she'd pushed her way through a narrow, unexplored passage on Lost River Cave's second level and discovered the Voices.

Nearly seven years had passed since the discovery. Now she had only six weeks left.

Impatiently Joy pushed aside the looming closure of Lost River Cave. Mourning what would happen in six weeks wouldn't help her today. She had work to do, years of effort and memories and dreams to wrap up, and she couldn't accomplish it with tears in her eyes.

Sounds from the screened back porch and laundry reminded her of all she had to do before she could enter the cave again. She hurried toward the huge industrial washing machines and a dryer that looked like something left by aliens on the crowded, worn cottage porch. Unless both generators were working—which was less than half the time—there wasn't enough electricity to run camp lights and the washing machines, so everyone tried to get as much cave gear washed as possible during the daylight hours.

Wearing shorts and sandals, Davy was already

sorting through piles of fresh laundry. Nearby a climbing rope rumbled and bumped in one of the washers.

"How's the computer program?" Joy asked.

"Still chewing it over." He gave a doubtful look to a pair of socks, then decided they probably had a few more miles in them. "The red rope felt a little stiff, so I'm rinsing it with a big dose of softener."

"Thanks. We won't need it today anyway. Fish did several loads of ropes before he went to the cave this morning."

"Thought so," Davy said, looking at the ropes stacked on a small table. "Nobody can snake-wrap those babies like he does."

"That's how he gets out of doing the dishes so often," Joy said. Braiding or coiling ropes so that they were easier to carry and wouldn't tangle getting there or while being used was as much an art as a science.

She looked critically at one of the clean ropes heaped on a counter, waiting for Fish's deft touch. Washing ropes wasn't done to make them look good, but to make them safe. Muddy grit left between the strands frayed and cut through them, dangerously weakening the rope itself.

"Remind me to run that one through again when we get back," Joy said, dumping the rope on the half of the floor that had been designated for dirty gear. "Did anyone find that backup Gibbs?"

Davy knew just enough about the technical aspects of climbing to get in and out of the cave safely. Since a Gibbs ascender was a basic piece of equipment, he didn't have to think about what Joy meant for more than a few seconds.

"It fell off its storage peg and landed under a pile of rope," he said. "Maggie found it and laid it out for you with your clean underwear. Of course, everyone else piled clean laundry on the same table, so . . ."

"That's what I like about Maggie," Joy said, flipping through a pile of mesh underwear until she found the ascender. "She's always thinking."

Davy grunted.

"Hey, sound more grateful," Joy said, stowing the mechanical ascender with her other gear. "Maggie knew if I didn't find the backup Gibbs, I was going to use yours and let you practice getting out of the cave one ascender knot at a time."

He made a face. "If I'd known that, I'd have turned this place inside out."

Quickly and thoroughly Joy checked that her special seat harness was in good condition, as were the various carabiners, figure eight descenders, extra narrow gauge lines—the climber's equivalent of a hiker carrying spare shoelaces—and all the other specialized equipment that went into cave exploring. Each curve of metal she packed had the subdued polish that came from use and painstaking upkeep. Each rope and line was clean, flexible, and smooth.

When your life depended on your gear, you took good care of it.

Besides, for Joy, working over the ropes and lamps, carabiners and ascenders, helmets and rappelling equipment gave her a sense of being part of history. Each smooth steel shape and various kinds of synthetic fiber ropes represented the end product of years of human exploration, risk, and achievement. Cavers spent their lives experimenting with and refining the equipment they carried down into the velvet darkness.

Her father and mother had been among them, as had her grandfather. Joy had entered her first cave when she was too young to remember. She'd learned to handle the equipment at an age when other children were playing with dolls and toy trucks. When she was older, other cavers had teased her about being her parents' "secret weapon"—the reason for their success in discovering new passages hidden within well-known caves. It was partly true. Being small was a real bonus when it came to exploring New Mexico's intricate, baffling, and astonishingly beautiful caves.

The washing machine switched to spin cycle,

made thumping noises, and started shimmying. Joy backed off and gave the machine a solid kick. The washer settled down into normal operation.

"Fish would smack you for that," Davy said. "He hates it when anyone abuses his babies."

"I won't tell him if you won't."

"It'll cost."

"How much?"

"You take one of my cooking nights."

"Deal," she said quickly. Davy was many things, but being a good cook—or even a halfway decent cook—wasn't one of them.

"These are yours," he said, handing over some more clothes. "They have 'shrimp' stamped all over them."

"Keep in mind, moose, that my written recommendations will follow you for the rest of your life."

"I'm shaking in my size thirteens."

She caught the wad of clothing he dropped in her hands. Though it all looked sleek and colorful, just holding everything made her sweat. Lost River Cave was always about 58 degrees Fahrenheit, and the lower two levels were wet. Staying warm meant dressing in special high-tech cloth, layer upon layer that wicked moisture away from the body and held heat against it.

But it wasn't cold in the summer desert, and that was where all her cave work began—in the desert.

She shook out the mesh long underwear, full-length pants and shirt, long-sleeved coveralls, pairs of socks meant to be worn one over the other, and lightweight, tough, high-tech boots designed to keep feet dry and right side up no matter what the conditions. The wet suits and scuba gear that were required on the lowest level of Lost River Cave hung in one of the empty cabins, waiting to be needed. But not today. Not even in the next six weeks. Cave diving was simply too dangerous to take on short-handed.

"Damn, I hate this part," Davy said, piling one hot piece of clothing on top of the other and shoving them into his cave pack.

"It could be worse," Joy said as she rolled and stashed her own gear.

"How?" Davy, even more than Joy, sweated just handling the caving clothes in desert heat.

"In my parents' day, wool was the cloth of choice. A lot of cavers still prefer it."

"Not this one. God, I itch just thinking about it."

"But when we're below, you'll—"

"Be grateful for every hot ounce of it," he finished. "It never seems possible when I'm up here."

"Just like the desert up above doesn't seem possible when we're down in the cave."

He reached for his hard hat, then hesitated when he saw that the battery pack sitting next to it was half empty. "Did Fish clean out the carbide lamps?"

"Yes, but we won't need them. The generators ran all night. The rechargeable batteries are topped off. Bet Maggie put them inside your boots, where you can't forget them."

"I only forgot them once and nobody's let me forget it since."

"Haven't forgotten them again, have you?"

With a grumpy sound, he checked his boots and found the batteries.

Joy grinned. "Like I said, that girl is always thinking."

She tugged at the webbing inside her own helmet, checked that the bracket holding the battery-powered lights was secure and that both lights were working at full power. The rechargeable batteries only lasted four hours if she used both lamps, eight hours if she alternated, but the light they gave was steady, strong, and clear. Since overnight explorations weren't possible with such a diminished group of cavers, keeping batteries charged wasn't a problem.

But just in case, she and Davy both carried chemical lightsticks, a spare flashlight and batteries, a simple cigarette lighter, matches, and candles. It made for extra weight, and no caver complained about a single ounce of it. Once beyond the twilight zone at a cave's entrance, the dark was seamless and absolute.

As soon as the equipment was assembled and stuffed into personal packs, Joy and Davy carried everything to the worn, battered Jeep that cooked quietly beneath the sun. The Jeep had been Joy's only legacy from her parents—that and caving skills and a shoebox full of family photos going back more than one hundred years. And love. Her parents had taught her to laugh and trust and love.

Then Gabriel Venture had taught her to hate.

Stop thinking about it.

But she couldn't, not when he would be here in a week.

Thank God I have at least a week's warning. I've got some serious work to do on my "game face" when it comes to that son of a bitch.

The Jeep's seats were hot enough to sear bare flesh. The lean-to that once had protected the vehicle had rotted beyond repair and blown down in March winds. There was no money for a new structure.

Silently Davy handed Joy one of the two-gallon jugs of water he had brought with him. Together they wet down the front seats and steering wheel. Everything dried immediately, but at least the evaporating water cooled the surfaces to the point that they wouldn't burn skin.

Joy wished she had something as useful to pour on her smoldering memories.

FOUR

After Gabe left the main highway and turned off onto a gravel road, there wasn't any traffic to keep him alert. He wished that he'd drunk more coffee to keep him going, and at the same time knew that even a stiff dose of minimart caffeine wouldn't have done much good. Making a dent in his weariness would have taken enough coffee to fill Lost River Cave.

For the past fifty-eight days he'd worked non-stop. He'd been awake for the last thirty-seven hours and had crossed so many time zones that he lost track of them.

The muscles of his left thigh and hip ached, then burned, then sent lancing pain messages up his back and down to his foot. It was time to stop, stretch, walk around, and baby the muscles that still reminded him of the climbing accident that had come within a quarter inch of taking his life. The quarter inch was the thickness of un-frayed rope that had remained after he finally dragged himself back up the crumbling face of the cliff.

It hadn't been easy. He'd spent an endless time dangling headdown over a two-thousand-foot drop, banging against granite with each swing of the rope, his weight entirely suspended from his left leg. But he'd been luckier than his guides. The landslide had swept them over and down and down until their screams were lost in distance and grinding stone.

His article on "Aerial Surveys and Mountain Trails" had nearly been his epitaph.

He'd spent a long time in the hospital wondering why he'd lived and his guides hadn't. In the middle of the night, he still woke up in a cold sweat, wondering.

The steering wheel bucked against Gabe's hands as the gravel road got worse, then a lot worse. Even slowing to fifteen miles an hour didn't improve the ride. One-handed, he opened a bottle of water he had bought at the minimart on the edge of town and drank deeply. After the humid Philippines, he had to keep reminding himself that a human being lost water in the desert much faster than seemed reasonable.

With each twist and turn of the road, memories sliced away at him, leading him back to a time when he'd been a whole lot younger in all the ways that mattered—and Joy had laughed in his arms.

Exhaustion hit him like a landslide. Even as he shook it off, he knew he should have stayed in Carlsbad, rented a motel room, caught up on his mail, found out what arrangements his editor had made for Lost River Cave, then memorized the names and accomplishments of the people he would be working with. And after he did all that, he should have slept around the clock before he took the rough road to Cottonwood Wells.

But he hadn't been able to wait. An irrational sense of urgency rode him, a feeling that he was racing toward something both unknown and unknowable, yet he had to race on anyway, before whatever it was got away.

So he drank bottled water and ate a stale "deli" sandwich while he fought the road. He was used to pushing himself physically, running on nerve and whatever food he could grab and eat without fuss. The difference now was he didn't enjoy working that hard anymore, but had nothing to put in its place.

As the road clawed up the rugged lower slope of the Guadalupes, cholla gave way to sotol, a plant that looked like an agave but was actually a cousin of the lily. Occasional junipers appeared in the northern creases of the land. He noticed the changing plant life only at the edges of his mind. He drove automatically, staring through the dusty windshield as though the answers to all his midnight questions were printed on the hood of his car.

No such luck. There was nothing but dusty paint and blinding brightness where the sun ran hotly over glass and metal.

More junipers appeared, and with them the small, rapier-tipped plant known as lechugilla. Curving yet stiff, the point of each "leaf" could wound a horse and punch through a tire or a boot with cruel ease.

The third time Gabe swerved to avoid a rock that turned out to be a shadow, he pulled over to the side of the narrow gravel road and turned off the ignition. The sun's thick, slanting light poured like honey over the hushed land.

Moving slowly, he got out of the car and walked a short way into the desert. It had been months since he had been this stiff. The doctor had warned him that long plane flights and tension would be harder on the tender muscles than anything but going headfirst over a cliff again.

The long plane flight Gabe could accept. But stress? He had no reason to be so tight. He'd wanted to come home to the States, to explore once again the velvet night of Lost River Cave, to . . .

What?

He didn't have any answer except the tension stealing through him, tightening him even as it drained his energy. He didn't know what had driven him from a hospital bed in Peru to the Great Barrier Reef, to Tierra del Fuego, to the steamy Philippines and then finally back to a stretch of New Mexican desert that few people knew existed and even fewer cared.

Memories drew you, whispered part of his mind.

Dreams, jeered the rest of him.

There was no end to the inner argument, no end to the tension aching in him, a tension that had begun when he crawled off that deadly Peruvian mountain asking himself every inch of the way why he'd lived and other men had died. What was there in his life worth saving?

Was he so fine and good and pure and kind that he should live when others died?

That answer was easy. **Bullshit**.

He was an ordinary man who'd been lucky in his career. Not as bad a person as he could have been. Not as good, either.

And still he asked **Why?**

He'd spent his last birthday in a hospital bed, his only present life itself. Trapped by injury, unable to lose himself in the wild lands of the world, he'd explored himself, reviewing the years and his own actions with the slicing, cool intelligence that made his articles crackle with insight.

But his life wasn't a mountain or a sea or a mysterious, impossible cave growing beneath the land. Emotions blurred his personal insights, reshaped memories into doubts, turned dreams into treachery.

Still asking **Why?** he'd come out of that hospital as tight as a rope in the instant before breaking. Then he'd accepted one assignment after another, his only requirement being that each place be different from the New Mexican desert and the wild, incredible cavern that haunted his dreams.

The woman, too, haunted him mercilessly. Another question without an answer. Another question that **must** be answered.

Why?

No answer.

Impatient, irritable, driven, he had raged to be in this place but didn't have a clue as to why it was so important to him. It simply was.

Finally he'd admitted that he could no more stop himself from coming back than he could walk on water. In some way that he didn't understand, Lost River Cave had become a mysterious symbol to him. He'd lost or found something there that he couldn't name, and he'd learned or forgotten something there that haunted his waking and sleeping dreams.

So he'd called the university to see if he could get into the cave, discovered that the exploration grant was running out, and offered to do another article. Then he'd called his editor at **Planet Earth,** suggested doing an article on the closing of Lost River Cave, and instantly had been offered the assignment.

Using the imminent closing of the cave as an excuse for his otherwise irrational need to be back in New Mexico, he left his last assignment unfinished and booked the first flight that would connect to Carlsbad.

Now the desert wind moved gently over him, ruffling his thick brown hair and tugging at the open collar of his blue cotton shirt. Stretching, he turned his face to the wind and the fiery, descending sun, giving himself to the moment with the intense sensual appreciation that was as much a part of him as his bones.

The smell of the untamed land swept over him, heat and dust and pungent plants. The spare, almost astringent scent of the desert pleased him more than the thickly layered perfumes of jungle flowers.

Called by the unique smell of drought and time, memories welled up in him, laughter and smooth skin and the taste of Joy on his lips. He fought the memories reflexively, savagely, as he'd fought them for nearly seven years.

The tension in his body increased until the muscles of his left leg knot. He walked stiffly, cursing the pain and the memories, haunted by desert scents condensing around him as delicately and relentlessly as time itself.

Abruptly he gave in, understanding at last that this was one of the reasons he had come back to Lost River Cave.

To remember . . .

. . . Heat and a fragrant wind caressing the land, whispering promises of the cool night to come. He and Joy were on their way to Carlsbad. Her father had given Gabe the keys to the Jeep, a warning about the difficult shift into third gear, and a grocery list as long as a driveshaft.

At the last instant Joy had jumped in, saying that if she didn't get out of Cottonwood Wells she would get cabin fever. In the interests of mental health, Gabe had instantly offered dinner and a show. Sam had ruffled her hair as if she was six instead of twenty and told her to have a good time.

Until that instant Gabe hadn't realized how hungry he was for Joy's smile, her laughter, her company. During the weeks that he'd been in Cottonwood Wells, Joy had first entertained, then fascinated, and finally compelled him.

Now, two weeks before he had to leave on another assignment, he knew that he'd never wanted a woman half so much as he wanted Joy.

From the way she responded when he'd held her beneath the brilliant desert moon and learned just a few of the secrets of her body, he knew that Joy wanted him too.

As soon as they were beyond sight of Cottonwood Wells he turned and slowly ran his fingertips over her cheek.

"I'm glad you came," he said.

Color rose beneath her skin. She turned her head quickly, brushing her lips over his palm. "So am I."

The rest of the day was a kaleidoscope of vivid, sensual images. The sun-colored flash of Joy's hair beneath the grocery store's cold lights. Her hand brushing against his fingers when they both reached for salt at the same time during lunch. Her tongue catching a drop of peppermint ice cream that had run onto her knuckle from the rapidly melting cone. Her laughter and sudden breathless silence when he'd neatly licked the minty mustache from her upper lip.

And the swift, hot flood of sensation that came when she returned the favor, licking every trace of ice cream from his lips, sending all the blood in his body rushing toward the flesh that strained suddenly against his jeans.

The movie was an exquisite kind of torture. He put his arm around her and pulled her close, drowning in her fragrance, her warmth burning against him hotter than any desert sun. She was watching him, not the movie, and at some point during the matinee she discovered that she wanted him. He saw it in her eyes, felt it in the infinitely yielding body so close to his.

He'd kissed her then, a kiss that had narrowed the world to the heat and hunger of their joined mouths. The honesty of her response, the small sound she made when his tongue stroked hers, was more exciting to him than any woman's touch had ever been.

As they left the movie Gabe thought about taking Joy to the motel at the edge of town. The idea of it left a sour taste in his mouth. She wasn't like the other women he'd known. It wasn't a matter of the three years difference in their ages. It was something more subtle. More elusive.

There was a transparency in Joy that simply didn't admit to the possibility of hurried sex in grubby motels. Maybe it was that despite her smoldering sensuality, she wasn't particularly experienced when it came to sexual play. Whoever her previous boyfriends had been, whether there had been only one lover for her or several, no man had ever truly set her afire and then burned deep inside her.

That was what Gabe wanted to do.

Burn with her.

He took Joy's hand, threading his fingers deeply through hers, squeezing, feeling her smoothness and warmth even as he let her feel his restraint and strength.

He didn't want to take her to a restaurant for dinner, to stare across the table at her with a hunger no food could touch. He wanted to be alone with her, away from everyone else. He wanted to feel like they were the only two people on earth, totally removed from all reality, knowing only each other.

Joy watched him with eyes as clear and luminous as rain. "How about a picnic dinner in the desert on the way home?"

"Hot dogs roasted over a salt cedar campfire?"

"If that's what you want." She grinned. "Otherwise Señora Lopez packs great tortillas and carne asada to go."

"You'd give up the steak dinner I promised you?"

"For a chance to eat in the desert alone with you and the sun and the wind, I'd give up six steak dinners."

He squeezed her hand and brushed his lips over her hair. "How did you guess that I don't want to be in a restaurant with everyone else in town?"

Joy's breath caught with a soft sound. "Because that's the way I feel too."

Her husky confession licked over him with tongues of fire. "Let's see how fast we can get the makings for our picnic."

Soon they were driving back out into the desert, following the faded road, lured by the thickly slanting rays of the late afternoon sun. Joy gave him directions to a tiny, mossy seep visited only by the wind and wary desert creatures. They parked the Jeep and walked the last hundred yards. There was no sign of other people, not even a faint trail. The land was untouched, trembling with light, newly created—the way he felt the first time he'd kissed Joy.

She made a tablecloth out of a bedroll she'd taken from the collection of camping gear that her parents always left in the back of the Jeep.

He put down the bags containing dinner and watched her small hands smooth the bulky fabric of the bedroll. He wanted nothing more than to feel her hands on his body, easing the hunger that made him ache. When he knelt in front of her, she looked up questioningly. He wanted to reassure her that he would be gentle, that he wouldn't hurt her, but he couldn't think of any words. He could think only of touching her.

"A kiss." His voice was almost hoarse and his hands trembled slightly as they curved around her face. "Just a kiss, sweetheart."

Her lips were soft, firm, unbearably sweet. He

wanted to sink into them, into her. He teased the inside of her lower lip until she gasped. Then he drove his tongue deeply into her mouth, groaning as he felt her fingers dig into the muscles of his upper arm. Her tongue moved against his, caressing and savoring and demanding more, always more.

Without knowing, without thinking, he pulled her down and covered her body with his while hunger raged through him, shaking him, and still the kiss hadn't ended. He couldn't force himself to pull away. He wanted to pour himself into her, filling her until she overflowed and turned to him with her own need, her own demand that he be part of her until they were one and that one burned with an endless fire.

Silently Joy told him that she wanted the same thing. She strained against him as her small, surprisingly strong hands searched over his back and shoulders and hips, caressing him, enjoying his strength.

The snaps on her western blouse gave way with a slow certainty that made her moan deep in her throat. It was the only sound she made, the only sound she needed to make. Her fingers dug into his hips as she met his kiss, matched it, and learned the heat and textures of his mouth.

The sensual, searching touches of her tongue excited him, telling him that she enjoyed the feel and intimacy of the deep kiss as much as he did. Her fingers speared beneath his waistband as passion surged through her body. She twisted against him, asking for more. Demanding it.

His hands released the catch on her bra. Despite the hammering of his need, he made himself go slowly, savoring each exquisite shift of her textures and responses. He held the sensitive flesh of her breasts, rubbed over their softness until his skin was on fire and her nipples were hard. She twisted against him and he tugged at her nipples with hungry fingertips.

Her response was a sudden, wild arching of her body and a cry that he drank from her mouth, wanting to share her with nothing, not even the desert silence.

Finally, lured by the pouting promise of her breasts, he pulled his mouth away from hers. He wondered if she wanted to know the feel of his tongue on her nipples half so much as he did. His teeth raked lightly over her neck, down the firm swell of a breast, and he nuzzled the peak with a teasing sweetness that brought a husky sound of pleasure from her. The sound quickly changed to a gasp and then a rippling cry of desire as he bent his head over her breast and drank from it as completely as he had drunk from her mouth.

She moaned his name into the silence and

moved against him with her whole body, urging him, inciting him. Her response was a wildfire raging through his self-control. While her husky words encouraged him, he took her even deeper, surrounding her breast with his mouth. With each shifting pressure of tongue and lips, he heard his name break on her lips. With each gasp of pleasure, her hands searched over his hips beneath his jeans.

Hungrily his hands swept from her shoulders to her waist to her thighs. She moaned and blindly sought more. His hand moved underneath her denim skirt and slid between her thighs. She shifted, easing his way, until he felt the steamy urgency of her against his palm and groaned.

So did she.

He caught her mouth beneath his again and thrust his tongue rhythmically against hers while his fingers slid beneath her silky pants to caress even silkier skin. She made a ragged sound and shifted again, asking and demanding in the slow movements of her body against his, giving him the sultry warmth he sought.

Fingers caressed, searched, sank into the incredible softness between her thighs. His thumb dipped, circled, rubbed the sleek button that rose to meet his touches. She answered with a twisting, sexy seeking of her hips that demanded more.

He hooked his fingers in her panties and pulled them to her ankles in a single motion. Kneeling, he lifted first one foot and then the other, removing her underwear.

"Gabe?" Her voice was ragged, like her heartbeat, like her breathing.

"I won't hurt you, sweetheart." As he spoke, he pushed up her skirt and kissed the skin around her belly button.

"I know. It's just that—" Words became a gasp as he bit her gently, sucked less gently, licked her.

"I've never—you're the first—oh, God—**again**."

Her fragmented words penetrated Gabe's hungry, urgent exploration of her secrets. He looked up and saw her flushed lips, her eyes dilated with passion until there was only a tiny rim of clear gray surrounding the black pupil, her blouse hanging open, her nipples hard and glistening from his mouth.

"Don't worry," he said, bending to her again. "I've never done this with a woman either."

She made a sound that could have been laughter and certainly was pleasure. "Not this. I mean, God, it feels—" She shivered, pushing against him as he teased her navel with his tongue and explored the hard bud hidden in her softness with his fingertips.

"Do you want me to stop?" he asked.

"No." She took a broken breath and moved slowly against his mouth, his fingers, giving and demanding and enjoying. "Gabe, I've never made love before. Not completely. That's all I was trying to say."

He went still. "You're a virgin?"

She smiled down at him as he knelt between her legs. "Not for much longer."

"Jesus."

He let out a breath that was another caress against her violently sensitive flesh. He saw the telltale shiver, the helpless seeking of her hips. She shared the desire that had claimed him as fiercely as the summer sun claimed the sky.

"I should stop," he said roughly. "I should put your clothes back on and—"

"No!" Her hands tugged at his T-shirt, opened his jeans, dove beneath, sought the living heat of him.

"You're sure?" he asked.

While he waited for her answer, he tasted her on his lips, felt her passionate heat sliding against his fingers, and prayed that she wouldn't change her mind. His fingertips traced her layered softness with maddening delicacy.

"Yes," she said hoarsely, twisting against his knowing touch. "Don't you dare stop, Gabe. **I want you.**"

Smiling, he watched Joy in the pouring golden

sunlight, savoring her abandoned movements as she responded to his touch. Every breath she took was his name, her need, her demand that he keep caressing her, learning her desires, teaching her his own.

A wild kind of calm came to Gabe, a certainty that was like nothing he had ever experienced. He would touch Joy in ways he had touched no other woman. He would equal her generous sensuality. He would melt her to her bones, and when she came back to herself in the aftermath of ecstasy, she would never again be touched by anyone without remembering her first time, and him.

"Gabe?" she whispered, eyes closed, body shivering with the intensity of her response.

"I won't stop."

He peeled away their remaining clothes until they wore only the shimmering gold light of late afternoon. Then he sank down to the bedroll, kneeling between her legs, asking her once again.

"You sure?"

"As sure as you are," she said, stroking his erection.

His breath hissed in.

She lay back and held out her arms in silent demand. As he bent over her, he hesitated, wondering if his caresses would shock her; and then knew that it would be all right, that despite her innocence she would understand, accept, glory in her own sensuality as he did. She was a lover to match his dreams.

"I have to show you how perfect you are," he whispered, kissing her lips, the frantic pulse in her throat, the nipples thrusting against his tongue, the shadowed navel, the triangle of molten gold hair. His tongue flicked over her, tasting her. "So sweet . . . so damned sweet."

The words ended in a husky sound as he gave in to his own sensuality, caressing her with an intimacy that he had never known with other women. Nor had he known his own need rising fiercely to meet feminine demand, he urging, she requiring, driving each other upward in a wild spiral of passion that transformed both of them.

When he finally moved back up her body she was crying and twisting against him, offering him everything that he'd ever dreamed of in a lover. She was hot, tight, deep, and if there was pain when he took her neither of them ever knew, for fire knows nothing but its own pulsing flames . . .

The hot dream memory faded, leaving Gabe aching in ways that had nothing to do with the fall he'd taken nearly a year ago in the Andes. He stood motionless as the echoes of passion clawed through him, leaving a seething hunger in their wake.

You bloody fool, he raged silently at himself.

Did you come halfway around the world for a piece of ass?

You bloody fool, he answered himself acidly. **Do you really think what's bothering you is that easy?**

There was no answer but the one that had driven him halfway around the world: lust was easy. It demanded nothing but its own satiation.

After Joy, he'd quickly learned the limitations of lust, the depression that came when he realized that sex was over but the hungry emptiness and need went on and on. He hadn't liked learning that lesson, because it meant that Joy had touched him much more deeply than he'd touched her.

That was why she had haunted him through the years.

Of all the women he had met, she was the only one who enriched his silences as well as his sensuality. She was the only woman who left him feeling complete rather than hollow. She was the only woman whose mental and physical response to him had made him reach down to the deepest parts of himself, satisfying needs that were less tangible and more enduring than lust.

But it had taken him seven years to admit it.

Fool, he told himself wearily. **You lost something before you knew what it was worth. By now some man who isn't as stupid as you were will have discovered her worth.**

By now she's happily married and has a batch of kids.

The thought made Gabe's mouth flatten. He couldn't stop remembering the baby that had never been born.

She said she loved me, but she was too young to know what love is, said the bitter part of him that had never gotten over her betrayal.

You left her.

I didn't know she was pregnant! I left her every bit of money I had and then some. And even if I'd known she was pregnant, what the hell was I supposed to do? Turn my back on my brother and mother—again—and on a career I needed in order to support myself and my family, much less a wife and child?

What other decision could I have made but to take the assignment and then come back to her?

There was no answer.

There hadn't ever been, even when he circled round and round the question in his hospital bed in Peru. He'd searched, but he hadn't found the answer in the South American mountains, beneath the Australian seas, or in the jungles of Asia.

The answer wouldn't be in New Mexico's desert either.

He'd been a fool to drive himself to exhaustion just to come back here as quickly as possible.

Time went in only one direction: forward. He'd endured the pain of remembering Joy for nothing, nothing at all.

Fatigue settled on Gabe, and with it a chill that didn't come from the increasing coolness of the evening air. He walked back to the car, started it, forced his mind to deal with the necessities of the moment. He should hurry. There were several turnoffs before he reached Cottonwood Wells. If it got too dark, he'd miss the subtle natural signposts that marked the route.

The way you've missed other things?

Shut up, he told himself savagely. **Just. Shut. Up.**

The car leaped forward, tires spinning, sending dust and gravel boiling upward in a confused cloud.

FIVE

The entrance to Lost River Cave was a slit barely seven feet by three. The black opening was all but hidden in a jumble of rock and brush a few hundred steep yards up the slope. When Joy turned off the Jeep's engine and climbed out next to Fish's Toyota, the sound of voices floated down over the rugged land to her.

Although she hadn't really been worried about the other cavers, she was always relieved when she saw them. Being responsible for groups of students varying in age from eighteen to twenty-four, plus some dedicated amateur cavers, was rather like being a parent. It aged her in subtle ways.

The first one out into the hot afternoon sun was Maggie O'Mara, a tall graduate student who had the body of a showgirl and a mind like a steel trap. Above ground, Joy envied the girl her height and stunning curves. Below ground, Maggie frequently and loudly envied Joy's lithe, petite grace. Maggie should have been an undergraduate, but she had skipped grades when she was younger. As a result, at barely twenty years old, she was a grad student in the university.

Maggie turned off her light, took off her helmet, and shook out chin-length auburn hair that curled wildly from the humid cave air. Her smile flashed in her muddy face.

"Hey, Davy, looking **good**!" she called, giving him a laughing once-over glance.

Davy paused in the act of pulling mesh underwear over his thick, powerful legs. He leered comically at Maggie's muddy, clothes-wrapped body. "Better than you, babe."

"Stick around," she said, reaching for the mud-plastered zipper. "It'll get hot."

The three other cavers behind her called out encouragement that no one took seriously. By the time Maggie stripped to muddy underwear, no one was watching. They were all too tired and dirty and chilled to be eager for anything but a hot shower, hotter coffee, and dry clothes.

Davy gave the redhead a brotherly swat on her rear as she went past him. She swatted him right back, yawned, and turned to Joy.

"I wish you'd been down there," Maggie said. "For once I was the smallest one in the group, so I had to try that new passage we found on the second level."

"Did it go?" Joy asked.

As she spoke, excitement suddenly animated her delicate features. She didn't notice Davy's quick look or the admiration in his eyes.

Maggie did. It had bothered her when she had first joined the cavers a month ago. Then she realized that a lot of men admired Joy and she treated them all the same, like first cousins or brothers or friends. Even Davy didn't turn her head, and as far as Maggie was concerned, Davy was an impressive hunk of male—brains and brawn both.

If it wasn't for Kati, Maggie would have sworn that the beautiful Dr. Anderson didn't know why God had put men on earth.

"The passage was awful," Maggie said. "I got stuck and Fish had to jerk me out. I stripped, greased up with mud, and tried it again." She shrugged. "No luck. I don't think even you would fit."

Despite her disappointment, Joy said warmly. "Okay. Thanks for giving it all you had."

"What I needed was a little less to give," Maggie said wryly, but she smiled, pleased by Joy's approval.

Joy looked at the compact, muddy man who was just now coming down the trail. Jim Fisher, or Fish as his friends called him, was an amateur caver and full-time mechanic who arranged his work schedule so that he could give every spare moment to Lost River Cave. Without him Joy would have spent a lot less time underground and a lot more above, waiting for repairmen.

"That old passage was a real pig," Fish drawled. "By the time I shucked Maggie out of there, I thought she was gonna be mashed down smaller than you. Try it if you like, Dr. Joyce, but I'm telling you, that lead don't go worth a damn."

She nodded and turned back to Maggie. "Thanks anyway. I'll take the next squeeze."

The girl grinned and slapped the lush line of her hip. "No problem, Dr. Joyce. Keeps me trim. After a month of cave crawling, I've never been in better shape."

That brought a chorus of remarks from the last two cavers, both of whom were male grad students with excellent vision, quick tongues, and only a few days left before they had to leave the cave.

Maggie paid no attention to their comments. She had five older brothers, which meant that male teasing didn't ruffle her one bit. She added her coveralls and long underwear to the growing pile in the Toyota. When everyone was down to shirts and mesh underwear, or underwear alone, they packed themselves and the rest of their mud-encrusted gear in the Land Cruiser and took off for Cottonwood Wells.

"That poor washing machine is going to have a real workout," Davy said, pulling on a long-sleeved undershirt.

"That's what it was built for. Just hope Maggie remembers to hose everything off before she puts it in the machine this time. I'm out of filters until Fish goes into town again."

Davy grinned. "Yeah, that was some mess, wasn't it? First time I've ever seen Maggie blush."

Joy gave him a sideways glance and silently hoped that he was finally noticing Maggie in the way she so obviously noticed him. Not that Maggie was embarrassing about her preference. She simply didn't bother to hide the fact that she thought Davy Graham was one very attractive man.

Just as Joy had once let Gabriel Venture know that she found him exciting. Twenty was such a vulnerable time. You were a woman in the eyes of the world, you were eager to explore that world, and yet you were still a child in the eyes of your parents. Open as a child, fragile as a child . . .

Joy's fingers tightened around her bootlaces until her knuckles ached. She had to stop thinking about Gabe. She knew all there was to know about love, despair, and Gabriel Venture.

But Lost River Cave remained to be explored.

She settled her helmet in place, checked the

lights, and picked up her rucksack and ropes. "Ready?"

"Willing and able."

As they approached the cave, Joy tried very hard not to remember the many times it had been Gabe by her side, Gabe who had explored beauty with her, Gabe who had tapped the heat and sensuality deep within her, Gabe who had taught her about love.

And betrayal.

SIX

Joy scrambled up the last steep pitch of Lost River Cave on her way to the desert night. Part of the uneven ground she stepped carefully over was made up of huge blocks of limestone that had once been the cave ceiling. Part of the ground was a trench through a thick layer of ancient bat guano that had been mined for fertilizer more than a century ago. Part of what she walked on was a slick flowstone deposit that covered both old guano and older limestone boulders. No matter which part of the trail she was on, it required attention and balance.

With muddy fingers she unclipped herself from the rope she'd used to steady herself on the slippery climb up and out of the entrance. Now she was surrounded by a soft, dry wind and the luminous shades of darkness that was desert night. The Milky Way swept overhead like a vast river of diamonds. Other stars sparkled in subtle colors and variations of silver. Like the cave below, the darkness overhead was a miracle of beauty.

Joy switched off her light, removed her helmet awkwardly because she was favoring her left arm, and shook her head. The air was cool, heady, crisp, like a fine white wine. She heard a noise behind her, turned, and saw a patch of light bobbing and glowing out of the cave's mouth. There was a clear metallic sound as Davy unclipped himself from the rope, then the softer, slurred sounds as he hauled the rope up and wrapped it carefully.

"Ready, Dr. Joyce?" he asked, coming up behind her. He lifted his wrist into the cone of light from his helmet. "We'll have to hurry to make it back on time."

"Ready." She bit back a groan as she pulled off her muddy gloves.

"Want me to drive? You banged up your arm pretty good on that slope."

She hesitated. "If you don't mind . . ."

"No problem." He turned off his helmet light and resettled the heavy, muddy rope with a casual motion of his shoulder.

The thought of that heavy rope dragging on her bruised arm made Joy doubly glad that Davy was along. "Thanks. If I baby the arm tonight, I'll be able to go caving tomorrow."

For an instant she wished she had Davy's

abundant strength. Then she admitted it wasn't her body that was worn out and dragging, or even her sore arm. It was her mind. She'd been pushing frantically against the knowledge of Gabe's return, acting like it was a tight passage she could put behind her if she just struggled long and hard enough. But all she'd done was wear herself out.

She rubbed the back of her hand across her forehead, leaving behind a dark streak. Cave mud was so fine that it worked into everything, even gloves and layers of clothing, like the damp chill that seeped into flesh and bone. The thought of the hot bath that was waiting for her made her groan again, this time in pleasure.

"Dr. Joyce?" Davy's voice was deep and anxious.

"Just thinking of a hot bath."

"Oh." He chuckled and stretched until he towered against the starry sky. "Yeah, I know what you mean. No matter how many times I go down in that cave, it still tires me out."

They piled everything in back of the Jeep, adding another coating of dirt to the vehicle. After the absolute blackness of Lost River Cave, the night around them was alive with light— stars of every intensity, the brilliance of the rising moon, and the warm yellow glow of the headlights.

When they drove into Cottonwood Wells it, too, was alive with golden light. Mantles burned incandescently inside lanterns, sending rich yellow illumination spilling out from the cabins.

Davy parked in back of Joy's cottage and looked around. "Generator's down again. There goes your bath, unless the solar unit is enough."

Joy sighed. "Poor Fish. He swears that second generator we got from the army was old when his great-granddaddy drove a mule team into New Mexico."

"That's not all he swears."

She almost laughed. The mechanic's creative profanity was a matter of envy among the other cavers.

"If cussing will make it go," she said, "then Fish—"

The rest of her words were lost beneath the ripping snarl of the generator coming to life. White light flickered, faded, then caught and held, flooding Cottonwood Wells with an electrical sunrise. The sound of the generator went up and down raggedly before settling into a steady noise that was somewhere between a purr and a growl. The sound diminished even more as Fish shut the door to the generator's shed.

Davy laughed. "Fish must have cussed it something special. Hasn't sounded that good since I got here two years ago."

"At least I'll be able to recharge the headlight batteries," Joy said. She had a carbide helmet lamp for emergencies, but she preferred the clean electrical headlamps in the virgin cave. "Not to mention keeping your energy-sucking computers going and having a mechanical slave to wash the clothes for us."

"Amen." Davy had drawn the short straw on the washboard often enough to dread it.

Together they carried their equipment to Joy's screened-in back porch, which was half as big as the cabin itself. She flipped on the light and began fighting with the muddy zipper of her coveralls. She had tried using buttoned coveralls, but Gotcha Passage had a way of twisting off even the most carefully shielded buttons.

The zipper didn't budge.

Joy swore under her breath.

"Stuck?" Davy asked.

"Stuck."

"Hang on." His reply was muffled, because he was peeling out of everything but his normal underwear.

She didn't really notice the brawny, mud-streaked, nearly naked perfection of Davy's body. The only thing she felt when she looked at him was hope that his strong, blunt fingers would have better success than hers had with the stubborn zipper.

"Let's have a look," he said, turning her into the light. He frowned as he bent over the zipper. "Mud."

Joy's answer was a cross between a snarl and a laugh. "Davy, you have a gift for—"

"Restating the obvious," he cut in, finishing the sentence before she could. "Yeah, I know. Comes with being a cartographer, I guess."

With one huge hand he held the collar of her coveralls. With the other he grasped the small zipper tongue and tugged. His muddy fingers slipped. He tried again. Slipped again. He started talking to the zipper the way Fish talked to the generators.

Neither of them noticed the man walking up through the darkness beneath the cottonwoods toward the cottage.

SEVEN

Silently Gabe walked up to the back porch of the cottage a master of cursing called "Fish" had directed him toward. According to what the laconic yet fluently profane mechanic had told Gabe, Dr. Anderson was just coming back from several hours in Lost River Cave, last cabin on the left. That and "Pleasedtameetcha" had been the mechanic's only comment when Gabe had driven up and spoken to the first person he spotted. It wasn't that Fish was unfriendly; obviously his whole mind was concentrated on cussing the generator back to life.

It had worked, too.

From the yard all Gabe could see inside the screened porch was the silhouette of a huge, nearly naked man. He assumed that it was Dr. Anderson, director of exploration, Lost River Cave. The bare porch bulb cast a harsh glare over the man, emphasizing his height and powerful build.

Gabe decided that the heavily muscled Dr. Anderson would be an asset to any shot-putting or weight-lifting competition. Young and handsome, too. With a rather cynical smile, Gabe pictured the response of Dr. Anderson's female students to their muscular professor.

Then Dr. Anderson moved and Gabe saw the outline of a much smaller person still encased in caving gear. Illumination washed over the petite form, revealing short, pale blond hair and delicate features.

Gabe's body clenched like he'd just taken a kick in his gut. Even as he told himself that it was impossible, that he was hallucinating, **It can't be Joy!** he was reaching for the screen door. He let it bang shut behind him and glared at the nearly naked young giant who was tugging unsuccessfully at Joy's zipper.

"I'll take care of her," Gabe said.

It wasn't an offer. It was a command.

Davy took one look at the man who had appeared out of the night and instinctively backed away from Joy.

Her head snapped up when she heard the voice from her memories. She felt every bit of blood drain from her face as the father of her daughter walked toward her out of the night, his expression dark, unreadable. All she could think was, **I was supposed to have a week to get ready before I had to see him. Damn it, it's not fair. I need that week. I don't want him to see me like this. Tired, dirty, off balance.**

Vulnerable.

Even as the frantic thoughts stabbed at her, Joy all but laughed out loud at herself. Life never turned out the way you expected it to, and certainly life made no promises about being fair along the way. Surely she should have learned that lesson after Gabe's seduction, her pregnancy, and the helicopter crash that had killed her parents and left her floundering alone in a situation she'd never imagined in her worst nightmares.

She'd survived a lot in the past. She could survive one more unpleasant surprise. She had to. There was no other choice.

No matter what, she had to protect Kati.

Automatically Joy used the survival lessons she'd learned at such great cost in the past. She simply put away the storm of conflicting thoughts/emotions/memories and concentrated on the single instant she lived in. Now. All that mattered was **now**.

Later she would sort through the tangled mess that passed for her rational, reasoning mind. For now it was enough that she control herself, reveal nothing, and protect her vulnerable core—the ability to love that had barely survived her twentieth year.

Joy turned away from the hands reaching for her, hands she once had kissed in passion and still remembered in her dreams.

"That's not necessary, Mr. Venture." She

reached for a bottle of liquid soap that she kept over the washing machine. "I can take care of myself."

Gabe froze. Listening. Staring. The voice was the same one that spoke softly in his memories and whispered through his dreams.

The same, yet different.

Where emotion once had shimmered and enriched her voice to the point of music, there now was only neutrality and precision.

Her eyes were the same, a luminous gray, haunting in their clarity. Yet her eyes were also different. She had learned to draw veils over their beautiful transparency, shutting out the world.

Shutting out him.

Or perhaps they were shadows rather than veils, a legacy of disappointment and loss.

"Joy." His voice was soft, urgent.

She stiffened as though someone had slapped her. Gabe was the only one who had ever called her Joy. It had started the first time she'd met him. She'd been laughing at something a caver had said. She was still laughing when she turned at her father's call and went to meet Gabe.

He'd looked at her for a long moment and said, **With that smile, I can't call you Joyce. Hello, Joy. I'm Gabe Venture.**

"My name," she said distinctly to Gabe, "is Dr. Joyce Anderson."

Gabe was shocked into silence. When he'd

known her, she was Smith-Anderson and not a doctor. Automatically he glanced at her left hand. Even muddy as it was, there was no sign of a wedding band. But then, maybe she didn't wear rings while she was caving.

Joy turned her back on the light to conceal the tremor of her hand as she squeezed liquid soap onto the zipper.

"Davy, go take the first shower before you get chilled." The words were like Joy's voice, careful and very controlled. She tugged experimentally at the zipper's metal tongue. Nothing gave. "Just be sure there's enough hot water left for me or the next time you're stuck in Gotcha I'll leave you there."

Hearing the odd tension in Joy's voice, Davy hesitated.

The zipper came halfway down before the tab slipped from Joy's soapy fingers.

With the lightning quickness she had almost forgotten, Gabe picked up where she had left off. The zipper opened obediently beneath his dry, steady hand.

She bit back what she wanted to say and spoke quietly. "Thank you."

The words were as stiff as her back. She stepped away from Gabe without looking at him. She couldn't bear to look at him. He was standing too close and she was too tired, too frayed to control her conflicting emotions much longer.

Hate him. Hug him.

Scream at him. Soothe the lines of exhaustion from his face.

Take a piece of muddy rope and strangle him. Kiss him like the world was burning down around her.

The tug-of-war was endless. The result was an emotional limbo of neutrality, an unstable calm in the center of a hellish storm. It was where she'd lived for seven years.

With luck Gabe would be out of her life again before the storm tore loose. At the very least she had to be alone with the storm, nothing but the walls and the unspeaking night to witness the emotions raging beneath Dr. Anderson's calm exterior.

Joy noticed that Davy was still hovering at the edge of the porch. She controlled her irritation at his protectiveness by reminding herself that Davy had no way of knowing who this strange man was, much less what intimate strangers she and Gabe were.

"Davy, this is Mr. Venture." As Joy spoke, she stripped out of her mud-encrusted coveralls, revealing almost equally muddy layers of cloth beneath. "He'll be with us for a few days while he updates an old magazine piece on Lost River Cave."

"Gabe, not Mr. Venture," Gabe corrected as he

held out his hand to the younger man. "And I'll be here several weeks, not a few days. I hope to find enough material to do a book on the art and science of caving. There hasn't been a virgin cave like this to study since Lechugilla."

Davy looked at his muddy palm and hesitated before offering to shake the other man's hand.

"I've done my share of miles on hands and knees," Gabe said, smiling. "A little dirt won't offend me."

Davy shook hands. "Mr. Venture, Gabe, pleased to—" The automatic flow of polite words stopped abruptly. "Are you Gabriel Venture, the writer?"

"Guilty."

"Son of a bitch! I can't believe it!" Davy's smile widened into a big grin as he shook Gabe's hand. "I'm a real fan. You're the only natural history writer I've ever found who was as accurate as he was exciting to read. The story you did on the discrepancies between aerial and foot surveys of that peak in the Andes was nothing short of brilliant."

"Thanks. It nearly killed me."

"Yeah? What happened?"

"Landslide hammered us right off a cliff face. I was lucky. My guides weren't."

Davy winced in unspoken sympathy.

It went deeper than sympathy with Joy. Eyes

closed, she fought against remembering the cold, spinning nausea that had hit her when she heard over the radio that the famous adventurer and writer, Gabriel Venture, had barely escaped death in the Andes and might be crippled for life. She'd been shaken by an irrational pain, a helpless sharing of what it must have been for someone like Gabe to lie in a hospital bed in a foreign country, wondering if he would ever walk again.

She'd forgotten the incident until now. She'd shoved it into the Dead Issues file under **Gabriel Venture, hated lover**. Her connection with him was like her parents' sudden death—an experience she'd finally, painfully, learned to accept without understanding it at all.

So she'd stopped asking questions, stopped trying to cope in any way at all except to get through one second, one minute, one hour, one day at a time; and if the Dead Issues file bulged and churned like two pigs fighting in a sack, well, too bad. She had a life to lead and she couldn't do it with her eyes fixed on the past.

"You okay, Dr. Joyce?" Davy's concern was clear in his voice. "Maybe you better let me see your arm before I go."

Gabe turned swiftly, looking at Joy with searching green eyes. She was very pale beneath the rich cave mud streaking her face. "What's wrong with your arm?"

"Nothing a good night's sleep won't cure."

She bent over, sending blood back into her face as she unlaced her boots and stacked them to one side. She stepped out of her coveralls and stuffed them into a washtub to be rinsed off with Davy's discarded caving clothes.

Davy hesitated by the door, obviously wanting to help Joy but not knowing how.

"Shower," she reminded him. "Solar heating doesn't work worth a damn by moonlight."

"Right you are." He half saluted, relieved to return to their normal kind of conversation, a combination of scientific exchanges and wry jokes. "I'll get my towel and be right back."

"Your towel is behind you in the bin," she said as she unzipped her damp, long pants. "Right where you left it last night. Good thing the desert is dry, or your towel would have mold on it thick enough to shave."

Gabe stood very still, literally frozen by the emotions slicing through him as he confronted the fact that Joy and this muscular young man were . . . close. Rationally, Gabe knew that he'd forfeited any rights to Joy years ago, when he'd gone out on assignment without knowing if she was pregnant. The irrational part of his mind—the primitive, deepest, strongest part of him—raged that she had no right to stand around on her porch at night with a brawny, nearly naked, potently masculine student.

After a few minutes of rummaging around in

the bin filled with odds and ends of clothing, Davy found his towel and trotted off into Joy's cottage. Within seconds the sound of the shower filtered out into the back porch.

"Does he live with you?" Gabe asked, his voice as coolly neutral as the moonlight pouring over the empty land.

Ruthlessly Joy clamped down on her first impulse, which was to tell Gabe to go to hell and take his questions with him. But doing that would invite an argument. Right now her emotions were too wild, too reckless, for her to risk a fight.

"No more than the rest of my graduate assistants," she said.

"The professor and students that play together stay together?" he asked sardonically.

"Davy's shower is plugged solid." She glanced up at Gabe. Her eyes were like Lost River Cave's deepest pools. Cold. "Why don't you go use your caustic tongue on it?"

"Joy—"

"Dr. Anderson or Dr. Joyce. Take your pick." Then, despite her effort not to speak, more words tumbled out. "No one calls me Joy anymore."

Gabe tried to bite back the angry words he wanted to say, but he wasn't completely successful. He was desperate for sleep and cut to his soul by the contempt that seethed just beneath the neutral surface of Joy's voice.

He should have been prepared for the possibility that she'd still be at Lost River Cave.

He wasn't.

"I can see why no one calls you Joy. You've turned into a sharp-tongued, flat-lipped woman who has about as much joy in her as a squeezed lemon."

His words cut her like razors, a pain more intense than any she'd known since he'd left her.

"Thank you," she said huskily, hating him, wanting to hurt him as badly as he'd once hurt her, as badly as he still was hurting her.

"Don't thank me—"

"Oh, but I must," she cut in, her voice vibrating with emotion. "You made me everything I am today."

For a few instants her eyes were no longer veiled. Gabe looked into their transparent depths—and for the second time that night felt like he'd been kicked in the stomach.

He'd wondered many times what might happen if he saw Joy again. He'd imagined anger, laughter, shock, sensuality, tears, elation. He'd imagined every emotion but the one he saw staring out of her eyes right now.

Hatred.

EIGHT

Emotion shook Gabe, a fury he hadn't felt since he'd discovered that Joy had aborted their baby. He took a swift step forward and opened his mouth to tell her what he thought of a lying bitch who had pleaded with him to stay with her because she loved him so much, and then she got rid of his baby as soon as she found out he wasn't rich.

Joy stepped away from Gabe so quickly that she stumbled, hitting her bruised arm against a shelf. A stifled cry tore from her throat. The room spun around her in a dark haze of pain. She would have fallen if he hadn't caught her by her upper arms.

"My arm," she said raggedly.

Instantly he shifted his grip to her waist. She sagged against him and fought past the nausea that had come on the heels of agony.

"Joy, sweetheart," he said against her hair, cradling her in his arms, rocking her gently against his chest. "God, I'm sorry. I didn't mean to hurt you."

She couldn't answer. She just leaned dizzily against his chest for a few moments until the room stopped spinning. When she breathed in deeply, his scent went through her like a shock wave, dragging widening rings of memories in its wake.

He'd made love to her so gently, so wildly, so perfectly. That was the way she had loved him, gentle and wild, everything she had to give.

Then he'd walked away without a backward look, never calling, never writing, tearing out her heart and leaving her to bleed in silence.

Weakly Joy pushed away from Gabe.

"Are you sure?" he asked. "You're white as salt."

"Let go of me."

His hands hesitated for a moment before they relaxed. But he watched her carefully, ready to catch her if she looked dizzy again.

"What happened to your arm?"

"I tripped."

With that she turned away from him, reaching for her familiar routine, pulling it around her like darkness around a cave, concealing everything inside a perfect, timeless midnight. Her fingers plucked at the waistband of her long leggings. She had the cloth partway down over her hips before she realized what she was doing.

She was accustomed to stripping down to her muddy underwear with anywhere from one to a dozen other people crowding around, jostling and cracking jokes about the state of their clothes and their aching muscles, making bets on whether the washer would quit on the first or third cycle. When Gabe had gone caving with her, it had been the same—no hesitation, no useless modesty, nothing but the camaraderie that was unique to cavers.

It was different now.

But to show that would be like announcing to Gabe that his mere presence disturbed her in ways that had nothing to do with hatred. Like his voice calling **Joy, sweetheart. Oh God, I'm sorry. I didn't mean to hurt you.**

Once she would have sold her soul to hear those words from his lips. That was years ago, centuries ago, when she was young and believed in life and love. Now she believed only in what she could touch—Lost River Cave's unearthly beauty and Kati's small arms wrapped around her in a big hug.

With numb fingers Joy peeled off her muddy pants and went to work unzipping the equally damp, gritty pullover. She worked her right arm out without difficulty, but not the left. She couldn't control a wince of pain.

Instantly Gabe reached for her, wanting to help.

"No." She pushed away his hands with cold fingers, her voice as exhausted as her eyes.

"Let me help you." Then he added softly, "I won't hurt you, sweetheart."

The words echoed in Joy's mind, returning to her slightly changed, a voice from seven years in the past reassuring a shivering, demanding, passionate virgin. **It's all right. I won't hurt you, sweetheart.**

She looked into Gabe's pale green eyes, saw them darken, heard his sudden intake of breath, and knew that he was remembering the same words and the same wild afternoon when he and she had burned together as hotly as the sun.

"No," she repeated, and she met his eyes without flinching.

"Joy—"

"Don't touch me." Her voice was low, raw.

The sound of Davy bumping into a piece of furniture in the living room and swearing roundly reminded Joy and Gabe that they weren't alone. Moments later, wrapped in a blue bath towel that was as oversized as he was, Davy walked into the screened porch.

"Arm stiffen up?" he asked, seeing that Joy wasn't out of her wet clothes yet.

She nodded.

"Need some help?" Davy asked.

"Please," she said, turning toward Davy with obvious relief. "If you could just peel off the top layers, I can handle the rest."

With a feeling halfway between helplessness and anger, Gabe watched Davy's big hands reach for Joy.

"No point in you getting all muddy again," Gabe said roughly, stepping between Joy and Davy. "Which arm hurts, Dr. Anderson?"

Joy looked into her former lover's hard green eyes and knew that she could let him undress her or she could start an argument that would end up telling Davy exactly why she didn't want Gabriel Venture's hands anywhere near her.

"My left." Joy's voice was as expressionless as her face.

"Will you be able to handle cooking dinner?" Davy asked, looking anxiously at her pale skin.

"I'll take care of it for her," Gabe said.

Davy heard the intensity beneath the simple words and looked uneasy.

"Don't worry," Gabe added, forcing himself to smile easily at Davy. "I'll take good care of her. Joy—Dr. Anderson—and I go back a long way. She was closer than my right hand when I did the first **Planet Earth** article on Lost River Cave. Couldn't have done it without her."

"No shit—I mean, no kidding?" Davy whistled softly. "She never said a word to us about that, and your article on Lost River Cave is required reading for anyone who wants to get into that cave."

"Mr. Venture is making a mountain out of a molehill," Joy said with forced casualness. "Many people helped him with that article."

"You're too modest," Gabe said dryly.

Before she could answer, he was deftly removing her muddy pullover.

"She sure is," Davy said, opening the back door and letting it slam behind him. "Thanks for the help tonight, Dr. Joyce. I get three times as much done when you're along."

"Any time."

Davy's hopeful voice floated back from the darkness. "Tomorrow?"

"We'll both go with you," Gabe answered.

"Great!"

Whatever Joy might have tried to say was muffled as he deftly eased her head through the opening of her pullover without disturbing her left arm, which was still covered in clinging, muddy cloth. Before she could brace herself for the pain that would inevitably come when she pulled her bruised arm free, she realized that it was already done.

"There, that wasn't too bad, was it?" Gabe's voice was subtly challenging.

"It didn't hurt at all," she said through stiff lips. "Thank you."

"You're welcome." He dumped the outer layers on the floor and eyed the mesh underwear that was every bit as damp and almost as muddy as the rest had been. No zippers. No buttons. Just a stretchy fabric and a tight fit. "The next part won't be so easy. In fact, unless you let me cut it off you, it will hurt like hell."

"Cut it? No way!" Her tone said she thought he was crazy. "For a broken arm, maybe. For a bruise, never." With a grimace she bent at the waist and held both arms out over her head. "Do you know how much this high-tech gear costs?"

His answer was lost in Joy's gasp as he peeled off the undershirt in a single smooth motion, leaving her standing in the cool air wearing nothing more than the practical black cotton underwear she'd discovered was perfect for caving.

In the instant before she turned away, Gabe saw the graceful curves of the woman who had haunted his dreams for thousands of nights. Like her eyes and her voice, her body was the same and yet different from his memories. The swell of breasts and waist and hips was still firm, still begging to be caressed by a man's hands. Yet there was a difference. She was no longer a girl. Nothing of her body was unfinished, nothing was in transition. All past promises had been fulfilled. She was every inch a woman.

And she couldn't turn her back on him fast enough, couldn't pull on a cotton shift quickly enough. She was acting like he was no more than a rude stranger who had wandered in off the desert.

It really pissed him off.

"You can stuff the blushing maiden act. I've already seen what's under the muddy bra and pants."

Joy's only answer was a stiffening of her body that made him regret that he hadn't waited until morning to meet "Dr. Anderson." Jet lag and exhaustion had reduced his normal self-control to little more than impulse and apology. Yet worse than any physical weariness was something deeper, much more painful.

After seven years all that remained of his haunting love affair with Joy was hatred.

What did you expect, fool? She's the one who flushed your child. Remember?

Joy turned around in time to see the contempt on Gabe's face. It confirmed the fear that had burned in her for seven years. He'd never cared for her at all, not really. For him she'd been just a passing amusement, an unsophisticated native of New Mexico's desert boondocks.

And easy, so easy, falling into his arms like sunlight.

Yet was that any reason for him to hate her? The only crime she'd committed was being naive enough to fall in love with a man who was completely out of her league—**the great Gabriel Venture**.

Joy didn't realize that she'd spoken the last four words aloud until she heard the echoes of her own contempt and outrage quivering in the small porch.

"What did you expect?" she asked.

Before Gabe could answer, she smiled with a cynicism that surprised him.

"No, don't bother to tell me," she said. "You expected the green little native to fall all over herself again on the way to your bed. April Fool, big shot. The little girl grew up."

"Little girl? Bullshit. You were twenty, just three years younger than me."

Joy didn't answer. It was the truth. It just wasn't a truth that she spent a lot of time remembering. Just as she didn't like to remember how she'd begged him to take her when he'd hesitated.

"I didn't even know you were still at Lost River Cave," Gabe continued, "so how the hell could I expect anything from you? As for being in my bed, when I want a female viper I'll go out in the desert and get one."

"Be sure to get her young, before she grows teeth," Joy shot back, stung by the knowledge that Gabe had come back for the cave, not for her. "Otherwise you'll wake up with fangs in your throat."

"You'd like that, wouldn't you?"

"Actually, I'd prefer that you not wake up at all."

Even as the furious words left her mouth, Joy knew that they weren't true. She remembered her pain when she found out that Gabe had been badly injured, dangling at the edge of death in a foreign hospital. Whatever else he was or wasn't, whatever his accomplishments and failings, this man was the father of her child.

"I'm sorry." Her voice was like her. Empty. "I didn't really mean that."

"You could have fooled me."

"Not as easily as you once fooled me," she retorted. When she saw anger burn across his cheekbones, she said almost desperately, "Gabe, this has to stop. We both have a job to do, and to get it done we'll have to go down into Lost River Cave together. If we're slashing away at each other, it won't work. You can't go down into darkness with someone you don't trust."

"Oh, I trust you all right." His voice was cold enough to burn. He was thinking about the abortion she'd purchased with his money. Not being a single mother must have made it a lot easier for her to work her way up the academic ladder. "You won't let anything personal get in the way of something important like your career."

Joy's eyes narrowed. She started to speak, but

he was still talking, still ripping strips from her pride.

"Without me," he said distinctly, "you don't have a snowflake's chance in hell of getting more money for Lost River Cave, **Dr.** Anderson. When I'm on a rope down there, I know you'll take very good care of me."

"How odd that you see me only in terms of yourself."

"What does that mean?"

"It means that you're exactly what you accused me of being—someone who puts career first and everything else last."

Her words slid through his angry defenses like light slicing through darkness. But unlike darkness, Gabe felt pain.

It made him furious that she of all people had the ability to hurt him. She was the woman who had casually aborted his child. She knew nothing about love.

Who was she to lecture him?

"But none of that matters," she continued, her voice unnaturally calm. "We're adults. We should be able to control ourselves long enough to get this job done."

Gabe bit back any reference to her abortion. If he opened that subject, he damn sure wouldn't be able to keep the discussion civilized, much less adult. It had happened years ago. He should be over it—and her.

But he wasn't.

"Does that mean you trust me?" he asked after a long silence.

"As long as it's directly related to your career, yes," she said, turning away wearily.

For the first time Gabe saw the blue-black bruise spreading from Joy's elbow to her shoulder. He forgot the angry words crowding his tongue and remembered the moment when his fingers had closed over her arms and she had cried out in pain.

"Joy." His voice was hoarse with exhaustion and helpless agony that the beauty of the past should have become so ugly in the present. "Your arm."

Surprised, she looked down at herself. The firestorm of her emotions had overwhelmed the pain signals from her bruised flesh.

"Is there any ice inside?" he asked. "I'll get a towel and wrap—"

"Don't bother," Joy said, walking away from him, back into the peace and loneliness of her empty cottage. "I was bruised long before you arrived."

The door to the house swung shut, leaving Gabe alone on the porch. Exhaustion, pain, and futility closed around him more darkly than any night.

NINE

The next morning Gabe walked through blinding desert light to the shadowed heat of Joy's back porch. Fourteen hours of sleep had restored his usual self-discipline, even though the hours had been as riddled with dreams as Lost River Cave was with hidden passages. But unlike the cave, there had been no beauty in his dreams, simply shapes looming out of darkness, voices calling his name in anguish and passion and regret.

And hatred.

That was a new voice added to old dreams, a cold thread of darkness stitching through re-membered light.

Deliberately Gabe turned his attention away from his emotions and toward his work. Four people were already in the screened porch and spilling out into the yard. One of them was Joy. She was sorting through caving gear and teasing Davy about needing whale oil to get through Gotcha.

The honey-and-sunlight flash of Joy's short hair was like a beacon to Gabe's eyes. With an effort he controlled a rush of warring emotions. He was a professional. An adult. It was time for him to pull his head out of the painful past and concentrate on the present.

His work was all he had left.

He paused, gathering first impressions of the people he would go caving with and write about. Davy looked as big in daylight as he had in darkness. Though only a few inches taller than Gabe, the grad student was nearly half again as thick. His broad, blunt hands made the climbing ropes look frail.

The young woman standing next to Davy came up to his jawbone and was as generously built for a woman as Davy was for a man. Like the black bikini she wore, the word "statuesque" barely covered the tall redhead's presence. Gabe hoped that she was keeping Davy's mind—and hands—off Joy. The redhead looked like all the woman any one man could handle, and then some.

The third person looked vaguely familiar. Medium tall, compact, wiry, athletic build, a face that was both shrewd and calm. It was the mechanic from last night, the one who had directed him to Joy's cottage. Gabe searched his memory for the man's name. **It's something odd for a** desert man—Waters? Finn? No, but close. Fish. That's it.

Fish was tinkering with a battery pack. Sweat gleamed on his naked back as he bent over a toolbox. He looked up as Gabe opened the porch door.

"Mornin', stranger." Fish stood and held out his hand. "Sorry I wasn't real sociable last night. That old generator can be right trying at times. Other one is even worse."

Smiling, Gabe shook Fish's hand. "I wasn't feeling real talkative myself. One way or another, I'd been on the road for seventy-three hours just to get here."

"Myanmar or Cambodia?"

"Yeah. Via the Philippines." He gave Fish a searching look. "How did you know?"

"Come in from halfway around the world once or twice myself when I was in the service." The skin around his brown eyes crinkled in an almost invisible smile. "Took damn near eighty hours the last time. That's when I decided being a world traveler was a mighty big pain in the butt. I mustered out, bought into a service station in Carlsbad, and commenced swearing at machines other than airplanes."

"He's real good at it, too," the tall redhead put in. "You ever want something talked to, you just holler for Fish."

"Now you know I never spoke poorly to nothing that didn't have it comin'," Fish drawled. He looked at Maggie. "You met Gabe yet?"

"Nope." She looked up from a pile of coveralls and smiled. "Hi."

"This here is Gabe Venture," Fish said. "Gabe, Maggie O'Mara." Fish winked at Gabe. "If you go to fallin' down in that cave, you just be sure this here gal is underneath when you land. She come factory equipped with some right nice cushions."

"Whisper it, Fish. Davy might hear," Maggie said. She looked over her shoulder to where Davy was carefully coiling ropes. "If that mountain of muscle fell on me, I'd flatten like a drop of water."

Davy smiled slightly but otherwise ignored the teasing.

Gabe held out his hand to Maggie.

"Are you really Gabriel Venture, the writer?" she asked, taking his hand. Her eyes were wide. Disbelief was clear in her voice.

"Disappointed?" he said.

"No way! I expected you to be old and ugly. You're a long way from either." Grinning, she looked at him with open approval.

"You're half right," Gabe said.

"Which half?"

"Both. I'm half old and half ugly. Looks like you got my shares of young and beautiful."

"Oh, I'm falling in love." Maggie gasped theatrically, staggered, and clutched the general area of her heart.

"Don't fall on me," Joy said crisply, stepping out of the way. "I don't have any cushioning to speak of."

Davy looked up suddenly. "Now that just isn't true." He gave Joy a brief, intense look before he went back to wrapping a rope. "Some cushions just aren't as **stuffed** as others."

Maggie turned quickly and confronted Davy, her fists on her firm hips. "Are you calling me overstuffed?"

He glanced up again, smiling. "Do I look like a man with a death wish?"

She feinted with her fist. He blocked it with his broad upper arm. Her fist smacked against his biceps. It was a teasing blow, hard enough to be felt but not hard enough to hurt.

"Someday, shrimp," she taunted, "I'll take you home to meet some really big men. Roy would make two of you, and he's my smallest brother."

Davy cocked a blond eyebrow at Maggie, handed her a tangle of rope, and said, "Since you aren't decorative, be useful."

Joy thought that she was the only one who sensed Maggie's flash of hurt at Davy's words. Then she turned and caught Gabe looking thoughtfully from Maggie to Davy.

Gabe's sensitivity surprised Joy. She didn't remember him as being aware of other people's emotional nuances—unless his family was involved. Or sex. Then he had an instinct as hypersensitive as a seismograph. Maybe that was why he was tuned in to Maggie. Maybe he wanted her.

When I want a female viper I'll go out in the desert and get one.

Be sure to get her young, before she grows teeth.

Maggie was fresh and young, the way Joy once had been.

The thought slashed through her, catching her unaware with its raw pain. Echoes of last night broke around her, cutting her with razor edges.

Sharp-tongued. Flat-lipped. As much joy in you as a squeezed lemon. Female viper.

"Don't listen to him, Maggie," Gabe said in a casual, teasing voice. "You're a knockout and Davy is just too tongue-tied to admit it."

Maggie didn't look up from the rope she was wrapping. "Nice try, but I know better." Her voice was almost casual. Almost, but not quite. "I've spent my whole life with five older brothers telling me what I look like. I know I'm 'overbuilt and underpretty.'" She hesitated and smiled up at Gabe almost shyly. "But thanks anyway. It was nice to hear."

Davy's intense blue eyes narrowed and he

looked at Maggie as though seeing her for the first time, hearing the wistfulness and sensitivity beneath the constant clowning that was her usual manner.

Gabe, too, heard the vulnerability in her voice. "You tell your brothers they wouldn't know pretty if it tripped them and laid them out flat. You're more than pretty, Maggie. As for being overbuilt," Gabe grinned, "I don't know a woman who wouldn't kill to be put together like you."

"Amen," Fish muttered.

"Such wonderful lies." Maggie sighed deeply, clowning again, but this time there was pleasure rather than wistfulness running through her voice. "Or maybe you've just been out in the wilds too long?" she teased, slanting a blue-green glance at Gabe.

"Don't slander him," Joy said. "Didn't you know he's a world-class expert on women? And his specialty is the barely twenty girls. A real connoisseur of them."

Joy heard her own words and all but winced at what they revealed. She would have to guard her tongue so that her bitterness wouldn't seep out like acid with every word she spoke. It wasn't Maggie's fault that Gabe was gentle with her and cold with his former lover. It wasn't Maggie's fault that she was young, stunning, and innocent, and that Joy was not.

So Joy smiled brilliantly, turned to face Gabe's glittering green eyes, and discovered just how angry her crack had made him. Her eyes stared back at him, as transparent as spring water—and as cold.

"I know you're very experienced in many areas," she said, speaking in a casual, low voice that belied the clear ice of her eyes, "but it's been a long time since you were in a cave, so I—"

"Six years, eleven months and thirty days," Gabe cut in.

He gave her a smile that lowered the temperature on the hot porch by about half. When he saw the look of surprise on her face echoed on Maggie's and Davy's, he half turned to them.

"Oh, yes," Gabe said softly, including everyone in his words without releasing Joy. "I remember to the exact day how long it's been. Lost River Cave was a unique experience for me."

"Why?" Maggie said. "I mean, you've been **everywhere.**"

He answered without looking away from Joy. "Yes. I've climbed some of the world's tallest mountains until I blacked out from lack of oxygen. I've nearly drowned in the warm storms of some very exotic seas. I've come close to succumbing to the hot seductions of a few deadly jungle flowers. But I have never been as fooled by anything as I was by the transparency of Lost River Cave's waters. So pure, so perfect, so innocent, seeming no deeper than my hand." The line of his mouth was grim. "But if you believe that innocent, sweet, deceptive surface, you'll stumble in and drown. If you don't freeze to death first."

Fish gave Gabe a swift, shrewd glance and went back to tinkering with the battery box.

Joy saw the look and felt heat rise on her cheeks. Fish knew that Gabe was talking about exploring women as well as landscapes.

And so did she.

She supposed she deserved it for her crack about connoisseurs and twenty-year-olds. The fact that her words were true didn't make the comment any less acid.

But he had no right to call her deceitful and cold. She'd never lied to him, and Kati was living proof of a heat that still haunted Joy's dreams.

"Since you're aware that what little you know about Lost River Cave isn't trustworthy," Joy said into the silence, "you won't object to being treated as a total novice."

"Would objecting do any good?" Gabe asked.

"No."

His smile was a razor slash of white. "Then by all means, **Dr.** Anderson, teach me whatever you think you can."

Davy looked up sharply, disliking Gabe's tone. "Why don't I show Gabe the ropes?" he said to

Joy. "We can catch up with you later in the cave. Or maybe you should stay here this morning. Your arm must be giving you fits."

Gabe remembered the instant when he'd grabbed Joy and she gasped in pain. He turned to her with a swift, almost violent movement. "Is it still bothering you? Didn't you put any ice on it?"

"There wasn't any."

"Let me see your arm."

"It's fine."

"The hell it is," he said. "I'll have a look at it, Dr. Anderson, or I'll know the reason why. If you think I'm trusting my life on a rope with a belayer whose arm is half dead, you're—"

"I'm not a fool, Mr. Venture," she cut in. She pushed up the sleeve of her loose gauze shirt. "I wouldn't go caving at the risk of someone else's life. Even yours."

Gabe swallowed his response to her last words and looked carefully at her arm. The bruise that had seemed so huge last night looked much better this morning. Without the added dark streaks of mud and the livid color that came from cold, it was obvious that the bruise wasn't serious. She would be able to go caving safely. The blue-black area was barely half the size of his palm.

What made seeing it like a blow to Gabe was the fact that there were two blurred yet unmistakable bars where his fingers had closed over the bruise, further damaging the tender flesh. He'd only meant to help her stand up, but instead he'd hurt her.

Very delicately he stroked his fingertips over the discolored skin, seeking any hard knots that would point to true injury.

There weren't any.

He cupped the bruise gently against his palm, restraining Joy with a hand on her wrist when she would have flinched away.

"I'll be careful of you," he said calmly, watching her gray eyes, seeing the pupils expand, sensing the sudden intake of her breath. "I just want to see if it's hot." He ran first his palm, then the back of his hand, then his fingertips down her arm from shoulder to wrist. "Feels fine," he said, his voice husky. Then, too softly for anyone but her to hear, "Very fine."

Joy felt her pulse accelerate and knew that in another instant he would feel it too. She wanted to snatch her wrist from his grip, but didn't. Yanking herself back from his touch would be as revealing as anything she could do except slap him . . . or return the caressing motion of his fingers with her own.

"Are you taking notes, Davy?" Her voice was light, her eyes icy. "This is how a connoisseur acts. Of course I'm not twenty, I don't have a shape other women would kill for, and I'm, shall we say, **shopworn,** but Mr. Venture is willing to overlook a few defects in the interests of civil intercourse."

When Joy heard the rage seething beneath each cold word, she wished she had bitten her tongue before she opened her mouth. She was afraid that the others would sense her fury and wonder why.

Gabe certainly had sensed it, and knew precisely why. Yet despite the answering contempt in his eyes, his touch remained gentle on her wrist and arm.

She had a crazy impulse to tell him that she understood, that she knew he wouldn't have grabbed her arm last night if he'd seen the bruise. But saying that would reveal too much to him.

And to the other people.

She could fairly feel everyone's curiosity about her reaction to Gabe. In all the time she'd worked with them, she'd never showed anger, no matter what happened.

"Well," she said, "I'm afraid our secret is out." She rushed on before the surprise in his hard green eyes could translate into words. Forcing a wry smile, she looked over her shoulder at the other three people. "You see, Gabriel Venture and I struck sparks off each other seven years ago. Obviously that hasn't changed. But we didn't let it get in the way of caving then, and it won't get in the way now." She looked back at him. "Will it, Gabe."

It wasn't a question. It wasn't a demand. There was a wary overture in the softness of his name on her lips, and a silent, not quite defiant apology buried in her offer of half-truth and truce.

"Struck sparks." His smile was off center, hard. "Yeah, I guess you could say that. In bloody spades." He looked past her to the three people watching them. "The good doctor and I will probably fight like hell on fire from time to time. When we do, just take cover." He looked directly at Davy. "That way no one else will get hurt." Gabe held Davy's eyes for a long, measuring moment before the younger man looked away. "Isn't that right, **Joy**."

She sensed the same ambivalence in Gabe's soft-voiced offer of truce that there had been in hers, but his eyes were green stone. For some reason he was furious at Davy. She opened her mouth to assure Gabe that Davy hadn't meant to hurt Maggie with his words, then thought better of it. She didn't want to embarrass Maggie.

Joy decided to keep Gabe away from Davy until things cooled off. Davy didn't need to be distracted by the kind of icy male anger Gabe projected so easily, so devastatingly.

"Right, Mr. Venture," Joy said crisply.

"Gabe. Just Gabe."

The threat was soft and very clear, as hot as his fingers stroking her captive palm.

"Gabe," she said, her voice husky.

"That didn't hurt, did it?"

He caressed the softness of her palm and inner wrist until he felt the wild beating of her pulse beneath his fingertips.

She hated herself for the betraying race of her heartbeat beneath his touch. Part of her pulse rate came from anger, pure and hot. But not all of it. Joy was honest enough to admit it.

"Think of it as a little practice in the fine art of civil intercourse. You need it, Doctor," he said. "You need it bad."

She flushed, jerking away from Gabe's too-knowing touch.

Davy swore and took a quick step forward, only to collide with the even faster Fish.

"I think it's time to take cover, children," Fish said, deftly using Davy's momentum to head him in the direction of the Toyota. "Lots of room to hide in that old cave." He turned and gave Joy a level look. "Unless you changed your mind, Dr. Joyce?"

Joy knew that Fish was asking if she felt safe with Gabe.

Gabe knew it too, and it infuriated him. He turned on Fish with a poised speed that the combat-trained mechanic noted and understood. Even so, Fish didn't back up.

"Just take all the blunt instruments with you and we'll be fine," Joy said quickly, her voice determined and light. "We'll catch up with you in the Voices in ninety minutes."

Fish nodded. "Ninety minutes and counting. Grab your gear, boys and girls. We're leaving now."

He herded Maggie and Davy out the door. As he passed Gabe, Fish spoke in a low voice that Joy couldn't overhear.

"Luck, man. You'll need it. In the six years I've known her, ain't nothing male been able to get near her. Damn shame, too. That's a whole lot of woman going to waste."

TEN

Too surprised to do more than let Fish's parting words sink in, Gabe watched the mechanic walk to the Land Cruiser, herding Maggie and Davy ahead of him. When the vehicle drove away in a flurry of dust and grit, Gabe turned to look at Joy, hardly able to believe what Fish had told him.

Six years.

My God. Did I hurt her so badly that she refused to trust anyone after me?

Did she really mean it when she cried out her love in my arms?

Yet even as the questions came, he rejected them. He'd learned long ago that you can only trust what people **do**, not what they say. A woman in love doesn't casually have an abortion.

Joy had done just that.

When Joy saw the speculative expression on Gabe's face give way to contempt, she felt worn thin, exhausted, unable to continue the battle. It was hurting her too much.

She spoke before he could. She knew she

couldn't take any more verbal shots without revealing how very vulnerable she was. All the emotions she thought she'd overcome—love, hate, fear, fury—boiled up with each cutting remark he made. She was a breath away from losing control.

She'd felt like this after her parents died and she discovered that she was pregnant, abandoned by Gabe with no more notice than a check to pay for an abortion. Not even a few gentle lies about how he was sorry he couldn't be with her to help her. Nothing.

It had nearly destroyed her.

That was when the searing determination and comfort of hatred had come to her, driving out love. Finally she'd forced herself to leave behind the hate, because it threatened to eat away her very soul.

She'd wanted her unborn child to know only love.

Joy had never regretted her choice. Kati was worth every agonizing moment of her mother's ordeal. Rightly or wrongly, in love or in lust, Gabe had given Joy a beautiful child. If for no other reason than that, she had to stop tearing at him and at herself.

In the end it would be Kati who would lose more than anyone.

"Truce," Joy said raggedly, rubbing her arms like she was cold. "Either that or go caving with

Fish right now. I'm not as cruel as you, Gabe. I can't survive this kind of battle."

His face hardened even more. He opened his mouth, a harsh retort on his lips. The words died when he noticed the shadows of exhaustion and lines of strain on her face, a fury of emotions she could no longer conceal. She'd never looked less like the name he had given her—Joy.

"Please," she said, hating the tremor in her voice but not able to control it. "No more."

Shocked by the tears she felt closing her throat and burning behind her eyes, she turned away swiftly. She hadn't cried since she'd looked at the tiny, perfect scrap of life that was her baby and realized that Kati would never have grandparents or a father to tease and love, cherish, and protect her.

"Which is it?" she asked, her voice raw. "Cutting me or going caving?"

"Are you going to stop clawing at me or are you suggesting just a one-way truce?"

"It hasn't been deliberate." Unable to meet his eyes, she sorted through her caving gear. "I guess there's more of the betrayed lover left in me than I realized."

"Betrayed?" he asked, his voice as harsh as his face. "I never promised you I would stay. And when I found out—"

"You're right," she cut in, just wanting the anger to end. Or at least not to be spoken aloud.

"You're right. There was no betrayal. You delivered exactly what you promised me."

Nothing.

Though neither one spoke, the word hung between them like a water drop suspended from a stalactite, shivering before the moment of release.

Gabe swore softly, violently, a single word that slipped past his control. "**Fuck**."

"I'm sorry," she began, "I didn't mean—"

"No more," he interrupted. "Your so-called apologies are worse than your insults."

Despair darkened Joy's eyes. It wasn't going to work. They couldn't say three words without slashing at each other.

And what would happen when Kati returned? When Kati grew up and Joy told her who her father was, would her daughter's only memory be of a man who hated her mother?

"Gabriel," she said desperately, "what do you want from me? What can I do to make you hate me less?"

His first thought was of the hunger that still swept through him, memories of what it had been like to feel Joy moving in his arms. Then he remembered the I-love-you lies, the baby she'd refused to have. He wanted to strike out at her, to wound her as deeply as she'd wounded him by rejecting his child.

Then he saw Joy's despair and knew that somehow he'd hurt her more than he ever realized.

Just as she'd hurt him.

Even though he'd never said he would stay with her or marry her—in fact hadn't even said that he loved her—despite the lack of promises, when he'd left Joy he'd cut her to her soul.

Is that why she aborted our baby? Revenge? Did I take a young woman's love and twist it into hate?

Suddenly he felt old, tarnished, spent. The despair in Joy's clear eyes was echoed in his own.

"What happened is in the past," he said, his voice hoarse. "There's nothing either of us can do about it now. Except live with it."

She wanted to cry out **What have I done to make you hate me?** but didn't have the strength to fight Gabe anymore. It was enough that for a moment he had looked at her with sadness rather than contempt in his eyes.

"Then let's see if we can't create something now that's better than the past," she said wearily. "No matter what did or didn't happen between us, I respect your ability to share new worlds with people through your writing."

Gabe looked into Joy's bleak gray eyes and felt an impulse to comfort her, even though anguish and anger still made his heart beat hard and fast.

"And I," he said softly, "respect the expertise

that has made New Mexico's Dr. J. Anderson one of the foremost speleologists in the U.S."

Surprise showed clearly on Joy's delicate face.

"Oh yes," Gabe said. "I finally did what I should have done the instant I accepted the assignment—my homework."

If he'd done it sooner, he would have guessed who Dr. J. Anderson was, no matter that she had dropped the Smith from her name.

If he'd known ahead of time that Joy was still at Lost River Cave, she wouldn't have been able to get past his guard so quickly, so painfully. And he wouldn't have been able to get past hers.

It would have been easier that way. For both of us.

But he didn't say that aloud, because it would have shredded the fragile threads of the truce they were both trying to weave from the ragged betrayals of the past.

"The package my editor sent me was very impressive," Gabe said. "You've had articles published in the most prestigious scientific journals on two continents, including a monograph on the effects of differing ratios of sulfuric acid and carbon dioxide on solution rates in the limestone of the Guadalupe Mountains."

Joy waited, too surprised to speak.

"Your work is the scientific cornerstone of a new understanding of how a certain type of cave is formed," he continued, "and how long it might take similar caves to develop. Then there's the treatise you did on deducing paleoclimates in the Southwest through analysis of Lost River Cave's formations. I'm told that is fast becoming known as the definitive work on cave formations and ancient climates."

She allowed herself to breathe. "I've been fortunate to work with dedicated people."

"And they've been fortunate to work with you."

She moved uncomfortably. "You're looking at me like you don't know me."

"In many ways, I don't." The Joy of Gabe's memories had been very intelligent; that was a big part of her fascination for him. She'd loved the cave, loved exploring and learning, but she hadn't had the drive or unflinching discipline the last seven years had brought out in her. "What you've done is very impressive," he said simply. "Your parents must be proud of you."

The pain that darkened Joy's eyes lasted only an instant, but it was long enough for Gabe to see it.

"My parents are dead." She turned back to her caving equipment.

"I'm sorry. I didn't know."

He hesitated, wondering if their deaths had been recent, if that was what had taken the laughter from her. The death of his own father had shaken Gabe. He still missed him. He always would. So much of childhood died with a parent. Joy had no brothers or sisters to share memories of those early years with. Gabe had his older brother, his port in many storms, and his mother's welcoming hugs whenever he managed to get home.

He couldn't imagine how it would feel to be totally alone.

"It must be very hard for you," he said slowly. "Was it . . . recent?"

"They died ten days after you left Cottonwood Wells." Joy hoped she kept her voice even, but doubted it. "Helicopter crash. Afterward . . . I changed my name. I wasn't the same person."

The sound of Gabe's quick intake of breath was clear in the silence. Without thinking, he touched Joy's cheek with gentle fingertips, but his emotions were reeling. **My God, to lose your first lover one week and your parents the next.**

No wonder she felt abandoned, betrayed. Life had turned on her and knocked her flat—and then had rolled over her again for good measure with a pregnancy she wasn't emotionally or financially equipped to survive.

"I'm so sorry," he whispered, regretting more than the death of two people he'd respected and liked. "Why didn't you write me? I would have helped you."

Yet even as he heard his own words, he wondered what else he could have done beyond what he'd already done—leave a check with his brother and Dan's telephone number with Joy. By the time mail would have caught up with him on the Orinoco, Joy's parents would have been dead for months and the abortion an accomplished fact.

"Somehow," he whispered as much to himself as to her, "I would have helped you."

Her only answer was a short, harsh laugh as she remembered the check for an abortion. "No thanks. I'd had all of your 'help' that I could survive."

She sensed Gabe's anger in the sudden clenching of his hand and the stiffening of his body. She looked up and saw rage darkening his face and making his eyes glitter like cut glass.

"The truce won't work if we talk about the past," she said painfully. "Somehow we both feel we were wronged. Well, too bad, how sad, life's a bitch and then you die. We'll just have to pull up our socks and get over it. Or we'll have to call it quits on Lost River Cave. Take your pick, Gabe. I won't talk about the past if you won't."

"Just a mutual professional love feast? I admire your work and you admire mine?"

"Love feast? **Love?** The Great Gabriel Venture? Ain't hardly likely, cowboy," she drawled. "Would you believe an armed truce?"

"Would you believe a bridle on the bitchy repartee? Or are you pushing me to put on the bridle for you?" he asked coolly, looking at her mouth.

A recent memory quivered between them—Joy trembling with something more than anger as he stroked her soft wrist and palm.

She flinched away from both the memory and the man. Taking a deep breath, she worked to damp down the rage that had come when Gabe used the word **love**.

The sensual threat in him was vivid, as hot as her own fury.

Too many memories whispering to her, telling her that she'd responded to this man before. He'd been the man who explored the secrets of her virginal body.

Perhaps she could still respond to him.

Perhaps she could finally escape the numbness in her core, the utter absence of sexuality that had made it impossible to love another man, and had ensured that Kati would always be what her mother had been—a lonely-only child.

The possibility of another child was as dazzling as it was terrifying to Joy, because it meant being Gabe's lover again. She didn't think she could survive his sensuality any better than she could his contempt.

Yet, somehow, she had to get along with him.

She'd endured too much to get where she was today. She wouldn't let it all go to hell simply because she couldn't control either her antagonism or her sexual response to her former lover.

"You don't want me, so please don't play this kind of power game." Her voice was quiet, ragged, as she looked into the green eyes that were too close, too familiar, dreams and memories combined. "No matter what you do to me, or I do to you, it won't change what happened when you left Cottonwood Wells. What we do can only affect this instant, **now**, and the future of a place that is very special to me."

She drew a long, jerky breath and made the only offer she could to appease Gabe, even though the thought of missing out on the last weeks of Lost River Cave made tears gather in her eyes.

"I'll leave Cottonwood Wells," she said huskily, "and I won't come back until you're gone."

He saw the tears that she fought so hard to hide and knew how much the offer had cost her.

"Christ, you really hate me, don't you?" he asked hoarsely. "Lost River Cave is your life, yet you'll walk away from your last chance to explore it just to avoid being around me."

"And you can't look at me without wanting to hurt me."

Her voice was as empty as her eyes. Too spent

to say or do anything more, she waited for his decision.

He saw the soul-deep weariness in her that mirrored his own. Whatever he'd hoped for when he flogged himself halfway around the world to rush back to Cottonwood Wells, it hadn't been what he'd found.

Fury. Hatred. Despair.

Anguish.

Well, fool, what now? And don't bother bitching about life's little surprises. The men who screamed for two thousand feet before hitting bottom would be glad to trade surprises with you.

Besides, look at it from her point of view. You made love to a virgin and left without knowing if she was pregnant. Ten days later her parents died. Then she found out she was pregnant and you were way beyond reach. For this you expected her to throw roses at you when she saw you again? What would you have done in her place—pregnant, twenty, parents dead, nowhere to go, no one to turn to, no money and no way to earn any?

It wasn't a question Gabe wanted to answer. It cut him in places he didn't know could bleed.

He hadn't meant it to turn out this way. He hadn't meant to leave her alone in a world that didn't give a shit whether Joy survived or went under.

He hadn't known her parents would die.

He hadn't meant to hurt her like that.

Just one of life's lovely little surprises, like a landslide and a grave two thousand feet deep.

Broodingly he looked at the woman who waited in front of him, all her laughter quenched, not even a glimmer of hope to ease the exhausted lines of her face or soften the bleak clarity of her eyes. The young woman he'd made love to so long ago was dead, killed by time and circumstance and a lover who hadn't meant to be cruel. If he'd come halfway around the world to resurrect the sweetness and innocence of a past affair, then he was indeed a fool.

And if he made this woman pay for his folly a second time, he would never again be able call himself a man.

"Stay." His voice was like Joy's, flat and hopeless. "If I'd known that your parents died so soon after I left . . ."

He couldn't finish. He felt sick at what he'd unintentionally put Joy through. He regretted the abortion deeply, bitterly; but he no longer hated her for it, no longer felt so utterly betrayed. "We'll explore Lost River Cave together and we'll leave the past where it belongs. In a grave two thousand feet deep."

She shuddered visibly, caught as much by the echoes of agony in Gabe's voice as she was by his last words.

"We'll have to start all over," he said. "I haven't been in a cave since I left here seven years ago. Treat me like a novice and you won't go far wrong. Can you handle that?"

"Yes," she said huskily. Then, so softly that he almost didn't hear, she added, "Thank you."

"For what?"

"Letting me stay. I know you don't understand, but—"

"I think I do," he cut in roughly, watching her with eyes that were almost opaque, like jade, translucent without being clear. "Lost River Cave is all you have left of your childhood, your innocence. Life took everything from you except the cave's beauty, its mystery, its dreams condensed into incredible, living stone."

She searched his face like a stranger had appeared in place of the Gabriel Venture she thought she knew so well. "How did you know?"

"Because I feel the same way about Lost River Cave. But I'm damned if I know why."

A gentle kind of silence grew between them, as though they had both discovered themselves lost in the same place at the same time; intimate strangers. Joy had an irrational desire to comfort Gabe, as though he'd never hurt her, never abandoned her, never taught her to hate.

In a way, it was true. The person who had hurt her wasn't this tall, weary, jade-eyed man who radiated questions and pain and . . . loneliness. This was a man she didn't know.

Just as she was a woman he didn't know.

Maybe he never had known her. Maybe she never had known him either, never truly loved him. Maybe she'd simply loved a young woman's dream of love.

"Maybe you'll find out once we're down there," Joy said.

"What?"

"Maybe when we're down there you'll discover why Lost River Cave is special to you."

His off-center smile was as unexpected as his words had been. It was the smile of a man who had stopped running and only then realized that he'd run himself to exhaustion.

"That would be too much to expect of life," he said. "I'll settle for finding the same kind of beauty in Lost River Cave that I remember. That's all I want now. A memory that isn't a lie."

ELEVEN

The road to Lost River Cave's trailhead was nothing more than ruts winding over the rocky, rumpled skirt of the Guadalupe Mountains. Joy drove the rugged track with the same casual expertise she handled climbing ropes and carabiners.

Mesquite and prickly pear, agave and tall, bloomed-out stalks of sotol gave a sparse shade for the baking land. Not until the highest elevations of the mountains did spiny, spiky plants give way to bushy evergreens.

"Carlsbad Caverns is over there, about four miles away as the raven flies," Joy said, waving toward the south and west. "What we're driving over, and what makes up the Guadalupe range, is the remains of a huge reef complex that grew in late Permian times and through the Triassic and Jurassic."

"Translation?" Gabe asked, whipping out a palm-sized computer and taking notes with a stylus on its screen, using his own cryptic code.

"Some of the limestone formations that make up the Guadalupes—those are the same formations where all the local caves are found—are more than two hundred and fifty million years old."

"But the caves aren't that old, are they?"

"No. All that happened back then was that a series of fissures grew between the reef and the backreef. That's what we call Stage One of cave formation. Stage Two came when the sea retreated and the reef complex was buried by an outwash of debris from higher land. Groundwater riddled the limestone with cavities until it was like a sponge."

She glanced over and saw him frowning in concentration while he tried to take notes during the bumpy ride. She half smiled. This was a Gabe she remembered, fierce intelligence and concentration equally matched.

"That stage lasted until about a hundred and thirty million years ago," she said. "For the next forty million years, a shallow sea covered what we call the Delaware Basin today." She waved toward the flat, searing desert that spread out from the lower flanks of the mountains, indicating the basin. "Then the Laramide Orogeny—"

"I surrender," he interrupted.

She surprised both of them by laughing. "Sorry. Your articles are so technically accurate that I forget you aren't an expert. Let's just say that there was a round of mountain building about ninety-five million years ago. As a result, the land slowly rose for about the next forty million years. As it did, water sank through the fissures between the various parts of the reef—remember them?"

"I'm still with you. Running hard, but hanging in."

"The water picked up carbon dioxide from decaying plants, which turned the water into a dilute form of carbonic acid, which dissolved away some of the limestone, which meant that the spongework caves got bigger and started meeting each other. Then the land stopped rising and things started to get really complicated, cave formation wise."

He made a sound very close to a whimper. But he was smiling.

So was she.

"Let's just say that the hydrocarbons that had been buried beneath the reef along the way 'matured' into oil fields with the help of the heat from a big body of magma—molten stone—beneath the Delaware Basin," Joy said. "Then the basin tilted and the hydrocarbons migrated up and met the groundwater coming down, and at the same time the Guadalupes were on the rise again. Presto. Hydrogen sulfide forms, is dissolved, and becomes a nifty kind of acid that really goes to work on the limestone. This is hot acid, remember. All that magma roiling around down there like a giant stove. That's why we call the result of Stage Three thermal caves."

"Hydrogen sulfide." He clamped the writing stylus between his teeth and braced himself on the dashboard as the Jeep hurtled over a particularly rough spot. "Of rotten egg fame?"

"Same stuff."

"God, it must have stunk."

"If you could have gotten down to the caves, it wouldn't have bothered you. You'd have been dead long before you noticed the smell. No oxygen. We're talking a really, really different place than it is now. That's Stage Three cave formation, driven by geothermal heat."

Gabe went to work with the stylus again. "I'm listening."

"I know. That's why you're so good at what you do. You really listen."

He glanced up, but she was looking at the road, not at him.

"Somewhere between twelve million years ago and five million years ago, Stage Four got underway. That was when dilute sulfuric acid rose upward—driven by heat from below—and ate out huge rooms, and in doing so started a chemical reaction that made gypsum and feldspar and a host of more exotic things settle out of the hot soup. Still with me?"

He grunted.

"The Stage Four sulfuric acid caves cut across all three earlier stages of cave development."

"Wait," he said. "You mean you have all four stages of cave development happening simultaneously?"

"Yes and no. What happens is—"

"Did you publish a paper on it?" he interrupted quickly.

"That's one way of describing a doctoral dissertation."

"Good. I'll read the monograph. Anything else?"

"Just the usual ups and downs of the earth's crust and sea level, which means that sometimes various caves were actively growing and sometimes they weren't. When the water table dropped, leaving the solution cavities dry, groundwater percolating down from the surface decorated them."

She braked to a stop next to the battered Land Cruiser. Except for the other vehicle, there was nothing that looked worth investigating for miles in all directions.

"Did they break down?" Gabe asked.

"Nope. The trailhead begins here this week."

"This week?"

"We switch approaches once a week to avoid marking the cave's entrance."

"No unregistered visitors, is that it?"

She nodded. "Careless cavers or specimen collectors could destroy millions of years of growth in just a few hours. Not to mention lousing up our samples of pristine cave water. We're very careful of our cave."

"So you aim for zero-impact caving?" he asked as he got out of the Jeep.

"We aim, but realistically there's always some impact." She got out. "Even our breath adds chemicals and bacteria to the cave."

"Not to mention what your feet do."

"We've laid out paths with orange tape to keep everyone on the same trails, but . . ." She sighed. "The trails are over, through, around, and between virgin cave formations. In some parts of the cave, we take off our boots and put on rock-climbing slippers so that we don't damage the flowstone any more than absolutely necessary."

Gabe handed Joy her rucksack from back of the Jeep. "Minimum-impact caving, then," he said.

"Yes." But she was looking at the rugged slope ahead, not at him, and her look was filled with yearning.

"What are you seeing?" he asked softly.

"Lost River Cave was formed from the same thick limestone beds as Carlsbad Caverns,

Lechugilla, Slaughter Cave, Spider Cave, and all the others. We've discovered more than one hundred and fifty kilometers of cave in Lechugilla, and more than one hundred and thirty-seven in Lost River Cave." She watched the unforgiving landscape as though trying to see through it to the honeycombed limestone beds lying beneath. "I can't help believing that somehow, somewhere, someday, Lost River Cave will connect with its more famous cousins."

Gabe whistled. "That would be quite a story. Is there really a good chance of that?"

"There's nothing that makes it impossible. But finding the connection could take years, maybe even generations, of exploration to untangle the skein of these caves. I only have six more weeks."

In the short time Gabe had been in Cottonwood Wells, he'd heard the same words from every other caver. "The cutoff in funds is really driving all of you, isn't it?"

"If you mean do we spend every possible minute in the cave trying to wrap up projects and experiments that have been in the works for years, yes, the closing of the cave is a real goad for us."

"Is that why you and Davy or you and Fish have gone caving with just two of you?"

Joy hesitated, then shrugged. "Two is the absolute minimum number of people required to enter a cave safely. Three is better, because someone can stay with an injured caver while the third goes for help. Five people leaves a decent margin for error or accident. That's why we abandoned the lowest level. Just too dangerous with the number of people we have on hand."

"My editor will be sorry to hear that."

"If he wants to pony up an extra five thousand dollars a week, I'll see what I can do."

Gabe shook his head. "Not likely."

"Talk to Davy. He has a bunch of photos of the lowest level on his hard drive, plus the most exquisitely rendered map program for caves that I've ever seen."

Gabe made a mental note to do just that. "Where are we going today?"

"Down to the second level. As Lost River Cave goes, it's a safe level—open and relatively dry. There are several routes, but we'll take the long way. It doesn't have long vertical descents or deep water or any really tricky passages across slippery walls or breakdown. Once we're down on the second level, we'll be in touch by two-way radio with the others."

"Sounds good."

"Then let's do a final check of the gear."

Joy went through her rucksack quickly, checking off each item against a mental list. With automatic movements she repacked everything but her cave clothing into the heavyweight nylon rucksack, which could be slung over her shoulder or around her hips.

"No backpack for you?" he asked, reaching for his own stuff.

"Nope. When I'm climbing on a standing rope, I do better slinging the pack from my hips. Keeps my center of gravity where I want it—low and close to the rope."

As always, the warm caving clothes looked and felt insufferable under the desert sun. She wouldn't put on a single piece of it until she was ready to enter the cave. Right now it was bad enough just holding the clothing. She stripped to her bra and pants and a light gauze shift that had no sleeves and just enough fabric to be legal. Even that felt too hot.

When she turned toward Gabe, he'd peeled down to his briefs and well-used hiking shorts. His backpack was at his feet.

"Ready to go through my equipment?" he asked.

"You're sure you want to act like you've never been caving before? You're going to get awfully bored hearing what you already know."

He looked up and gave her a sad, off-center smile. "I've learned that I don't know nearly as much as I thought I did."

*I didn't know your parents had died. I'm
sorry, Joy. For so many things*.

But the words went no farther than his mind.
He'd promised to leave the past in a grave two
thousand feet deep. He would keep that promise.
It was the least he could do for the woman who
watched him with shadows and no laughter in
her clear gray eyes.

The regret in Gabe's voice made Joy ache. No
matter how intently she searched his eyes, his
face, the nuances of his expression, she could
find none of the contempt he'd shown for her
before. Bitterness, yes, but not focused on her.
Somehow the knowledge of her parents' death
had taken away his hatred of her.

She wanted to ask why that had made such a
difference to him, but didn't. She had no more
desire than he did to burn her fingers stirring
through the ashes of their mutual past.

A grave two thousand feet deep.

That's the way it had to be.

"All right." Joy drew a deep breath. "We'll go
through the checklist. Helmet?"

Gabe dug his helmet out from under a pile of
high-tech clothes and placed it in her hand.
When she saw the dents and gouges on its surface
she was too shocked to speak. She simply looked
up at him, eyes wide, horrified.

"What . . . ?" she couldn't finish.

"Landslide. Peru."

"My God." Her fingers trembled as she measured the damage to the tough helmet. "You're lucky to be alive."

"That's what they tell me."

Carefully she checked the helmet, ignoring the faint shiver of her hands. Despite the dents the helmet was in good shape. Nothing was cracked. Nothing pressed on the network of straps and padding that cushioned the skull. She looked thoughtfully at the leather chin strap and went to the Jeep.

"I've got an extra elastic strap," she said, rummaging in the glove compartment. "I'd rather you use it. That way if you get jammed descending a tight chimney, you can tip your head out of the helmet and there's no chance of strangling yourself."

"Elastic it is." He took the strap from her fingers. "Can you really strangle yourself on a helmet strap?"

She almost smiled at the change in his voice. This was the man she remembered—asking questions, assembling facts, transforming them into words and insights that crackled with intelligence. She'd meant it when she told Gabe that she respected his work. She did.

Despite the pain it caused her, she'd read everything he'd done in the years since he left her.

"About the second or third time that someone accidentally strangled because their helmet wedged in a narrow slot during a descent," she said, "elastic chin straps became real popular."

Gabe eyed the new strap with interest.

"Helmet lamps?" Joy asked.

He dug out his electric lamps and battery pack. The lamps were new, almost startling in their polish against the battered helmet. The bulbs fit snugly in their sockets and the filaments were intact.

"All right?" he asked.

"Fine." She pried into the battery pack. As she'd suspected, the pack was as new as the lamps. No one had modified the battery pack for the special demands of caving.

"Problem?" he asked, peering over her shoulder.

"Nothing huge. This will be okay for today, but tonight you'll want Fish to put some masonite spacers in. Otherwise the batteries will slip away from the contacts and you'll be—"

"Left in the dark," he finished.

She made a muffled sound of agreement and began laying out the contents of his backpack on the Jeep's hood. "Flashlight, extra batteries, extra lamp bulbs, waterproof matches, candles, cigarette lighter—oh good, you have the chemical light sticks, too."

"They looked like a safe bet to me."

"They are," she said, holding up one of the slender plastic tubes. "Twist this and you'll get a surprisingly strong light. As long as the chemical reaction inside the tube lasts—usually twenty-four to forty-eight hours—this is a nearly inde-structible source of light." She set the stick down. "Where's your pocketknife?"

Silently he reached into his climbing shorts and produced the knife. It had a serrated blade as long as his index finger that could cut through anything but steel cable.

Joy tested the blade's edge, nodded approv-ingly, and put the knife with the rest of the equipment on the hood.

"Nice compass," she said, admiring it before setting it aside. "Mmm, Swiss chocolate. Better not let Fish see that. He has a passion for the stuff. Raisins," she muttered, moving aside a plastic packet with her index finger. "Bleh."

"Still hate raisins, huh?"

"With a passion."

"But they make great—"

"—emergency food," she finished. "I still don't like 'em. No matter how you pack, smash, drown or otherwise abuse raisins, their taste and texture doesn't change. Bleh!"

He laughed softly.

"Peanuts," she said, going through his food. "Soon to be peanut butter, compliments of

Gotcha. Tablets to purify water. First aid kit." Her eyes widened as she opened the small kit. It was like a miniaturized surgery, everything in place from sutures to disinfectant. Reverently she closed the tiny case. "What a beauty."

"Worth every penny I paid," he agreed.

The canteen was all it had to be: tough, waterproof, and small enough not to be in the way more than half the time. He also had a compact survival kit that was a miracle of modern advances in materials that would keep a human being warm and relatively comfortable under conditions that were neither.

"Space blanket, extra wicking socks, shoelaces, change of clothes, paper clips, and safety pins." She looked up suddenly, almost smiling. "Useful little devils, aren't they?" Before he could answer she was concentrating on the equipment again. "Ensolite pads for knees, elbows, and seat, more batteries, peppermint hard candies." This time she did smile. "Oh, boy, you're in trouble. Better hide these."

"Why? Fish has a thing for them, too?" Gabe asked, amused.

"Nope. I do. After a few hours down there, peppermint is like having sunshine dissolve on your tongue. Problem is, I like them when I'm on top, too. Can't keep them around." She gave everything on the Jeep's hood a final, quick look.

"That's it for the personal gear. On to the climbing equipment."

While he refilled his backpack, she opened his rope sack and began pulling things out. She was satisfied with everything until she came to his climbing rope. It was designed for mountains, not caves. It was nearly half an inch thick and had never been used.

"Damn," she muttered. "We should have washed this last night. It would have been much easier to handle. Then there's the stretch factor." She frowned and mentally went through alternative routes down to Lost River Cave's second level. She shook her head. "Won't work. This rope is great for belaying the leader on a mountain, but it's too stretchy for caving. If anything goes wrong on the long route, we'd have to use one of the others. We've got one vertical descent of nearly a hundred and fifty feet—if you fell using this rope, it would stretch so much before it stopped you that it would be like having no rope at all. You'd end up ten feet wide and an inch thick at the bottom of Surprise."

"Surprise?"

"That's our name for the slot. It has what looked like a floor fifty feet down. It wasn't. It was a very thin cave formation that had closed the slot partway down." Joy smiled crookedly, remembering. "Good thing Fish was belaying me. I didn't even have time to call out a warning before the floor gave way, but he didn't let me slip more than six inches."

Gabe could all too easily picture Joy standing on a fragile sheet of rock more than one hundred feet above the true bottom of the slot—and then going through, falling, her life dependent on her rope and the skill of the person belaying her.

Even though he knew that she was a careful, experienced caver, the image of her falling left a queasy hollowness in Gabe's gut. He'd learned that no matter how carefully life or an expedition was planned and executed, things went wrong. What looked like a floor was really a fragile ceiling, and what looked like solid mountain was really a lethal rockslide waiting to be triggered.

And ropes, even the best, contained flaws that couldn't be discovered short of the final test, when a human life dangled over a bottomless void.

"Anyway," she said, "there's too much stretch in this rope for the longer descents. We'll use my backup rope for you."

"May I see your rope."

There was no question in Gabe's voice. He would inspect the rope very carefully before he trusted his life to it.

"Sure." Yet even as Joy agreed, she sensed the

unyielding steel beneath the polite request. "If you're that concerned about my judgment, maybe you'd feel better if—"

"It's nothing personal," he cut in. "I check my own ropes. Always."

She searched his face but found only the contrast between his dark, thickly curling lashes and the luminous green depths of his eyes. "It's in the gray bag."

With that she went back to sorting through Gabe's rope sack. She found another rope, this one thinner, an emergency rope. There was the usual assortment of backup equipment such as webbing loops and spare carabiners.

Then her groping fingers found a piece of rope that was less than a foot long. When she pulled it out, she saw that both ends had been neatly cut, as though it had once been part of a longer rope. But the segment itself was useless. The outer surface of the nylon rope was badly abraded, almost furry looking. In one place the structure of the rope itself had been frayed until all but a quarter inch of the inner core had been worn through.

She stared at the ruined rope, wondering why he bothered to carry it with him.

"It reminds me of how narrow the margin between survival and death can be," he said, watching her, "and how important a good rope is. That was new, top of the line, and I used it only once. In Peru. If the rope had been cheap or worn, I'd be dead."

Joy looked at the frail strands that were all that had held together the rope and Gabe's life.

"This?" she said in a raw voice. Then, "How far?"

"Did I fall?"

Her mouth was too dry to speak, so she nodded.

He shrugged. "Not far. Under twenty feet, for sure, or the force of the rope stopping me would have broken my back. Even so, I fell far enough to bounce like a yo-yo on an elastic string. Far enough for the chest harness to break and part of the Swiss seat to give way and leave me dangling by one leg and a chicken loop. But the piton held during all the time the rockslide broke like a stone wave over the cliff we'd been climbing. My rope held, too. It tore hell out of my hip and leg, but I survived."

She closed her eyes and drew an unsteady breath as she imagined Gabe dangling helplessly on a rope while a rock slide ripped through piece after piece of his safety equipment. The strain on his leg must have been terrible.

"No wonder they thought you might never walk again," she said, her voice ragged. "It's a miracle you survived at all."

His eyes narrowed as he saw the depth of her

reaction to the knowledge of his past danger and injury. She hated him, but the thought of him hanging at the end of a fraying rope, battered by falling rocks, brought her no pleasure.

She looked up at him, her eyes as clear as spring rain, searching. "Does your leg still bother you?"

"Not nearly as much as the questions."

"The questions?"

"Why me? Why did I live? Why did other men die? Why—" He made a curt gesture with his hand. "Questions without answers."

"Ah, those questions," she said ruefully. "The ones we all ask on the way to growing up."

At that moment Gabe knew Joy had cried out those same questions after her parents had died in a helicopter crash.

He should have been there with her. He hadn't been.

It was something he would regret for the rest of his life.

"The questions were a little late coming to me," he said. "I'm thirty."

"Some people never ask those questions at all, no matter how long they live."

"And the answers? When do they come?"

She sensed the urgency beneath his controlled exterior. Whatever was driving him came from deep inside, all the way to his soul.

It was exactly that intensity which had drawn her to Gabe from the first instant they met. She'd known instinctively, certainly, that he was a man who would demand a response as intense as his own.

She'd never met another person like him. No one else had had his combination of wide-ranging curiosity and sensual involvement with life. No one else had shared her eagerness and consuming wonder in the world around her as he did. No one else had been able to release the primal response of her body and mind as he had.

But the questions Gabe was asking concerned emotions rather than earth sciences. That was new.

"There's a world full of answers," she said. "The trick is to find one that satisfies you."

"Have you?"

"Sometimes. And sometimes . . . not. Some nights are longer than others."

That, Gabe thought, **is the understatement of the century.**

TWELVE

"We'd better get going," Joy said to Gabe. "I want to have plenty of time for you to get used to being in a cave again before we try exploring any new leads."

Without a word he reassembled the contents of his rope bag and climbed into his thermal underwear. The same clothes he'd used for mountain climbing would serve for caving. Right now the underwear was hot enough to pull sweat out of him, which the efficient cloth promptly drew away from his skin.

The sun was like a torch.

He pulled on his pants quickly, left his thermal shirt unbuttoned, and stuffed his climbing gloves in a pocket. He put on the battery pack and helmet. The caving coveralls he'd bought seven years ago were still tight enough not to get in the way and loose enough not to be uncomfortable. He put the pads in the seat and knee pockets and elbows and pulled on the coveralls, leaving them unzipped. The wire leads from battery pack to helmet stayed beneath the coveralls, where nothing could snag on rocks. Socks, jungle boots, and leather-palmed gloves completed his outfit.

He tested both lamps, even though he would probably use only one at a time. They worked. He was ready to go. More than ready. He was getting hotter by the instant.

"All set?" Joy asked.

"God, yes. Anything to get out of the sun."

Laughing, she led the way into a brush-choked ravine and down a steep descent to the mouth of the cave. The entrance was concealed by brush. No one could see it until they forced their way past the dry, prickly barrier.

At the mouth of the cave there was a doubled loop of rope with a carabiner attached. The anchor loop was slung around a huge boulder. A rope attached to the loop trailed down like a thin, bright tongue into the cave's beckoning darkness. Cool air stirred caressingly, whispering of the moist cave hidden beyond the reach of the scorching desert sun.

Joy dressed quickly. The last thing she put on was a specialized harness, called a Swiss seat. At the moment she wore it reversed. That way the seat became an ideal restraint for anchoring a belay. Automatically she checked that the rigging around the boulder hadn't frayed or tangled since its last use. Only when she was confident of the anchor did she snap herself to it.

"I'll belay you into the cave," she said to Gabe. "After you get through the short trench cut into the guano floor—"

"Guano?" he interrupted quickly. "I don't remember that."

"Like most of the caves around here, this was a fertilizer mine back in the nineteenth century." She yanked on the rope. It didn't budge. "They went broke real quick. The guano was so old that it had about as many nutrients as gravel. The bats have long since gone to other roosts. Mom and Dad probably didn't mention it to you because they didn't want to pinpoint the entrance too closely. We didn't have a steel locking grate for the entrance back then."

"Gotcha."

She grinned. "Gotcha comes later. After the trench, it's nearly two hundred feet of a real steep pitch over loose rubble and fresh flowstone. Before you start down, holler to make sure no one's on the way up. Ready?"

He visualized her instructions and his own memories and nodded his head. He went to the black opening, cupped his hands around his mouth, and yelled, "Yo!"

He waited a long ten count. No answer came up out of the darkness. No one was below.

Joy carefully pulled up the rope that was trailing down into the cave. As she wound the line into a neat coil, she examined it for fresh cuts or abrasions.

Gabe stood right beside her, checking the rope for himself.

She wasn't insulted or irritated. After seeing the horrifying piece of rope he carried in his pack, she wouldn't have objected if he'd insisted on going over every inch of every rope with a six-power magnifying glass.

In fact, she wanted to do it herself.

"Okay?" she asked.

He finished examining the last bit of rope, nodded, and pulled on his gloves. "Ready when you are."

"When you get to the bottom of the rubble slope, you'll see a path laid out between two strips of orange tape. Off to your right there's a big block of breakdown. Ceiling rubble. Wait behind it while I descend."

He nodded.

Joy put on her own gloves and sat down facing the mouth of the cave with her legs partially extended. The newly coiled rope was at her left. One end of the rope went around her lower back, and from there to Gabe.

Gabe put on his Swiss seat and attached himself to the rope so that he would be able to climb freely unless he slipped. Then the rope would spring taut under Joy's hands, preventing him from falling. She herself would be anchored against the pull of his weight by her own attachment to the massive boulder.

Although he could see plainly that she was in position to belay him, he went through the necessary ritual of voice signals—necessary because he wouldn't always be able to see her. That was when communication would be critical.

"Belay on?" he asked clearly.

"On belay."

"Ready to climb."

He waited, poised on the brink of the cave, his helmet lamp looking very pale in the blaze of desert light.

"Climb," she responded.

"Climbing."

With that he began his descent into Lost River Cave, his life quite literally held in her hands. He didn't hesitate, a fact that astounded him when he realized it. Despite all that had happened, despite the violent emotion he'd seen lurking at times within Joy's gray eyes, he knew at some deep level that she wouldn't deliberately harm him.

It was one of the few certainties that remained to him after the accident in Peru, yet he hadn't even discovered it until this instant.

As he walked backward down the slanting

trench, the cone of the one light he was using picked out the deep layer of ancient bat guano. Tiny, needlelike shadows poked out of the reddish deposit. They were the bones of bats that hadn't lived for thousands of years. He looked at the fragile remains wonderingly before moving on.

The last of yesterday's stiffness left his hip as he came to the end of the guano mining trench and entered the steep, slippery part of the descent. Here sunlight thinned into the "twilight zone" of the cave. He worked his way deeper into the darkness with every backward step. The reassuring tension of the rope moved with him, neither too tight nor too loose. He had an impulse to call up praise of Joy's belaying skill through the deepening well of velvet darkness folding around him.

He kept silent. When a climber was on belay, only a few words were used. **You're doing a great job!** weren't among them.

Coolly, caressingly, Lost River Cave's seamless night condensed around Gabe. That was when memories spun up out of the well of darkness like ghostly ropes attaching him to anchor points in the past.

The first time he came down to the cave alone with Joy, they turned out their lights and stood hand in hand, adrift in the limitless, magic

night of Lost River Cave. With sight gone, every other sense leaped into razor focus. The subtle lemon-and-rose scent of her perfume. The warmth of her breath washing over his lips. The heat and peppermint taste of her tongue. The exquisite textures of her mouth revealed to him in a kiss that had no end.

The memory sliced through Gabe even as his body moved more deeply into Lost River Cave. His breath came in hard and fast, then settled into its usual steady rhythm as his muscles responded to the demands of the descent. Soon he was at the end of the steep pitch, looking up toward the small, brilliant spot where the mysterious cave world ended and the New Mexican desert began. He removed the rope and stepped back.

"Off belay," he called.

Joy's response carried easily down to him on the damp air. "Belay off."

He fastened his shirt and zipped up the coveralls against the coolness of the cave. Air stirred past him, a damp breeze that promised a large cave lying in endless darkness, waiting to be discovered. Nearby the rope shifted and slithered, responding to movements beyond the reach of his cone of light.

He looked around quickly, spotted the block of breakdown Joy had mentioned, and walked behind it. There he would be protected from any rubble she might accidentally kick loose during her descent.

Up on the surface Joy finished connecting the rope to the boulder again. She reversed her seat harness and positioned the climbing rope so that she could in effect belay herself down the steep pitch. After a final check, she stepped off backward into Lost River Cave's cool, welcoming darkness.

"Coming down," she called.

"Yo!" he answered.

Moving with the easy rhythms of an expert technical climber, she fed rope across her body, using the friction of rope against her clothes to slow and control her descent.

Gabe could have climbed down into the cave the same way, but if he'd fallen—or if she fell now—the shock of landing against a static anchor like the boulder would be enough to break bones, even if the fall was only a few feet. With a belayer in place, the shock of hitting the end of the rope was softened by the unavoidable slipping of rope through the belayer's hands. The slippage was only a few inches, but it was the difference between an abrupt, brutal stop and a more gentle end to the fall.

When Joy reached the bottom of the rubble slope, she released herself from the rope and set it aside. In a few hours they would need it to climb out of the pit. As she moved, she was very careful not to step on the rope, forcing sharp-edged grit into the strands. The only thing worse than walking on a rope was hacking at it with a knife.

"Ready?" she asked.

Gabe turned slowly, letting his light play over the room. "Ready," he said absently. Then softly, gratefully, "The route down might be different, but this hasn't changed—the point of light, the darkness, the mystery calling in silence."

Joy looked up where collapsed ceiling had broken through to the ground above, revealing the presence of Lost River Cave to the outside world. The breakdown surrounding them contained blocks of stone as big as houses that leaned every which way. Smaller rocks of all sizes filled in the cracks. Debris had sifted down from the surface, sand and dirt and pieces of desert plants, even a few white bones left by animals that had fallen into the cave and not been able to get out.

Though beautiful, Lost River Cave wasn't any place for the unlucky, the foolish, or the weak.

Slowly Gabe swept his light over the cave floor. Without tape marking the path, he quickly would have been lost. It took an experienced eye to pick out the smudge marks left by earlier cavers' boots, especially when there was no single obvious path over the immensely jumbled floor of the cave.

The floor was dry, as were the walls and ceiling. There were few formations visible, and none of them were the kind of fantastic stone decorations that made a person stand and stare in disbelief.

"It seems drier than I remember," he said finally. "Or is it just that this is a different route than the one we used to take?"

"It's drier. We're in the ninth decade of drought. The past five years have been especially dry."

"Not what most people expect of a cave."

"The highest levels of our New Mexico caves are often like that. Without water, caves die."

"Is the drought man-made? Global warming?"

"Doubt it. In this area the groundwater level has been fluctuating for millions of years. At one time this was all below the water table. That's when carbonic acid from the groundwater above and sulfuric acid from the hydrocarbon field below went to work dissolving limestone."

She looked up, directing her helmet lamp at the ceiling of the cave. "As the water table sank, air filled the rooms and passages that were left behind. Sometimes there was enough groundwater to make waterfalls and rivers running through the caves. Sometimes water simply seeped through cracks and gathered in drip pools far below."

"So there aren't any cave formations up here because it's too dry now, or because there hasn't been enough time?"

"Oh, there are formations up here," she said. "I could show you tiny draperies and ribbons of flowstone. Even a few miniature stalactites and stalagmites."

"But nothing like the formations farther down."

"Right. It's the rate of water movement through the ground, not time alone, that determines how fast cave formations grow. It's a lot drier today than it was a few hundred thousand years ago, so a lot less decoration takes place."

Joy turned and spotlighted the nearby cave wall with her headlamp. She left the trail and began picking her way over to the wall.

"Should I stay here?" he asked, looking at the orange tape she had stepped over.

"No. Just be careful. A lot of stones are loose."

Gabe followed, curious. He couldn't see any other tracks, any other sign that anyone had ever walked on this particular stretch of cave floor before.

Joy stopped near a knee-high boulder, shining her light on the surface of the rock. The angle of the light revealed a stalagmite no bigger than a fingernail. The stone growth was dry, almost powdery looking.

"I don't know how old this little stalagmite is," she said. "In the years I've come here, I've never seen a drop of water on this stone. Maybe some year it will rain and rain until the ground is too full of water for it to be carried down into the cave in the usual ways. Then the ceiling will drip here, and water will fall on this little nubbin, calcium carbonate will precipitate out on impact, and the stalagmite will come to life again."

"I thought that evaporation was what caused stalagmites, not precipitation."

Joy almost smiled. It was good to hear curiosity instead of hostility or sadness or regret in his voice. It was good to sense his quick mind fastening onto words and phrases and facts, shaking them until a new insight fell into place.

"That's what speleologists used to believe," she said. "We've all seen the salt formations left when one of the local runoff lakes dries up. We thought it was the same when groundwater broke through to a cave: water evaporated and left its mineral content behind as a layer of new stone. Very logical. Very neat. Except for one small, insurmountable fact."

"What's that?"

"Evaporation isn't possible down beyond the twilight zone. In the darkness, the humidity is one hundred percent all day, every day, year after century after millennia."

"So?"

She adjusted the cone of her helmet light and let it sweep across the jumbled room. "So the air simply can't hold any more water vapor. Which means that water drops can't evaporate and enter the air as vapor. And if water can't become vapor, then all the lovely cave decorations we'll see farther down must have another source."

The sidelight from Joy's lamp washed over Gabe's face, highlighting his thoughtful frown.

"Okay," he said, "water percolates down, gets to a cave ceiling—and then what?"

"I've written a paper that—"

"Translate it into layman's English," Gabe challenged, a smile in his voice.

She laughed softly.

The sound went through him like an exquisite knife, slicing open areas of memory that he'd spent years covering over in scar tissue.

"I don't know if I can translate," she admitted. "That's your department. You take new, esoteric worlds and translate them into universal experience for everyone to share. And you do it beautifully."

Her compliment was like her laugh, bringing Gabe both pleasure and pain, memory and regret. He felt at peace with and understood by Joy as he had by no one else, anywhere, even his own family.

And yet . . .

The past was always there between them. Like the shattered beauty of the underground room where they stood, the past was beyond hiding, beyond healing.

"Without being too technical about it—" she began.

"Thank God."

She ignored him. "The amount of dissolved limestone that water can hold is directly related to the amount of carbon dioxide that is already dissolved in the water. Are you with me so far?"

"So far, so good," he said cautiously.

"Now imagine that you're a water drop pressing down through the earth, pulled by gravity and pushed by the weight of other water above you. Okay?"

"Um. Yeah."

"There you are, under pressure, stuffed with dissolved limestone and gases like carbon dioxide and you're hanging on to them with everything you've got. You push through the ceiling of a big hole in the ground. Instead of being surrounded by water-impregnated stone, suddenly you're surrounded by air. Sort of like what happens when you open a can of soda—fizzzzz."

"Still with you," he said when she paused.

"Great. Get ready for the moment of truth. The instant you push through stone into air, there's less pressure keeping you together. Some of the carbon dioxide you've been holding in your arms fizzes up and out, which means that you can't hold on to all of the dissolved limestone, either."

"It does?"

"Trust me. Complex chemistry at work."

He smiled. "Okay. What next?"

"You lose some of the dissolved limestone, which becomes a very thin coating of stone on the ceiling—the beginning of a stalactite. And then"—amusement lurked in Joy's voice—"much lighter, you fall to the floor and go splat, helping to build up a stalagmite."

"But if limestone has already precipitated out of my water drop to make a stalactite, how can there be any left over for stalagmites?"

"Because when you hit the floor, your hands and arms fly open, releasing more pressure and allowing even more carbon dioxide to escape. Which means—"

"More limestone precipitates out," he finished thoughtfully.

As he spoke, he swept the cave floor with his helmet light as though seeking evidence of what Joy had described.

"Right." Her eyes followed his light beam, searching as he was. "And, if you're very lucky, after hundreds of thousands of years, millions of years, stone is built by tiny layers into shapes more fantastic than any man's dream, creations as incredible as anything in art or nature."

His headlamp shifted from side to side almost impatiently, wanting to see what she had described.

"Oh, we're about a million years too late for this chamber's glories." Her voice was both brisk and oddly wistful. "If there were any cave formations here, they're buried beneath the breakdown."

"Why did the ceiling collapse?"

"Lots of theories."

"Pick one."

"Think about all that water percolating down, happily dissolving stone as it goes," she said. "It widens natural joints and seams in the structure of the ancient reef itself. Eventually there's not enough integrity left in the limestone to hold up the ceiling against the pull of gravity."

"How long does that take?"

"There's no rule. Sometimes the ceiling falls as soon as the water table drops, draining the room, leaving the ceiling unsupported. Sometimes the ceiling doesn't fall until much later, and then it all comes crashing down, burying the beautiful formations that have been built drop by drop beneath it."

"Pity." He tried to imagine what the room

might have looked like with fantastic spires and columns and draperies of glistening, multicolored stone. "So much beauty destroyed."

"In some ways, yes. In others . . ."

She hesitated, searching for words that would help him to understand that in the natural world there were no absolute beginnings and endings. Just a timeless **becoming**.

"In others," he prompted.

"It's simply change, not destruction. The water is still at work below the original chamber, leaping from ceiling to floor across a bridge of air, creating new beauty. And below the level of cave decoration is the saturation zone, where the chambers themselves are still being formed, waiting for the earth to shift and lift them up so that they, too, can be decorated."

Caught by the intensity of her voice, he looked away from the cave to her face. It was a study in golden skin and fluid shadows and focused intelligence. At that moment she was so beautiful to him it stopped his breath.

"Maybe only one level exists down there, filled with water," she said. "Maybe there are as many levels as there are beds in the limestone to form chambers. We don't know. We only know that a cave is there, now, forming beneath our feet. Not destruction. Just change. And often, creation. In an eerie, magnificent way, caves are alive. Like us."

Slowly he played his helmet light over the ceiling and down the wall, trying to imagine the room filled with water in an era of great rain. Then the coming of drought, the water table shifting down, down, taking with it the power to dissolve stone.

And finally the dripping of groundwater into caves. The slow, slow creation of beauty within a stone hollow. The eventual collapse when the ceiling fell, smashing everything that had been so painstakingly built through time spans incomprehensible to man.

Like life, changing in an instant, rearranging everything.

A sudden roar as a mountain gave way, and a grave as deep as time. A helicopter crash that devastated a young woman seven years ago, and a man today.

He wondered if the cave felt the smashing instant of change echoing through time, reshaping everything, even the cave's understanding of itself.

The fanciful thought both amused and saddened him. He hoped that Lost River Cave wasn't alive, not like that. He wouldn't wish a million years of questions and regrets on anything.

Even stone.

THIRTEEN

Nothing was visible in the vast darkness but two cones of shifting, bobbing light and two stripes of orange tape. The floor beneath Gabe's and Joy's feet was rough, treacherous. As he followed her deeper into Lost River Cave, the rock surrounding him closed down. The chamber became a twisting, ever-shrinking passage.

Earlier his helmet lamp had been lost in the immensity of the chamber. Now, nearby pale limestone walls threw back his light from all directions. Soon he could touch stone on both sides simply by raising his arms. The ceiling pressed down even as the floor slowly began to slant downward.

"Watch your head," Joy warned, tilting her helmet light just enough to highlight the ragged rock overhead. "The ceiling comes down to five feet four inches real quick."

Moments later Gabe was crouching to avoid banging his head.

Joy didn't have to bend one bit. Even with the added height of a helmet, she didn't scrape the ceiling.

He grunted and bent lower. It wasn't long before his legs were complaining about having to walk in such a cramped, awkward way.

She never even slowed down.

"You're enjoying this, aren't you?" he said.

"You bet your ass I am. Up on top I have to buy my clothes off the kiddie rack and stand on my tiptoes to see over everything except jackrabbits. But down here the world has to bend over and look at things my way."

In spite of his discomfort, he laughed. "I'm going to take you to see the sequoias someday. You'll get a crick in your neck looking up."

"I get a crick in my neck looking up at Davy. Oops, going down," she warned.

While she stooped, he doubled over and rested his hands on his knees, his elbows bent outward. It worked for a while. Then both of them were forced down to their hands and knees as the passage kept on sinking deeper and deeper into the earth.

Now the walls showed stains of black or brown or orange, depending on which minerals had been dissolved in the groundwater. Here and there patches of moisture showed through, shining in the lamplight.

Gabe's breath came easily but more deeply than normal. His curiosity remained in full force. "I don't remember this route from seven years ago."

"New," Joy said, ducking even lower.

"Who discovered it?"

"Me."

He grunted as he banged his helmet and then his elbows on the shrinking passage. His caving gear protected him, but he took the warning and slowed down.

"You found it? Figures," he said.

"How so?"

"Small."

"Yeah? Just wait until you try Gotcha. Had much practice crawling long distance on your hands and knees?"

"Does six miles down a mountain trail count?"

"It's a start," she said, but her voice wasn't nearly as light as her words. The thought of Gabe injured and crawling down a mountainside made her stomach twist. "Ceiling going up."

"Thank God," he muttered.

He was too busy keeping his feet—and keeping up—to do much more than note that the floor wasn't as rough as it had been. Even so, he sensed something changing around him, a quality of the air as much as anything else.

A few minutes later Joy stopped and directed

her light straight up, silently telling him that he could stand again. Gratefully he stretched muscles that were complaining from the unaccustomed use.

"And I thought rock climbing used every muscle in your body from every possible angle," he said.

"Caving is a lot like rock climbing. In the dark."

"No rain, though."

"Ever climbed up a cave waterfall?"

"Can't say that I have. Sounds cold."

"It is," she said. "Bell Bottom is one of the few caves I've met that I didn't like. You go in down a waterfall, which ensures a wet, cold time until you come out, climbing up the same waterfall."

"At least you don't have wind tearing at you, the way you do on a mountainside."

"Don't bet on it. Some caves literally breathe, with air flowing in and out at rhythmic intervals. Winds up to thirty miles an hour have been clocked. Not up to mountain storm speeds, but enough to tangle you and your rope real good."

"Wind inside the caves? What causes it?" he asked.

"I told you. Caves are alive." Amusement danced through her words. "Actually, no one knows for sure. Lots of theories, though. Most of them have to do with the movement of warm surface air replacing cold cave air and vice versa, or differing air pressures below ground compared to the surface."

"Any waterfalls or wind in Lost River Cave?"

"Yes, somewhere. We can hear them but we can't find them, damn it." More than anything else Joy wanted to find the waterfalls that gave the Voices its murmurous music. "As for wind, nothing serious in most Lost River passages. We get breezes, even some pretty good ones, but nothing to worry about."

"Worry?"

"Getting knocked off a ladder or a rope. Wind-chill factor." She turned her light away from the ceiling and led him farther into the cave. "Hypothermia. When the body gets too—"

"Cold to survive," he finished. "A common problem for explorers everywhere but the tropics."

"Was it cold . . . that day on the mountain?" The words were hesitant, her voice almost husky.

"Not really. That was the only thing that didn't go wrong. That and a quarter-inch of rope."

"Have you climbed since then?" When he didn't answer immediately, she said. "I'm sorry. I don't mean to pry. It's just that if you don't climb anymore, there will be a lot of places in Lost River Cave that—"

"It's all right," he said matter-of-factly, cutting

across her apology. "As soon as I physically could, I went back. That mountain took a lot from me and gave me only questions in return. I didn't want it to take my self-respect too."

Even as he said the words, Gabe knew that was why he'd been driven to return to Lost River Cave. Somehow, in some way that he didn't understand, he'd lost or left behind something of himself here. He didn't know what it was or if it could be regained. He only knew that he had to find out.

As the silence lengthened, Joy wished she could see his face. She wanted to ask what he was thinking. She wanted to understand him with an intensity that shocked her.

When she'd been with Gabe seven years ago, she hadn't felt it was necessary to share his mind, his fears, and his hopes, or to have him share hers. The mere presence of him had been overwhelming, like the moment when she'd pushed through the tight crawlway called Gotcha and found herself within the murmurous beauty of the Voices. That instant had so saturated her senses that she hadn't been able to think at all. She'd simply felt the immensity of the room, seen its beauty shimmering in the sweeping cone of her light, and heard its eerie, extraordinary voices whispering in the velvet darkness.

She hadn't thought of the forces that had

shaped the chamber or the explorations awaiting her. She didn't consider the dangers or the sheer hard work and unexpected rewards of surveying the new chamber. She didn't even think about the possibility that this room would lead to other rooms, other passages, other instants of overwhelming discovery. All of those thoughts had come later, after she'd absorbed the Voices into herself, growing and changing to meet the challenges of her discovery.

There hadn't been any "later" for her when it came to Gabe. There hadn't been any chance to absorb and grow and change to meet his challenges. There had been only the incredible rush of discovery, the sweet, hot, wild moments within his arms, and the endless chill of his loss.

Losing him had been like being caught down in Lost River Cave with no more than a few matches to light her way. That had happened to her once. As part of her training in cave exploration she'd been left alone in one of Lost River Cave's smallest rooms, with only seven matches for light. She'd managed to grope her way back to the entrance, but she'd never forgotten how unfamiliar the cave had become, how distorted by darkness and fear.

It was a lesson she learned very well. Never again did she enter a cave—no matter for how short a time—without thoroughly checking her light sources.

In the same manner she'd groped her way out of darkness and fear after Gabe left and her parents died. She'd learned from that too. Not once in the days and weeks and years since then had she allowed herself to trust and love another human being enough that his absence would cast her adrift in darkness without light or hope of it.

Only Kati had slipped inside her guard.

Only Kati, Gabe's daughter, a little girl whose smile was like her father's, lighting up any darkness.

For an instant Joy wanted to tell him about Kati, about the life that he'd so casually spurned. It wasn't the first time the impulse had come to her. Often in the past six years she'd wanted to send pictures to him, to share with him the trivial and transcendent moments of raising his child.

She'd never given in to the impulse before.

She didn't now.

Seven years ago Gabe hadn't been interested in anything but the sensual moment and the long term of his career. He'd had no room in his life or his mind or his heart for the woman who loved him. How much less would he have been interested in a baby who at first needed rather than gave love?

After Gabe met Kati, **if** he asked who her father was, Joy would tell him the truth. No man was Kati's father, except in the briefest, most meaningless sense: sperm donor.

The instant of conception wasn't the enduring relationship known as fatherhood.

When Kati turned eighteen, Joy would tell her who her biological father was. Until then, Kati would have no father except in her own dreams. It was better that way. Dreams were kinder than reality. It would crush Kati to know that her father had never wanted her to be born.

As for Gabe . . . he'd made his choice seven years ago. Joy had lived with it.

He had no right to complain.

"The next part starts out easy," she said, turning away from him, leaving him in darkness. "There's a steep scramble down, about a hundred feet of stooping, and then the ceiling pitches way down. Thirty feet later you're into Gotcha."

She hesitated. Never in the time she'd known Gabe had he showed any hint of claustrophobia. But that might have changed, like the change from a Gabe who rarely noticed other people's feelings to the man who not only saw Maggie's hurt but tried to ease it.

In Gotcha's tight passage claustrophobia could be fatal.

She turned back toward him. "Are you at all uneasy in close places?"

"No."

"You're sure? I found another way into the Voices, but it takes forty-five minutes and involves a vertical drop of one hundred and seven feet at the end."

"I'm sure. But if you're worried, take me the long way around."

That surprised Joy. Seven years ago he would have insisted on going through Gotcha just to prove that he could. And he would have been able to. Then, as now, he was both supple and strong.

In silence Joy moved her light slowly across Gabe's body, as though measuring him against both her memories of the past and the needs of the present.

"You're not as thick as Davy," she said, "but you sure are wide in the shoulders. Wider than I remem—" She stopped in mid-word, jerking back from the black pit that was the past.

"I spent a lot of time living outdoors, exploring rough country." He shrugged. "Strength was just one more survival tool."

"Living on the edge."

He started to disagree, then shrugged. "Yeah, I guess so. Adrenaline, the young man's drug of choice." He shook his head, remembering. "Hard to believe we all survive it."

Joy didn't say anything. She could see for herself that Gabe wasn't young like that anymore. The years of testing himself against the land had left him with a strength and physical assurance that was both reassuring and oddly exciting.

That hadn't changed. Gabriel Venture was an exciting man. He would still be exciting when he was sixty.

Abruptly she turned away. "Gotcha it is. I'll go through first and take our equipment. Then I'll come back and follow you through."

"Why?"

"So if you get stuck I can pull you out."

"You?"

"Believe it. I pulled Davy out once."

"Impossible," Gabe said, not bothering to hide his laughter. "You're too small."

"You'll laugh up the other sleeve after I yank you out of the third angle and get you headed straight again."

"Small but tough."

There was no laughter in his voice now. He was remembering what she'd gone through when she was barely twenty. Yes, she was tough. He'd known grown men who went under trying to carry less of an emotional load than she'd shouldered through her twentieth year.

"I'll try not to get stuck on you," he said. Then he realized his words could be taken more than one way.

Before he could say anything more, she did. "Don't worry. I'm a champion unsticker and you're a champion eel. Gotcha's little games will be no problem at all for us."

She walked off quickly. With the ease of long experience, she picked her way between the tapes across the uneven, often slick, downward-slanting floor. She kept her light pointed at the orange tape rather than glancing around at the cave formations that were appearing more and more often.

It was harder for Gabe to stay focused between the orange lines, but he didn't complain. He followed her at his own pace. He could have gone faster, but didn't. It was stupid to hurry through unknown territory for no better reason than the watch on his wrist. Accidents happened that way, and regrets.

He'd made enough mistakes in the past to learn that it was much easier to do it right the first time than to try to undo errors in the midst a storm of **if only**s.

"Pit ahead," she said.

"How deep?"

"Bo Peep's just a middling drop. Under forty feet. Straight down, though. Doesn't go anywhere useful that we've discovered. Doesn't blow, either."

"Blow?"

"Air movement. Cavers have a saying: If it blows, it goes. Bo Peep doesn't blow and doesn't go."

They skirted the pit's black mouth.

The farther down they went, the more signs of moisture there were—dampness on the walls, patches of very fine-grained mud between rocks, the vague glistening of stone surfaces. Every gleam of moisture proved the cave was alive, limestone dissolving and forming again in a new shape, drop by drop, millennia by millennia.

Beneath their feet, the cave was a mosaic of rubble and slick spots where water dripped and formations grew. Gabe wanted to stop and examine some of the cave decorations that his light revealed, but Joy showed no sign of slowing down.

Something at the edge of his light kept sparkling like a veil of diamonds. He opened his mouth to ask for a few minutes to look around, then shut it without a word. There would be time later to question and explore the fine details of Lost River Cave. For now it was more important to get some idea of its broader outline.

Joy's light stopped, then swept back over the cave floor to Gabe's feet. "Everything okay?"

"Just got caught in some of the small details."

Her smile gleamed beneath her helmet light. "Hard not to. There are galleries I could show you no bigger than a doll's theater and so beautifully decorated in miniature you're sure fairies go there to dance."

"Do you have file photos of those special places, or should I bring my camera next time?"

"We have more photos than you have pages to write about them."

"No problem sharing a few of them with the magazine?"

"Shouldn't be."

"Good," he said, coming up to stand beside her. "I can cover a lot more ground if I'm not stopping every few seconds to take an irresistible photo."

She laughed. "You sound like Gina, one of the grad students we can't afford anymore. She was a video nut whose husband was a video wizard. She had a digital camera that could do everything but make dinner."

"Really? What kind? I'm always on the lookout for a good camera."

"Ask Davy. He keeps all the digital info for his maps."

Joy moved her headlamp away from Gabe to the trail ahead. It was a steep scramble over flowstone, rubble, and breakdown that had fallen so long ago it was sprouting stalagmites like beard stubble. There was a sling anchorage for the belayer and a rope that had been used by the three cavers who had gone ahead to the Voices.

Unlike the first descent into the cave, this pitch was narrow, water-smoothed, and had almost no reliable hand- or footholds. Here belaying was not only a safety precaution, it was a necessity.

The chance of somebody slipping—especially somebody unfamiliar with the cave—was about one hundred percent.

Silently they prepared for the descent. Joy snapped herself into the anchor sling, settled in for the belay, and waited.

"Belay on?" Gabe asked.

"On belay."

"Ready to climb."

"Climb," she said, bracing herself subtly.

"Climbing."

For a time she could hear the soft scuff of his feet as he walked backward into darkness. Those small noises disappeared beneath the whispering sound of rope moving over her clothing when she fed out more of the coil as he needed it.

From where she sat she couldn't even see the glow of his lamp. He had dropped down over the lip so swiftly that he was invisible to her. Only the change in tension on the rope feeding through her hands told her that she wasn't alone. She felt smooth pulls and then sudden lurches when he lost his footing for an instant. Each time he regained his balance almost as soon as she realized it had been lost.

But not before her heartbeat raced. She found herself straining to hear the least noise, to sense the slightest change in the pressure on the rope.

Gabe could feel Joy's attention in her deft handling of the rope that helped him keep his balance. The steeply slanting rock face in front of his light showed faint traces of other boots. It also showed the glisten and shine of fresh moisture, the—

Suddenly his feet shot out from under him. In a heartbeat he was back on the deadly mountain again, hurtling out into the void while rocks and the screams of men battered him.

"Falling!"

FOURTEEN

Almost immediately the rope holding Gabe went taut, ending his fall. Even so, it took him a moment to understand that he was in Lost River Cave, not on a Peruvian mountain, that he was dangling from Joy's hands rather than from a piton hammered deep into stone, and that there was a steep, smooth slope rather than a two-thousand-foot drop beneath his feet.

Cold sweat slicked his skin. Adrenaline slammed through him. His chest was an aching void that both demanded and resisted breath.

With the discipline that had kept him alive more than once in the past, he brought his body and mind back under control. He turned himself until he was facing the wet, gleaming rock. An instant later he was supporting his own weight.

"Climbing," he called up to Joy.

"Climb."

She hoped that Gabe couldn't hear the relief in her voice. It wasn't just that he hadn't hurt himself—as long as the belay held, he hadn't been in any real danger. But after what had happened in Peru, she knew that he must have a bone-deep horror of falling. To feel himself out of control again, even for an instant, must have been terrifying.

Yet he'd kept his head, found his footing again, and resumed the climb as though nothing had happened.

Joy understood the kind of courage and determination required to overcome helplessness and raw fear. Once, three years ago, Kati had wandered alone into the desert picking wildflowers. Before Joy found her again, she discovered just how much she loved her little daughter.

It had been a terrifying discovery.

Until that instant Joy had believed that she would never love again—not like that, her whole being hostage to another life, a life that could be taken in an instant, leaving her alone once more.

The rope went slack in Joy's fingers.

"Off belay," Gabe called.

Her answer floated down in the darkness to him. "Belay off."

A few moments later the upward-tilted lamp from Gabe's helmet washed over the smooth, steep pitch. The small, gliding figure of Joy moved through light and darkness with dreamlike ease. When she touched the cave floor beside him, she gave him a quick glance and a reassuring smile before she led him deeper into Lost River Cave.

As he followed her, he found himself at first intrigued, then fascinated by her grace and assurance. He'd been with many men in many wild lands, but he'd never met anyone who so completely accepted a place for what it was. She didn't so much conquer the cave as slide between its spaces, its unique possibilities.

It wasn't her strength that gave her access to the cave's secrets, but her finesse. She knew herself, knew her equipment, knew her own abilities and limitations.

At twenty she'd been much more impulsive, much less accepting of the idea that she couldn't do anything and everything.

When she was twenty he never would have stepped off backward over a slippery stone lip while she held his life in her hands. It had always been the reverse. He had belayed her. She had trusted him.

The insight all but paralyzed him. Like the moment when he had first seen Joy's delicate features in the shadow of Davy's naked strength, Gabe felt as though he'd taken a blow to his gut.

Why should she trust you now, fool? asked the sardonic part of his mind, the part that hadn't let up on him since he'd crawled off that deadly mountain in Peru.

But I never meant to hurt her.

Bloody wonderful. Bet that just comforted her no end when her parents died. Bet it helped her all to hell at the abortion clinic too.

He stumbled and nearly went full-length on the cold stone.

"Gabe?" she asked, hearing the scrambling sound behind her.

"I'm fine," he said curtly.

With a savage inner curse, he controlled his thoughts and his body, focusing his attention on the demands of Lost River Cave's uneven surface rather than on the pitiless, unreachable past.

"Ceiling's coming down," she said.

"Fan-fucking-tastic," he said under his breath.

"What?"

"Oh frabjous day!" he amended quickly.

"Callooh! Callay!" she retorted, smiling.

He laughed. "You remember 'Jabberwocky.' "

"I read it at least twice a week," she said, ducking around a stalactite that had left more than one gouge on her helmet.

"Anyone ever tell you that you have unusual taste in reading material?"

She caught herself just before she said **Through the Looking Glass** was one of Kati's favorites. "It's a break from chemistry monographs."

Gabe's answer was a grunt because he was duckwalking again, grateful for every one of the viciously painful exercises the physical therapist had given him after the mountain had nearly killed him. Now, despite the strain of the awkward movements forced on him by the cave, his left side wasn't much worse off than his right.

It was small comfort, but better than no comfort at all.

The farther he went into the cave, the more he understood why Joy didn't use a backpack. Every time he tried to shift position to take the strain off his quads, the backpack snagged on the ceiling.

"Sit here," Joy said.

Thankful for the insulating pad in the coverall, Gabe put his butt on damp, cold stone.

"Sitting," he said wryly.

She made a sound that could have been a giggle.

It surprised both of them.

She shrugged out of her equipment sling and tied it to her ankle. Then she positioned the sack holding her rope so that she could push it along in front of her.

"Give me your backpack," she said.

"Giving you my backpack," he said as though he was still being belayed.

She laughed out loud.

He stripped off his backpack and watched her tie it just behind her own rucksack. "You're really going to take my stuff, aren't you?" he asked.

"I really am. You'll thank me on the other side.

Davy swears that Gotcha is only six inches across at one point."

"Can he get his helmet through?"

"You mean the old caving axiom?"

"Yeah. If you can take off your helmet and push it through a passage, your body can follow."

"Oh, it's true most of the time. But not always. Especially for someone with as much bone and muscle as Davy."

"Or hips like Maggie's?"

"Her hips wiggle through just fine."

Joy pulled the wire leads to her helmet lamp. It meant she was in the dark, but that was better than having the wires getting hung up on rocks as she wriggled through the passage.

Without being asked, Gabe directed his helmet lamp toward the discouragingly small opening to the crawlway that Joy had named Gotcha. He watched while she flattened onto her stomach and eeled into the passage, pushing the rope bag ahead of her and dragging two compact sacks of equipment behind.

Very quickly his helmet light stopped being much use for Joy. Her body almost filled the tunnel, leaving room for little more than random flashes of illumination from behind as she moved deeper into the passage. The sounds of cloth rubbing over stone, boots scrabbling against mud to find the rock beneath, and Joy's soft grunts of effort faded, leaving Gabe alone in Lost River Cave's immense silence.

As soon as Joy jackknifed through the first of Gotcha's seven major twists, the darkness within the passage was complete. The lack of light didn't bother her. She'd done Gotcha so many times that she usually did it by touch alone. It was impossible to get lost when there were only two ways to go—forward or backward.

After the fourth twist in the tube Joy rested for a moment. Despite the fact that Gotcha had been formed by water seeping through joints and seams in the limestone reef, and then widened by becoming the tunnel for an underground stream, the walls weren't smooth. The thin layer of cave mud was deeper in some places than in others. The ceiling dropped in some areas and went up in others, and the walls pinched in or flared out according to weaknesses in the ancient reef.

On top of that, moving water always had currents that wore away stone unevenly. The scalloped pattern that remained in Gotcha's passage snagged clothes, helmets, equipment bags, and boots. The scallops also gave good leverage for elbows, hips, knees, and feet. In all, getting through Gotcha was a workout that left even experienced cavers sweating and a little breathless.

Voices gradually drowned out the sound of Joy's breathing. Voices whispering, voices murmuring, voices in liquid songs teasing her mind. By the sixth twist in the difficult tube, she was wrapped in haunting sounds.

The first time she'd pushed through the unknown crawlway, the voices had frightened her. Gabe had been gone sixteen days, her parents had been dead less than a week, and she'd heard her mother and her father and her lover whispering to her, calling her name softly, tearing her soul with claws of grief and memory.

By the time she'd emerged into the Voices' immense room, she was crying too hard to see anything within reach of her light.

Today Joy wriggled out of Gotcha with dry eyes. Fine silt and memories clung to her. She stood quickly, searching for lights weaving among the unearthly voices. She saw only darkness. Automatically she connected the wire leads to her helmet lamp.

Light speared out, revealing the cave's muted shades of cream and rust, oyster and tan and charcoal. She walked first to the left, then to the right in a thirty-foot zigzag that led around a drapery of solid stone and into the room itself.

From her new perspective she saw a faint glow of light somewhat to the right and below her. There were no other light sources that she could see. Either Davy, Fish, and Maggie had stayed close together and their lights showed as a single source of illumination, or someone was hidden among one of the hundreds of deep alcoves, solution cavities, sponge-like mazes and overhangs that lined the room.

She pulled out her two-way radio.

"Fish?"

"Yo."

"Where?"

"Opposite end from Gotcha. Davy and Maggie are with me."

"Everything okay?"

"If okay means writing notes, holding string, writing notes, measuring string, cussing at dainty sonar and laser gizmos that don't work worth spit after Gotcha—yeah, things are okay."

"Sounds normal. I'm going back through Gotcha for Gabe. If I need you, I'll holler."

The little radio made a popping sound as Fish punched the send button once, which was shorthand for **Understood and out**.

The room Joy called the Voices was four hundred and six feet long, three hundred and fifty-three feet wide at its widest point, and so haphazardly shaped that at first the cavers had thought it was three rooms rather than one. Until you learned a few landmarks it was easy to get lost in the black velvet sweep and intricate stone formations of the Voices.

Joy peeled off equipment, stacked it neatly to

one side, and got back down on her hands and knees. Then she stopped, remembering the impact the Voices had on her the first time she'd heard them seven years ago. She didn't know the names of the ghosts who would claw at Gabe's soul, but she knew that he had them.

She had seen them in his eyes.

That was new. The Gabe of her memories had no shadowy hauntings, no dark regrets, nothing but the bright future calling to him.

Joy reached for her rucksack, untied the top, and plunged her hand in. After a little groping her fingers closed over one of her emergency light tubes. She brought it out and twisted it sharply. Pale green light glowed magically from her hands.

She propped the light tube against a stalagmite that was growing a few feet beyond Gotcha's beginning—or end, depending on which way you were going. The light would be a beacon for Gabe, a piece of reality to hold on to while the Voices sliced through his soul.

She unplugged her battery leads again and went back into the twisting passage. When she emerged there was only darkness. Hurriedly she plugged in her helmet lamp.

"Gabe?" she called, her voice frayed.

"Here."

The voice came from her right. Reflexively she

snapped her head around, bathing his face in light. He winced and closed his eyes.

"Sorry." She tilted her light away from his eyes. "You startled me. I didn't expect to find you sitting alone in the dark."

"Just getting reacquainted with the absolute lack of light," he said. "Better here than when I'm wedged in Gotcha."

"Are you . . ."—she hesitated—"all right?"

"I'm fine," he said softly. "I find the blackness very peaceful. It makes all my other senses come alive."

She couldn't see him smile but she heard it in his voice.

"I know what you mean," she said.

Her own voice was subtly vibrant. She was remembering a time seven years ago when she'd turned out both their helmet lamps in order to let him experience the seamless, flawless dark. He'd kissed her then, deep within Lost River Cave's eternal night, and she'd been all but overwhelmed by sensations that had nothing to do with sight. It was the first time she had truly felt the strength in his lean body, the heat, the hunger.

The memory went through Joy like the Voices, calling to her in ways she could neither fight nor understand.

"Give me your rope." Her voice was husky.

Silently he handed over the canvas sack with his rope in it.

"At about the fourth twist of Gotcha," she said quickly, tying the bag to her ankle, "you'll hear voices. You aren't going crazy. It's just flowing water and the chamber's eerie acoustics coming to you through the crawlway. Hold that thought and keep pushing forward."

There was a quality to Joy's voice that made Gabe wish his helmet light was plugged in so that he could see her face. She sounded as concerned for him as she'd been when he'd fallen on belay. It made him wonder if she somehow sensed the caustic interior dialogue in his mind as he tried to understand, or at least accept, insights about himself and the past.

"Spooky, huh?" he asked curiously.

"Very. When I forced the tube the first time, I thought I'd finally gone nuts."

"When was that?"

"Six days after my parents died." Her tone didn't invite comment or comfort.

He said nothing more.

Using the illumination from Joy's helmet lamp, he lined himself up just outside Gotcha's small mouth.

"Like most waterways formed below the water table," she said, "Gotcha is essentially circular. People aren't. If the going gets too tight, take off your helmet and push it ahead of you. If that doesn't change your profile enough, back up until you can pull one arm down along your side and lead with the other arm. That will give you a more circular profile."

"If Davy can make it, I should shoot through Gotcha like grass through a goose."

"Don't bet on it. He has more meat, but you have more width in the shoulders. It's the shoulder bones that get stuck on a man."

"And on a woman?"

"Pelvic girdle," she said succinctly.

"Poor Maggie."

The thought of Gabe noticing Maggie's firm, lushly rounded bottom irritated Joy even as she told herself that she was being foolish. Nothing had changed Gabe's sensual nature in the last seven years, and Maggie had a body to tempt any man.

Bleakly Joy hoped that Maggie kept her usually level head when Gabe's charm started to work, dissolving her barriers like superheated groundwater working on limestone.

He'd certainly dissolved Joy fast enough.

"I'll be right behind you," she said in a clipped voice. "Don't try to stay on your stomach all the time. Use your sides, your back, whatever gets it done. Make your body give in to the passage, because it sure as hell won't give in for you. Stone is stronger than any man. Don't fight it. Flex with it. If you get stuck, either holler or thump your foot three times. When you feel me grab your ankle, relax and **breathe out.** You'll be unstuck in no time at all. Okay?"

"Gotcha."

She groaned at the pun.

He gave her a triumphant smile and began slithering into Gotcha's mouth.

She waited until his feet were about two yards in front of her before she unplugged her helmet lamp and began to wriggle slowly after him. She paused from time to time, gauging his progress by the soft grunts and blunt curses that marked his efforts.

Although he had to back up on the second bend and try a different angle of approach, he didn't have any real problem with the first three twists. As near as she could tell, he ended up on his back coming out of the second turn. Davy had the same problem with that part of the tube and solved it the same way.

Silently Gabe kept mental track of the twists and turns of Gotcha's unforgiving passage. Somewhere on the way through the fifth turn, the aches and scrapes and complaints of his straining body dissolved in a soft rush of sound, spectral whispers washing over him, calling to him.

He froze, heart hammering. He knew that it

was his mind that was giving flesh and names to impossible ghost voices from his past.

He knew it, yet he couldn't believe it.

I love you, Gabe. I love you! Don't leave yet. Stay for another week, a day, a minute. Oh, Gabe, I love you so much! Stay with me, love me, let me love you. Please!

He didn't hear his answer.

He didn't have to.

Woven through the ghost-Joy's words, dissolving them, came the soft cries of a baby that had never been born.

FIFTEEN

Even days later, in the pouring light of late afternoon, the memory of the first time he heard the Voices was as real to Gabe as the hot water streaming over him while he stood beneath the only working shower in Cottonwood Wells. His body had gotten used to the physical demands of cave crawling, but the uncanny cries still haunted him. He kept reliving again and again the rushing Voices and the instant six years ago when his brother's much-forwarded message had finally reached him.

The New Mexican cutie was satisfied with $3,744 and an abortion.

Only now did Gabe question the white-hot anger that had consumed him while he held the letter that had waited for him for eleven months. Only now did he admit if it had been any other woman but Joy, he would have felt little but a determination never to be so careless again.

He certainly wouldn't have felt betrayal, contempt, and a rage that hadn't ended until she told him that her parents had died only a few days after he left for the Orinoco.

Whatever else did or didn't happen years ago, he knew now that she hadn't had the abortion casually.

The certainty that Joy truly had been as loving as she'd been innocent unknotted something deep inside Gabe, something that he'd never even admitted was there. He didn't know why he hadn't questioned his rage before or why he was seeking the truth of the past now. He only knew that he was doing it.

Each time he thought of the past, the conviction that what he'd shared with Joy wasn't a delusion or a lie gave him a breath of peace. Like a fantastic cave decoration forming deep within the earth, he sensed something growing within himself, moment by moment, memory by memory, something of unearthly beauty emerging where only darkness and emptiness had been.

He turned off the water and began toweling himself dry. The long, livid rope burns that had marked his leg so badly a year ago had faded to dense maroon shadows that he didn't notice anymore. He had a few new scrapes and bruises here and there, compliments of Lost River Cave's hard and slippery surfaces, but none of the damage was worth mentioning. Despite the three strenuous days of cave crawling he'd put in with Joy, he felt good. Very good.

He felt more alive than he had in years.

Seven years, to be precise.

His heart stopped, then beat more quickly. **When will she let us talk about the past?**

Don't push, he told himself roughly. **This time let her set the pace.**

He'd been very careful to give Joy as much space as possible while they were caving. They talked about Lost River Cave during the day, traded jokes with whoever else was in Cottonwood Wells over dinner, and then he went alone to his cabin to translate his notes and consolidate his impressions of the cave, the people, and himself.

If Joy felt the same relentless need to understand more about him and her and the past, she didn't give a single hint of it.

Go slow.

Don't fuck it up again.

Whatever "it" was.

And that, too, was something he didn't know. He only knew that it was as real as the fantastic cave growing beneath the violent desert sun.

His stomach growled. Fiercely.

He checked his waterproof, scrape-proof, shockproof watch. Quarter of five.

Unfortunately for Gabe's demanding stomach,

it was Davy's turn to cook dinner for the camp. That meant tacos and refried beans. Apparently Joy was the only one in Cottonwood Wells besides Gabe who knew how to bake biscuits or toss a salad, fry a chicken or barbecue a succulent rack of ribs.

But Joy was working on some obscure estimates of the importance of phreatic versus vadose water in Lost River Cave's formation. Normally she would have done the work at night, after dinner, but Kati Something-or-other was coming back to camp tonight and Joy wanted to have time to spend with her.

From what Gabe had gathered the few times Kati's name had come up, she was a camp favorite who had taken a week's vacation at a nearby ranch. Beyond that nothing much had been said. Among the cavers, conversation always revolved around caving in general, Lost River Cave in particular, government grants, and the latest advances in caving equipment. People were rarely mentioned, unless they were one of the early, almost legendary cave explorers.

In fact, until the ride back to camp today, Gabe hadn't even known that Fish had a wife, much less two kids in high school and an out-of-work live-in brother-in-law that he couldn't stand.

No wonder Fish spent so much time away from home.

Gabe stretched until the ligaments in his neck and shoulders shifted and popped. He pulled on underwear, a pair of walking shorts, and sandals. There was no need for any more, and a case could be made for wearing a lot less. The New Mexican summer was an endless cauldron of dry heat. He enjoyed it, just as he enjoyed the contrasting coolness and moisture of Lost River Cave.

He'd even come to love the Voices. He knew now that the yearning, accusing cries came from his own mind, not from ghosts whispering through darkness.

And he wondered what voices Joy heard in the cave, what ghosts called to her, tearing apart her soul. Though she'd never mentioned it, he was certain she heard them. How else would she have known the depth of the emotional shock that would overtake him the first time through Gotcha?

That was why she'd left a light burning at the tube's black exit, giving him a luminous bit of reality to hold on to while the Voices broke over him in a relentless, ghostly, overwhelming wave. Once they must have broken over her, too.

Had she heard a baby cry then?

Does she still hear it now?

That was one question Gabe would never ask. Just as she had known that he would be emotionally disoriented by the Voices and had left a light to help him, he knew that the abortion must have left a psychic wound on Joy that would never heal.

A wound he'd helped to inflict and had done nothing to soothe.

A wound that had now, too late, become his.

If only . . . began the familiar thought.

If nothing, fool, came the equally familiar response. **Time only runs one way.**

Tired of his thoughts, Gabe walked through Joy's cottage to the back porch, opened the door of the washing machine, and pulled out a rope. He looked at it critically before deciding that it would benefit from another rinse and a second dose of fabric softener.

When the rope was awash again, he checked the clothesline to see if anything had come off in the desert's playful wind. Nothing had.

After that there were no more excuses to delay going to the cottage next door and getting some scrubbing done. The fact that he had to haul water in a bucket because the plumbing was dead didn't excuse sloppy housekeeping.

On the other hand there wasn't much reason to straighten out a sleeping bag that only he would see and knock mud off boots that would only get muddy again in a few hours. Now, if he was going to be sharing his sleeping bag . . .

With a muttered word Gabe reeled in his

thoughts. It was bad enough to have Joy haunt his dreams as relentlessly as water haunted the Voices. If he allowed her into his waking thoughts, he would walk around in a permanent state of sexual arousal.

Which was pretty much how he felt anyway.

The more he was with Joy, the more his memories welled up, overflowing the barriers of his will, filling him with hunger.

He could remember all too vividly the contrast of her pale hands against the dark hair of his body, the pleasure of her touch so great that it was nearly agony, the incredible feeling when she caressed him as intimately as he caressed her, the soft heat of her lips and mouth teasing him, and the sleek fire of locking himself within her.

The worst of it was that he knew she was remembering too, and the memories were a fire burning beneath her calm surface. He could see it in her eyes, in her expression, in the fact that she avoided touching him in even the most casual way. He'd told himself that it was hatred that made her pull away from him.

Then he'd found himself doing the same thing, drawing back rather than touching her, because if he touched her once he didn't think he could stop. She filled his dreams the way whispers filled the Voices, completely, irrevocably, part of the very fabric of reality itself.

I know why she's drawing back, but why am I?

Gabe had asked himself that question many times before. Usually a whisper of fear answered him, a clenching in his gut that warned of danger.

This time what he felt was anticipation, not apprehension.

She might not like me worth a damn, but she wants me. I want her. We're both adults in a way we weren't seven years ago. There's no reason to pull back.

And some excellent reasons to go forward.

He needed to feel the incredible satisfaction of her response to him, to hear again her wild cries as he brought ecstasy to her. He would let her set the pace of talking about the past, but he would no longer allow her to slide away from the physical need they both felt. The next time she looked up at a man's naked shoulders, it would be Gabe bending over her, not Davy Graham.

Whistling softly to himself, Gabe went to Joy's living room and looked out over the sun-drenched brilliance of the unpaved driveway that joined the ramshackle cottages of Cottonwood Wells to the rest of the world. A car had just pulled up in a whirl of dust in front of Joy's cottage. She was standing on the front steps, laughing, her face alive with pleasure.

It was a face out of Gabe's dreams, a happiness that he hadn't seen in her since he'd come back to Lost River Cave. He felt a slicing instant of envy for the person who was able to transform the cool, contained Dr. Anderson into the laughing Joy of his memories.

Two children climbed out of the car and ran toward Joy's cottage. The first girl was dark-haired, quick, unremarkable.

The second girl sent the ceiling of reality crashing down around Gabe, changing everything in one explosive instant.

He made the hoarse, harsh sound of a man who had been hit from behind. He felt paralyzed. He forced himself to take a deep breath, to control his wild thoughts, to look rationally at the little girl who was taking the front steps two at a time despite her short legs.

Red hair. Slanting eyes. High cheekbones. Triangular chin. Dimple on the left side. A way of looking over her shoulder with her right hand on her hip.

He knew her.

Stunned, he watched the girl romp up onto the open front porch and call gaily over her shoulder to her friend.

The closer the redheaded girl got, the more certain he was. He didn't know her name, but he had a picture that looked just like her, a photo more than a half-century old, a snapshot of his mother celebrating her seventh birthday with a cocker spaniel panting at her feet and a new doll under her arm.

The driver of the car called out, breaking Gabe's trance.

"Laura! Get back here, honey. You promised to help me with dinner, remember?"

The dark-haired child stopped, pouted, and turned to go back to the car.

The redhead skidded to a stop and turned to follow. Joy stopped the child's headlong rush with a few words. "Kati, say goodbye and then help me bring in your stuff."

"Aw, Mom, I—"

"Kati." It was all Joy said.

It was enough.

Kati raced back, stood on tiptoe at the driver's side of the car, kissed the woman who was driving, and grabbed a sleeping bag and a ratty stuffed animal. Overflowing with energy, Kati danced back around the car toward Joy.

"Coming, Mom. See?"

Motionless, feeling like he was in the center of a cyclone, Gabe could only watch while reality took new shape around him.

Joy had loved him.

She had loved him enough to bear his child with no one to help her, no one to advise her, no one to comfort her, no one to share the burdens and the rewards and the responsibility of raising a child.

She'd loved him more than he had believed possible, more than he'd deserved.

And then she'd hated him enough to tell him that she'd an abortion.

She'd hated him enough to raise his child in silence, telling him nothing, not even that his daughter was alive. Love might have dulled with time, but hatred hadn't.

Even when they worked alone in the cave, Joy hadn't given a single hint of his daughter's existence.

If we talk about the past, Gabe, it won't work.

Joy's words came from the violent darkness of his emotions, whispers that had new meaning.

Hatred.

She hated him more than he believed possible, more than any man deserved. It was a miracle she hadn't dropped him down one of Lost River Cave's deepest pits and tossed the rope in after him.

It would be a miracle if he didn't do the same to her.

SIXTEEN

The front screen slammed and the little girl raced into the house. She skidded to a stop as soon as she saw Gabe standing motionless in the living room.

"Who are you?" she asked.

He searched Kati's face with a hunger he wasn't aware of, an intensity born of years of rage and grief. Nothing he saw made him believe that his first impression was wrong. **Kati was the image of his mother all those lost years ago.** The eyes were gray rather than green, but the rest was like seeing a picture come to life.

He sat on his heels to bring himself closer to eye level with the little red-haired miracle.

"I'm Gabriel Venture." His voice was rich with emotions held in check. "My friends call me Gabe. Would you like to?"

"Sure," she said easily. Arms full, she trotted past him toward a small closed room that was down a short hall off the main room. "I'm Kati. Are you a caver?"

He closed his eyes, caught by too many emotions to trust himself to speak.

Kati doesn't know her father's name.

"I'm a writer," he managed finally.

She opened the door and disappeared in the tiny room. "Oh, you're the one Mommy told me about."

"What did she tell you?"

His voice was too sharp, too demanding, but he could no more control it than he could the adrenaline that had slammed through his veins when the ceiling of reality caved in and he recognized his own daughter dancing toward him through the rubble.

Kati ran back to the main room and grabbed a sock that had jumped out of her armload of overnight gear.

"You're gonna write about the cave and then maybe we can come back here someday," she said, throwing the sock into the small room and shutting the door behind her.

"Back?" He held his voice carefully, as if it was too fragile to be trusted. "Are you going somewhere?"

Kati shrugged with a maturity older than her years. "Sure. When the cave closes, Mommy's got to get a job somewhere or we won't have any money."

He opened his mouth. Nothing came out. He didn't know what to say. Joy hadn't mentioned anything about what would happen after the grant ran out, so he'd assumed she would be staying on at the university.

To assume makes an ass out of you and me, he told himself sardonically. Again.

When it comes to Joy, all assumptions are wrong.

But then it's goddamn easy to be wrong when you're blindfolded and turned loose to stumble through a minefield.

Anger curled through Gabe, hot and eager. Before he could ask any more questions, the car out in front of the cottage honked twice and drove away in a wash of dust.

Kati ran past Gabe to the back porch. The screen door slammed and the girl's high, excited voice rang out.

"Gravy-bear, I'm back! Catch me!"

Gabe got to the kitchen window just in time to see Kati throw herself into Davy's arms. Laughing, shrieking, she was lifted and whirled over his head in a game that was obviously familiar and much enjoyed by both of them. Maggie stood at the sidelines, laughing as hard as Kati and calling instructions on dive-bombing with a live bomb.

Joy walked into the kitchen, expecting it to be empty. The house rules were simple: everyone shared the one working shower and no one hung around afterward except Joy.

But there was Gabe, leaning against her kitchen counter, staring out of the window with hunger in his eyes, in his face, in the very tension of his body.

She glanced outside. At first she thought it was Maggie that had called such depth of feeling out of Gabe. With that thought came a tearing emotion that Joy was forced to acknowledge as jealousy even while she told herself that her reaction was totally irrational. She had no hold on Gabe.

More important, she didn't want one.

He turned when she thumped a bag of groceries on the counter. She saw the fury in his eyes.

"Tell me, Dr. Smith-Anderson," he said, giving a sardonic emphasis to Joy's maiden name, "was yours a long marriage?"

In that instant she knew that somehow he'd discovered that Kati was his child. A storm of emotions swept through her—relief and anger and fear.

And curiosity.

She was the only living person who knew the truth of Kati's parentage. She didn't understand how he could have known so quickly. Kati didn't look anything like her father. She was fair where Gabe was dark. Her eyes were gray rather than green. She had a dimple and he had none. Her hair was red and she had golden freckles where Gabe tanned darkly, smoothly.

Kati didn't resemble her father at all, except in subtle ways that tore at Joy's heart at odd moments: Kati's wide-ranging curiosity, her physical courage, the way she had of looking over her shoulder with her hand on one hip and one eyebrow half-raised.

"No," Joy said, her voice husky.

"No what?" Then, in a low voice that vibrated with warning, Gabe said, "Don't lie to me."

"I've never lied to you."

"**Like hell you haven't.** Who is Kati's father?"

"No marriage. No father." Joy's voice was under control again, as cold as Gabe's was hot.

"That's not what I meant and you damn well know it!"

"Do I?" Carefully she began putting away the groceries that Susan had picked up for the camp. "Then what did you mean?"

"Kati's my daughter."

Joy shrugged. "Biologically, yes. In any meaningful way, no."

"**Meaningful?** Bullshit! It's damned hard to have a meaningful relationship with a child I thought you'd flushed as soon as you found out I wouldn't be supporting you."

It was Joy's turn to be shocked and furious. "What are you talking about? I never asked for a penny from—"

"I'm talking about abortion," he cut in. "I'm

talking about a lying little bitch who told my brother she'd an abortion, then went and had my baby and never told me about it. For six years I thought my baby was dead—but she was alive and growing and I didn't even suspect it. Sweet Jesus Christ, I didn't know you had that much hate in you."

Joy felt the searing pleasure of anger sliding beyond her control. She didn't even try to call it back. A vicious sweep of her hand scattered groceries across the counter.

"You didn't know a goddamn thing about me except that I was hot for you," she said. "All you cared about was a sweaty time in the backseat and no strings attached. I gave you just what you wanted, everything you asked for. Don't come whining to me if you don't like what you got. I paid the price of your precious freedom, not you."

"You didn't even tell Kati about me." His voice was controlled, savage, like a whip curling out, hungry for flesh to tear.

Joy's voice was the same. "What should I have told her? That her dear daddy didn't even want her to be born? That he gave me $3,744 for an abortion?" For an instant her voice cracked. "I wanted—oh, God, how much I wanted!—to tell you to take that blood money and shove it right up. But I couldn't. It would pay for vitamins and doctors and hospital costs. So I took the money and told your messenger he could tell you to go to hell, I was doing what was best for me, not for him."

Gabe remembered his brother's relayed message, so like Joy's—and the conclusion so opposite: **I'm doing what's best for me and to hell with your brother.**

Your new Mexican cutie took the $3,744 and had an abortion.

"So what should I have told Kati, **sweetheart**?" Joy asked acidly. "That the son of a bitch who was her daddy never even bothered to write and find out whether it was a boy or girl?"

Gabe made a husky sound as he realized the extent of the broken communications. And the cost.

His shoulder muscles bunched as his fist crashed onto the counter with enough force to make dishes in the cupboard leap. In the charged silence the sound was like an explosion.

"You never wrote to me about money or anything else," he said finally, his voice flat.

"Where would I have sent the letter—to Mr. Soon-to-Be-Famous Gabriel Venture, care of the Orinoco River?"

Gabe's eyes narrowed to jade slits. "Dan had my address."

"Your darling brother wouldn't give it to me.

He told me what I saw was what I got, that I should take the check and forget about you and your money." Her smile was like a knife sliding out of a sheath. "It was good advice. I took it."

The gray blaze of Joy's eyes told Gabe more than her words. She was telling the truth. She'd been telling the truth seven years ago. She'd wanted him, not his supposed wealth.

"Christ Jesus, what a mess," Gabe said in a low voice, thinking of how hard it must have been for Joy with no parents, no money, nothing, not even a hope that he would come back. "I'm sorry."

"For what? That I didn't have the abortion?"

"You know I didn't want—" he began furiously.

But she was still talking, years of rage honing her voice until it was as cutting as her smile had been. "You made your choice, Mr. World Traveler. You seduced a twenty-year-old virgin who was dumb enough to fall in love with you. You knew when you left that I might be pregnant, and you left anyway. But before you left you made arrangements for me to have an abortion, just in case I might need one. Any rights you might have had to Kati ended that instant. You're not her father. **You're nothing.**"

"That's bullshit, **sweetheart.** I didn't want you to have an abortion. I left money so if you were pregnant you'd have something to pay the bills until I could send you more. When I found out that you'd flushed my baby I wanted to—"

Abruptly Gabe realized that his fists were clenched so hard that his knuckles were white. Rage was a bitter taste in his mouth, a wild flush across his cheeks. He took a deep, shaking breath, appalled at the depth of his fury. It had lived within him for six years, eating away at him in unexpected ways—and then it had exploded.

Leaving him empty.

"It was eleven months before I got Dan's letter telling me about you and the money and the abortion he thought you'd had," Gabe said hoarsely. "After that, there wasn't much point in writing to ask you about the sex of our baby, was there?"

She saw through the aftermath of his rage to the weary exhaustion beneath, and felt her own fury slipping away. He hadn't wanted her to have an abortion. He hadn't wanted to kill the only thing she had left to remind her of how it had felt to be alive and in love and at peace within his arms.

He hadn't wanted to destroy her.

But he hadn't wanted to stay with her either.

When Joy spoke, her voice was as hollow and husky as his. "Let's be honest with ourselves this time around. Neither of us wanted an abortion.

Neither of us was prepared for a child. You chose your course. I chose mine."

"I didn't know you were pregnant," he said fiercely, pulling Joy into his arms. "Sweetheart," he whispered against her hair, her cheek, the corner of her mouth, **"I didn't know."**

He kissed Joy with consuming tenderness, his lips trembling as they brushed over hers, his whole body quivering when he felt her hands frame his face. Then he lifted his head and her sad smile sliced through him, telling him that he was only beginning to measure what he'd lost, what he would yet lose.

"Gabriel, Gabriel," she murmured, shaking her head slowly, feeling the warm, remembered silk of his hair slide between her fingers, her body trembling against his. "Let's be as honest with each other now as we were seven years ago. If you'd known that I was pregnant, you still would have gone away."

Once he would have brushed her words aside with the easy assurance of youth. He wanted to brush them aside now, but the attempt died in his throat. He was older, wiser, with the kind of self-knowledge that came from hanging head-down over a void and measuring the depth of his own grave.

"I tried to stay with you," he said. "Then Dan told me how tight money was, and how much I could help him and Mother with the advance money from the Orinoco assignment. He told me that my career, the career he and Mother had sacrificed for, was just getting started."

Joy closed her eyes and let herself be held.

"I shouldn't have let him talk me out of staying with you, knowing you might be pregnant. But I did."

"You wanted to see all the wild places."

He closed his eyes against the pain of understanding himself. "Yes. At twenty-three, I was young and eager for the world."

Joy was surprised by the hurt twisting through her. Despite her calm statement that he would have left no matter what, deep in her heart she'd always hoped that he would have stayed with her if he'd known she was pregnant.

Part of her had always hoped that he loved her as much as she loved him.

When Gabe felt her hands pushing against him, silently asking to be released, his arms tightened for an instant.

"Joy, it was nothing against you. It was simply the wrong time for me . . . too soon, too many other people depending on me."

She stepped away from him, her face pale. "I understand."

"It's not the same now. **I'm** not the same," he said, taking her hand.

"I know."

And even as she agreed she took her hand from his.

"Then why are you turning away from me?" he asked.

"Because you don't understand."

"What?" he asked, searching the crystalline shades of darkness in her eyes. "What don't I understand?"

"Me. I've changed too."

He remembered the black emotions he had seen staring out at him from her eyes. "You don't really hate me. Don't try to tell me that. I don't believe it. You were trembling when you kissed me."

"I don't hate you." Joy looked up at Gabe, her eyes as deep and unflinching as winter.

"Then what is it, sweetheart?"

"It was too soon for you to love seven years ago—and now it's too late for me."

He drew a swift breath. "Why?"

"Love requires trust. Trust requires innocence. I'm not innocent anymore."

"I took that from you when I left," he said, his voice raw. "Is that what you're saying?"

"Yes." Her smile was gentle, accepting, and sadder than tears. "Being left behind is very educational. And it wasn't just you." She closed her eyes for a moment, concealing the pain of her own new self-knowledge. "Losing my parents that way, no warning, no chance to prepare . . ." Her eyes opened, clear and certain. "I'm a long way from the girl I was seven years ago."

He stepped close again, stroked her hair, her cheek, and listened to her words as though his life depended on it.

"Looking back . . ." She hesitated, sighed. "Even if you had stayed, I don't think it would have worked. Your family was against it and you're close to your family."

Gabe couldn't argue that. When he was able to, he talked to his brother and his mother every few days.

But the next talk he had with Dan wouldn't be pleasant.

"Instead of simply not loving me," Joy said quietly, "you would have ended up hating me and resenting the child you never asked for. Bad timing all the way around. Too soon for us, Gabe. Way too soon."

"And now you think it's too late." His voice was as grim as his narrowed eyes.

"Not for you. All you have to do is find someone young and innocent and trusting. Like Maggie." Joy turned away, her expression tight, hidden, as she added, "And then, of course, you'd have to have the guts to follow through."

Before Gabe could say anything, the front door

of the cottage slammed, warning them that Kati was back.

Joy spun toward him and said softly. "Please, don't—"

"Tell my daughter who her father is?" His voice was low, challenging.

Joy took a ragged breath and braced for a storm she hadn't ever thought would come.

SEVENTEEN

"Mommy? What's for dinner?" Kati called.

Joy spun toward the kitchen doorway and held out her arms. "Hi, button. Hungry?"

Kati leaped up just as her mother's arms closed around her wiry little body. Joy settled her daughter's legs around her waist and looked eye to eye with her.

"Missed you," Kati said, giving Joy a noisy kiss.

"Even with the whole Childer family around you?"

"Uh-huh. I still want brothers and sisters and a daddy, but no one's as good as you. Love you."

"I love you too."

She hugged her daughter close for a few moments longer, then lowered her to the floor. Though Joy couldn't see Gabe, she felt his focus like the sun burning her.

"Bath before dinner." To underline her words, Joy traced the streaks of dust on Kati's fair skin.

"Fried chicken, huh, please?"

"Tacos and refried beans."

"Uh-oh, Gravy-bear is cooking again."

"Yes, but don't hurt his feelings."

"Oh, I won't," Kati said solemnly. "Gravy-bear is soooo nice. Are you sure he isn't my daddy?"

Joy struggled to keep her voice light. "I'm sure, button."

"Do you think he'd like to be?" Kati asked, her eyes and voice wistful.

"I think your Gravy-bear couldn't love you any more if he was your very own daddy." Joy's voice was teasing but her hands shook.

"Yeah," Kati said matter-of-factly, chewing on her lower lip. "That's what he told me. But then why doesn't my own daddy love me?"

Joy felt her control slipping away. She swept up Kati in her arms and turned so that her daughter's back was to Gabe. She desperately wished that Kati had chosen a better moment to talk about her ongoing search for a father. It was a conversation Joy was used to, along with her daughter's wheedling, teasing pleas for siblings.

But Joy wasn't used to having the conversation with Kati's father standing two feet away, his body taut, his eyes like green ice, his face fierce with a truth that no one had spoken aloud.

Oh, God, don't say it, Gabe, Joy pleaded silently, giving him a look as fierce as his own. **Please! Don't let Kati find out like this. She isn't ready for it.**

I'm not ready for it.

And you're not ready either. Don't you see? She can handle the reality she knows. But if you tell her you're her father, when you leave she'll feel rejected all her life.

Don't do that to her.

Please. Don't.

Gabe didn't have to be a mind reader to understand the unspoken appeal in Joy's eyes. And to feel it cutting through his defenses into his soul.

He'd never meant to hurt Joy by leaving. He'd never dreamed even in his worst nightmares that he'd hurt his own child, this lively, bright-faced little girl with yearning gray eyes.

"I'm sure your father loves you," Gabe said, while his face ached with the strain of controlling his expression.

Kati turned toward him so fast that her hair flew out in a fiery cloud. "Really-for-sure sure?"

"Really for sure."

There was a certainty in his voice that intrigued Kati. She looked at him with transparent eagerness. "Do you know my father?"

Joy closed her eyes and waited for Kati's innocent world to be shattered.

"I don't know any man who deserves a little girl as special as you," he said honestly, his voice husky.

For a moment Kati measured Gabe with unflinching gray eyes that reminded him very much of Joy's.

Then Kati gave him a breathtaking smile. "You want to help me make tacos with Gravy-bear?"

"Bath, young lady," Joy said quickly, carrying her daughter out of the kitchen.

"But Mommy—" Kati began.

"Mr. Venture has a lot of work to do," Joy said, overriding Kati's objections. "Say goodbye."

"Gabe," Kati retorted, pouting at her mother. "He said I could call him Gabe."

Joy's lips flattened as she opened her daughter's bedroom door. "Bath."

Kati read the danger signals from her mother and resigned herself to losing this round. But not without getting something in return. "Then I get to help with tacos."

"Depends on how fast you take your bath, doesn't it?"

The little girl frowned. She loved taking long baths.

Gabe listened to the voices floating back from the bathroom, followed by the muted thunder of water filling the ancient claw-footed tub, and then Kati's peals of uninhibited laughter when her mother tickled her. He visualized the bath ritual from his own childhood, his mother bent over the tub, washing him and his brother while they did their best to splash water over everything in the room.

Sometimes things had gotten out of hand. Then his father would come into the bathroom, lift his wife out of the mess, and begin washing squealing, splashing young bodies with equal parts determination and resignation. Whenever that happened, the brothers had looked at each other and laughed secretly, glorying in their power over their parents.

Gabe's smile faded when he realized that Kati had never known that delicious childish conspiracy with a sibling against a parent. She'd never had the sweet certainty that if one parent got fed up, there was a fresh one just down the hall. And if both parents were out of sorts, the siblings could ride out the storm together, secure in their attachment to a co-conspirator.

Kati couldn't do that. Except for her mother, she was alone.

Joy was alone, period.

No one to lean on. No one to take her place when her child's needs were greater than a single parent's energy. No one to relax and curl up with at night. No one to reassure her that she was doing a fine job under difficult circumstances. No one at all.

And she wasn't looking for anyone.

Kati might be searching for a father in the males around her, but clearly Joy wasn't looking for any man for any purpose at all. She'd meant exactly what she'd said to Gabe. She loved no man because love required trust and she no longer trusted.

It hadn't stopped with simply not loving any man. Her reaction when Gabe touched her—the automatic flinch, the surprise in her eyes—told him that she rarely allowed anyone physically close to her but Kati.

Yet Joy had trembled when he held her, shivered when his lips brushed over her mouth, sighed when her hands had sought and found the warm thickness of his hair. He might have killed her ability to love, but her body still responded to him. The shimmering sensuality he'd once discovered in her was still there, waiting to be released. All he had to do was get past her anger and distrust.

He could start by not telling Kati who her father was until her mother was ready to handle it.

Aching, Gabe turned and let himself out the back door of Joy's cottage. As he did, he hoped that he wasn't making another mistake, hurting people when all he wanted to do was make up for the wrongs of the past.

EIGHTEEN

Ten days later the voices closed around Gabe. They murmured softly, endlessly, haunting him with phrases from his past and his present. He pushed forward into the cave anyway, following Joy's lead, knowing that there wasn't any help for any of it.

No matter how many times he heard the Voices, they would always pluck at his soul.

At least now an unborn child no longer called to him through the cool darkness. He heard cries, yes, but they were a little girl's innocent questions as she tried to understand why a father she'd never known didn't love her.

Using knees, elbows, heels, and toes for leverage, he pushed deeper into Gotcha. There was no way for him to tell the Voices to be still, that he regretted the past as he'd never expected to regret anything in his life. There was no way to tell Kati that it wasn't her fault she didn't have a father. There was no way to explain that he hadn't even suspected Joy was a virgin until he was too gripped by passion to believe that any moment would ever exist except the one consuming moment when he found himself locked deep inside her.

The fact that Joy had wanted him as much as he'd wanted her, the fact that he hadn't known her innocence, the fact that he'd accepted the Orinoco assignment before he ever came to Lost River Cave, the fact that he'd done all he could for Joy by leaving her every bit of money he had—those facts described but didn't relieve him of his responsibility to her.

And to himself.

Love requires trust. Trust requires innocence.

Grimly he pushed against stone and wondered what forgiveness required.

Whatever it was, he needed it. Underneath the last ten days of professional questions and note-taking and cautious camaraderie, he was a single raw ache. He didn't know the way out of the trap he'd built in the past. He only knew that life lived like this, in silence and waiting and pain, wasn't life at all.

Does Joy ever wake up in the bleak hours before dawn and wish to hell that she could live the past all over again?

Like him. Aching.

Asking questions that had no answers.

Feeling loneliness and regret like a cold, hidden river dissolving away his soul while darkness closed around him in a seamless shroud.

Not once in the past ten days had Joy said or done anything to him that said he was the least bit different from the other cavers to her. Unfailingly polite and professional with each other, they could have been complete strangers.

Such bitterly intimate strangers.

With a whispered curse, he shoved free of Gotcha and stood again to plug in his helmet leads.

"Gabe?" Joy asked softly, seeing the unmistakable lines of pain on his face. "Are you all right?"

She touched his shoulder in the instant before she controlled herself and snatched back her hand. Since she'd found herself trembling in Gabe's arms, she'd been very, very careful not to touch him.

He simply looked at her, saying nothing.

"What's wrong?" she asked. "Did you hurt yourself coming through Gotcha?"

His brief smile tore at her. It revealed a defenseless agony that she knew too well from her own experience. She made a protesting sound and touched him.

"Gabe?" she whispered, one voice among the

Voices swirling around them in darkness. "What is it?"

"Have you ever been lonely?"

His words echoed in his mind as though someone else had spoken them. He heard the pain and the emptiness and the searching hunger. Then, even as his words sank beneath the murmurous sounds of the room, he flinched away from them.

"Christ, listen to me asking you about loneliness."

His bleak laughter stabbed through the Voices as he walked past Joy into the huge room.

She made a small sound and turned away, shaking with a sudden storm of emotions, torn apart by discovery.

And by anger.

What right does he have to be lonely? He's gotten everything he ever wanted—fame, respect, adventure, discovery. He's the Great Gabriel Venture. He explored the world while I explored abandonment.

It cost me too much to care about him in the past. I won't make the same mistake again.

I can't afford to.

Even though I sense loneliness in him, a hunger and a need that are like mine. Hunger and need aren't enough. Gabe hasn't changed in the most important way. He still cares more

about his career than about anything else, including his loneliness.

He proved it when he agreed without arguing to leave the past alone so that he could do what he came here to do—another article about Lost River Cave.

He proves it again and again every day with his cool, relentless professionalism.

He hasn't changed, not really.

I have. I'm immune to love, to him.

Be as lonely as you like, Gabriel Venture. It won't touch me.

"Coming through," Davy called. "I think. Damn, this last one's a real bitch."

Joy realized that she was blocking Gotcha's exit. Hastily she stepped aside.

Davy wriggled out of the impossibly small opening, pushing his wadded-up clothes and helmet ahead of him and dragging a string of equipment from his ankle. And cursing fit to blister stone.

Wearing only his underwear—and that just barely—he kicked free of Gotcha, stood, and stretched thankfully.

Joy nudged his clothes with the toe of her muddy boot. "Gonna freeze, boy."

"Nah." Davy whacked himself on his stomach with a broad palm. "Too much natural insulation."

Maggie emerged from the hole in time to hear

Davy's words. "Gravy-bear, you don't have a spare ounce of fat on you and you know it."

"Do tell," he said. He bent over and pulled Maggie to her feet as if she was no bigger than Kati. "Can't say the same about you, can we? You got a license for that trailer?" He swatted Maggie on the butt as he reached past her for his clothes.

Joy didn't need to see Maggie's face to know that Davy's casual comment stung.

"Tell you what," Joy said to Maggie. "You hold him and I'll cut his throat."

"Sold," Maggie said with enough emphasis to get through Davy's thick hide.

He looked injured. "What did I do?"

"Got an hour?" Joy asked sweetly.

"For you, Dr. Anderson, I have more than—"

"Would it be possible to get on with this bloody exploration?" Gabe asked from the darkness beyond Gotcha. "Or is Davy waiting for you two to tuck dollar bills into his muddy underwear?"

"For you," Davy said to Maggie as he pulled on his clothes, "the cost is ten bucks. Dr. Anderson, now, could—"

"Gravy-bear," Maggie cut in huskily, "did anybody ever mention that you have enough mouth for another row of teeth?"

Laughing, Davy stuffed his shirt in his pants, completely unself-conscious as he dressed. "Just you, Maggie, and you're too young for me to take seriously."

"Then you're a damn fool," Gabe said and turned away.

Wincing, Davy glanced from Gabe to Maggie. "Looks like you have yourself a champion. You got something going that I don't know about?"

"She's got brains," Fish said as he pushed out of Gotcha. "Not to mention heart, grit, and a body that would make a saint think about sinning."

"Fish," Maggie said, smiling widely, "would your wife mind horribly if I kissed you?"

He laughed and stood up as he plugged in his helmet light. "She'd mind like hell, Maggie. You see," he said, winking at her, "my wife knows I'm too old **not** to take you seriously."

"Old?" Maggie laughed. "You're not a day over thirty-five."

"You got that right," Davy retorted. "Fish is **hundreds** of days over thirty-five. Hell, **thousands**."

Maggie gave Davy a sidelong look. "Sometimes you're a real pain in the ass."

"Shut up, children," Fish said amiably, turning toward Joy. "What's on the program today?"

"I want you to referee while Maggie helps Davy with his survey," Joy said dryly. "Begin at the breakdown on the northeast quadrant of the Voices. I'm going to try to find a path through the Maze."

Thinking of the impossibly intricate, ceiling-to-floor mass of solution cavities and cave formations known as the Maze, Fish laughed. "A path, huh? Whatever you say, ma'am."

She smiled slightly. "I know, I know. But I can't help believing that there's a passage from the Voices into a whole new area of the cave. A big one. The water we're hearing has to come from somewhere and go to somewhere else. And the air in the Maze blows. You've felt it, Fish. You know you have."

"Sure have. Lost it, too. Time and time again. Speaking of time, who's keeping it today?"

"You."

He looked at his watch, rubbed off the muddy face with an equally muddy finger, and asked, "How long?"

"Call out the hours. And make sure Maggie drinks," Joy said. "She keeps coming back with her canteen half full. Just because it's cool down here doesn't mean your body isn't using a lot of water."

"I hear you," Fish said.

He made herding motions with his hands. Davy and Maggie walked ahead of him at a smart pace, keeping between the bright orange strips of tape.

Joy walked toward the pool of light cast by Gabe's helmet lamp.

"Is Maggie all right?" he asked quietly, following Joy as she walked deeper into the Voices.

"Yes." Joy's answer was soft, yet it slid among the murmurous cascading whispers like a knife.

"Davy's an idiot," Gabe said.

"Maybe."

Joy tried to focus on the cave's uneven floor rather than on her own seesaw emotions. She couldn't. Her feelings were too strong to be ignored. Hearing Gabe champion Maggie had bruised Joy in unexpected ways.

"And maybe," she said bitterly, "Davy's just smart enough to know that Maggie is too much woman for him."

"Do you really believe that?"

"Maggie has never had a lover, and it's not for lack of offers."

"Which means?"

Finally certain that they were beyond the hearing of the other cavers, Joy stopped and turned on Gabe.

"Maggie's first man will be her last," Joy said coldly. "Davy is only twenty-three. Do you think he's ready for that kind of relationship?"

"I wasn't, is that what you're saying?"

With an effort that left her throat aching Joy made her tone matter-of-fact. "That's what I'm saying."

"I'm ready now."

"Then what are you waiting for? Get moving before Davy wakes up and figures out that he's letting a terrific woman slip through his thick fingers. Of course, you might have a small problem," Joy added. "One or all of Maggie's brothers will do their best to kill you when they find out you've seduced and abandoned their baby sister. They just wouldn't understand how writing another article about the ass end of nowhere is more important than Maggie's happiness."

She heard the harsh intake of Gabe's breath, but she didn't see his expression. She was already turning away, already regretting her quick tongue and the emotions eating through her control as surely as acid ate through limestone.

If Gabe took her advice and pursued Maggie, Joy would hate him, hate Maggie, hate herself.

The thought that he might have learned enough to find and recognize love in another woman terrified Joy. She'd felt nothing like it since the moment she'd doubled over the steering wheel of the Jeep with labor pains and understood that she'd started toward town too late, that she would end up having her baby in the desert with no one to help her.

Gabe saw Joy stumble. He caught her, turned her toward him, and wanted to cry out in protest at the strain he saw in her face. He knew that she'd been thinking about the past, a past she refused to talk about.

As for the future, it didn't exist—for her, for him, for them.

He couldn't bear even to think about it, the days and months and years of regret and pain.

Past and future were out of reach. There was

only the time he would spend at Lost River Cave, exploring the earth and himself and the past Joy refused to discuss despite the small, red-haired tornado dancing through their lives.

With enough time, enough space, enough understanding, he kept hoping that Joy would talk to him. She simply had to. He didn't know how much longer he could go on this way.

No past. No future. Just now.

So don't fuck it up now.

Very carefully he released Joy. Even through the multiple layers of clothing the warmth of her called to his senses. If it was just desire twisting through him, he would have seduced her, satisfying both of them, relieving a torment that had begun seven years ago and had no end in sight.

But it wasn't that simple.

The longer he was with Joy, the more certain he was that he needed more than her body. He needed what he'd once had with her. All of her, mind and body and soul. The laughter and the tears, the heat and the silences, the luminous reflection of love in her eyes.

He wanted her love with a savage force that taught him how little he'd ever wanted anything before in his life.

And she wanted only to hurt him more.

"I think," he said carefully, "you should confine your lectures to the nature and formation of New Mexico's limestone caves. If you keep chipping away at me, something will happen that we'll both regret."

Appalled by the cruelty of her own words, Joy could only nod agreement. Though she'd forbidden Gabe to talk about the past, she kept making sideways references to it herself, digging away at his careful exterior, trying to discover what feelings lay beneath.

If any.

"I'm sorry," she said huskily. "It isn't fair of me to keep prying beneath your surface, trying to find out how you really feel. I already know. I know how important your career is to you. I understand. You've made a life for yourself that's very exciting, very fulfilling, a life that anyone would envy."

He looked at her curiously. "Do you?"

"What?"

"Envy my life?"

The question shocked her.

Then the answer came, more shocking than the question.

"Yes. Part . . . part of your fascination for me," she said, her voice halting, "was the places you'd been to, the places you'd go, everything fresh and exciting. I wanted those places. I wanted them as much as you did, and . . ."

Her voice frayed into silence. She gave up trying to explain and just shook her head slowly.

"And I knocked you up and took off for the

very places you would have cut off a hand to see," he finished softly. A shudder moved over him as he realized that he'd delivered Joy into a very opposite kind of life, single motherhood and necessity closing down around her in a cage that had no key. "I didn't know you wanted the wild places," he whispered, his voice one among the many Voices in Lost River Cave. "Believe me, sweetheart, I didn't know."

"How could you? I didn't know myself, until this instant."

It was Gabe's turn to be shocked.

"I couldn't let myself know," she said, "because there was nothing I could do about it except break my heart over it." She drew in her breath and released it in a long, ragged sigh. "But it's all right. I had Lost River Cave to explore. And Kati." Joy smiled through trembling lips. "She's a miracle. She trusts so easily, lives so completely, loves so beautifully." Joy laughed shakily. "She's also a stubborn little witch, but that just reminds me that she's real, that she'll grow up, that someday she'll love a man and . . ." Joy bowed her head against the ache in her throat. **"Oh God, let her love wisely,"** she whispered beneath the liquid sounds pouring through the darkness.

But Gabe heard.

He closed his eyes against the naked pain on

Joy's face, yet nothing could close out what she had said. He knew that her agonized prayer would come to him again and again in the bleak hours before dawn. In the darkness of his soul her words would be whispered endlessly among the Voices.

"Joy," he said huskily, reaching for her, needing to comfort her and himself.

His fingers closed on emptiness.

He opened his eyes. Joy's light was retreating from him silently, farther away with each breath, each heartbeat.

NINETEEN

In aching silence Gabe followed Joy through Lost River Cave. They left behind the orange stripes that marked previous explorations, but she never hesitated. Though he moved quickly over the uneven cave floor, he didn't catch up with her until she stopped and waited for him.

"We'll begin here," she said.

He listened carefully to the nuances of her voice. Controlled, professional, as though she'd never prayed that her daughter would be wiser in love than her mother had been.

"Do you see that drapery?" she asked, moving her head and at the same time turning on and focusing the second lamp as an intense, narrow beam.

Growing down from what had once been a sinuous crack in the ceiling was a huge sheet of creamy limestone striped by various earth tones. It was a decoration of the kind that cavers called "cave bacon." This particular formation had grown almost to the floor of the cave itself.

"Turn your back to it," she said.

He started to ask why, then simply did as she asked.

"Now stay there," she said. "When I call out, shut off your lamp and turn back around. But not until then. Okay?"

Part of Gabe wondered if she was going to just walk off and leave him to find his own way out of the cave, but all he said was "Okay."

Quickly yet very carefully, Joy picked her way over to and around the drapery on a path she had discovered by accident a few days ago. Despite the rarity and beauty of the huge formation, she hadn't laid down any orange stripes leading to it. She hadn't even told anyone that the formation existed.

Until now.

The cave floor was frosted with delicate formations growing among the more solid decorations. She tried to walk only where the path was over the ancient limestone bed itself rather than the newer, unique sculptures precipitated out of water and darkness. Finally she was behind the drapery.

Poised on tiptoe, she adjusted both of her headlamps to the widest possible beam. Then she turned toward Gabe. "Lights out and you can turn around."

He shut off his light. When he turned around, he sucked in his breath with a wondering sound.

For all its massive weight, the limestone drapery was translucent. Her lights spread through the stone, making it glow with an unearthly beauty. Subtle colors rippled in silence, a dream living in the mind of a nameless god. Graceful folds of stone shimmered with moisture. The drapery was vital, alive, growing.

Gabe hadn't seen anything to equal it in any of the places on earth he'd explored at such great cost to himself and others.

Joy's helmet lights stroked across the drapery, then away, leaving it in primal darkness once more. Light halved as she turned off one of her helmet lamps and headed back toward him.

He made a sound of protest that went no farther than his mind. He tried to tell himself that the stone drapery wasn't a miracle, it was the result of simple, rational physical processes working over long periods of time. A water drop zigzagging across a tiny crack in the slanting ceiling, the slow seepage of more water, the even slower precipitation of stone, more seepage flowing over the new stone, more precipitation, until the result was an extraordinary limestone drapery so delicate that light could slide through it in a subtle blaze of radiance.

Without a word Gabe turned toward the woman who was standing beside him. He realized that she'd been watching him, absorbing his reaction.

Only then did he understand that she'd given him those moments of beauty in silent apology for the mother's prayer that would haunt his dreams.

"Thank you," he said simply, wanting to touch Joy, afraid if he did she would withdraw again. "What do you call it?"

"You mean like Gotcha or Surprise or the Voices?"

"Yes."

She hesitated. "No one else knows about the drapery. It's not on Davy's survey. I discovered it a few days ago when you and I got lost in the Maze."

Gabe looked toward the jungle of cave formations and solution cavities known as the Maze. "I remember. We came at it from a different angle. It's an amazing place."

"If that's a pun, I'll have to kill you."

"What pun?" he asked immediately, deadpan.

Her grin flashed in the reflected light.

He wanted to hold her. He didn't. It was enough to see her spontaneous smile.

"So how did you find it?" he asked.

"When I turned back to see if you were following me, **I saw your light shining through stone.**" The memory of it was in her voice, and in the goose bumps marching beneath warm cave clothing. "I couldn't move. I couldn't even speak. It was the most impossible, most beautiful thing I'd ever seen."

The understanding that she'd just shared with him something that she hadn't showed anyone else transformed Gabe as surely as light transformed the rippling stone. Then he saw the same knowledge come to her, changing her.

She stepped back from him quickly, fear plain in the tight lines of her face. "We'll have to be sure that Davy surveys it. It's too beautiful to be lost."

"What will you call it?"

"Deception."

Gabe thought of the beauty, the impossibility, the light pouring through stone. "Why not call it Love?"

"Same difference." She kept on speaking, her voice precise, leaving him no opening. "There are four sections on the perimeter of this room that haven't been thoroughly explored. They're our best hope of finding a passage through to the cavern that is producing the water sounds."

"Like Honeycomb?" Gabe asked.

Joy thought of the section of limestone that had been dissolved away until all that remained was a largely undecorated lacework of stone that very much resembled a honeycomb. From it came an endless whispering of voices and a steady breeze, telling Joy that there was an opening—a large opening—on the other side of the large formation of lacy stone.

"Yes, like that," she said. "But to get through there would mean destroying some of the Honeycomb itself. No matter how much I want to find the source of the Voices, I won't do that. Lost River Cave has been growing for millions of years. I couldn't bear knowing that I'd destroyed part of it in a reckless search for its deepest secrets. The cave will either yield to me in the time I have left, or it won't."

Once Gabe might have disagreed with her, but no longer. He knew now the many ways that regret haunted ambition's deepest caverns, a cold black river running through layers of dissolving stone.

"I want to try the Maze again," she said. "I'm sure we can find a way through it."

"If we don't get lost again."

"Yes, that was something, wasn't it? On our hands and knees, listening for the other three cavers." She smiled slightly. "You should have let me call them on the radio."

"Me? You're the one who said something about not wanting Fish to have to pull you out of another hole. Did he help you when you were lost once before?"

"You could say that."

There was a tone to her voice that alerted him.

She was talking about the past. "What could **you** say about it?" he asked.

"I could say my damn compass is stuck again."

She rapped the face against her watch, jogging loose the stubborn needle.

Reluctantly Gabe accepted the change of subject. He reached into his backpack and brought out the compass that she had quite frankly coveted at first glance.

"Trade you," he offered.

"Yours is five times better than mine."

"Guess I'll just have to stick real close so you can't lose me," he said, switching compasses with her.

"I'll only borrow it for the Maze. And I brought a handful of extra light sticks too. We'll use them as markers."

She reached into her own rucksack and pulled out a notebook containing the crude map that she and Gabe had made and expanded each time they tried to unravel the Maze's secrets. Davy had fed the information into his computer, but the generators had been so cranky he hadn't tried to update his big map.

"We're here." She pointed to a snaky line on the paper that represented the translucent drapery.

"Where? I can't see it." He shifted until he could look over her shoulder. "Okay. Got it."

He was standing so close that each time he

exhaled, his breath washed warmly over her cheek. She breathed in sharply, trying to control the shiver of awareness that went over her when she realized how little space separated them.

He reached around her with both arms, took the notebook and pencil from her hands, and began to write, but all she noticed was the pressure of his chest against her back. She told herself to move away. She didn't. She wanted to give in to the delicious warmth stealing through her body. She wanted to lean against his strength and glory in it.

I've got to be crazy, she told herself wildly. **I haven't been able to let a man touch me in seven years. Gabe killed that part of me when he left, and I proved it when I tried to date other men.**

I can't kid myself that anything has changed. I've just got a bad case of memories, that's all. That's the only way I can respond sexually—in memories. That's why Kati will be a lonely—only the rest of her life.

If Gabe made a real pass, I'd freeze solid. So quit tormenting yourself and teasing him. That kind of revenge is contemptible.

When her eyes focused again on the map, she saw that Gabe had labeled the stone drapery "Love."

"Naming is the prerogative of the one who discovers, isn't it?" he asked calmly, seeing the sudden tension in Joy's face. "According to you, it was my light that picked out the formation first."

"Yes," she said in a faint voice.

She took a deep breath to steady herself. With the air came the warmth and scent of his body, triggering an extraordinary burst of memories. For a timeless instant she was in the desert rather than in the cave, and the Voices were Gabe's love words caressing her as he merged with her for the first time, making both of them whole. It was a moment that often returned to her in dreams and memories, the exquisite sliding instant when his body first moved within hers.

"Joy?" He steadied her as she swayed. "Are you all right?"

No! I'm going crazy!

Don't stand so close to me. Neither one of us can take what you're offering, so just back the hell up!

The desperate words went no farther than Joy's mind. Stepping away, she shook off the hands that were burning through layers of cave clothing to the vulnerable flesh beneath.

"I'm fine," she said curtly. **Or I would be if you and my damn memories would just quit teasing me, reminding me of what I felt once and never can feel again.**

She found a light stick and twisted it sharply. Eerie green illumination pooled in her hands. Using a shoelace from her pack she looped the light around the slender tip of a head-high stalagmite. She tried to take a reading from Gabe's compass, but her hands weren't steady enough for the delicate instrument.

Without a word he took it from her. When he called out the numbers she wrote them on her map. It was a routine that had become familiar in the last ten days.

Together Gabe and Joy eased into the Maze, trying a new route. They paused frequently to describe cave formations on the map, to take readings on the compass, and to stack bits of natural debris as direction markers. Twice she added new light beacons, leaving behind unearthly glows as she and Gabe pushed deeper into the unexplored Maze.

After Fish's second **"Yooooo!"** came to them from the Voices' immense darkness, marking the passage of another hour, Joy called a halt. Despite the strenuous cave crawling she and Gabe had already done, they didn't take a rest break. They simply stayed in one place long enough to eat a handful of high-energy food and drink deeply from their canteens.

There was no way for them to know how wide the Maze itself was, how long it would take to find the wall of the cave and work their way along it in their search for passages that might lead to other rooms. Proper exploration was a time-consuming job. Two precious hours below-ground had already passed.

Gabe shrugged into his backpack again. "Ready?"

Joy muttered something as she groped through her rucksack for some hard candy. Her fingers closed around several circular, paper-wrapped shapes. She didn't remember packing anything like them. She pulled out her hand and looked.

Pink-and-white peppermint pinwheels gleamed on her palm. It was Gabe's candy, the sweets she once had told him to hide before she stole them. He'd given them to her and she hadn't even known.

"Thank you," she said, looking up suddenly, sensing that he was watching her.

"My pleasure." His voice was deep. He was remembering how much better peppermint tasted from her lips.

She glanced away quickly. With clumsy fingers she unwrapped the mint, put it in her mouth, and tucked the wrapper deep inside her rucksack where it wouldn't spill out to litter the virgin cave.

"Let's try this direction," she said, blindly heading off into the Maze.

Walking carefully over the rough, often slippery floor, always trying to avoid the most delicate formations, Gabe followed Joy deeper into the unknown. The Maze was a fantastic forest of cave formations, a beautiful obstacle course made of draperies, flowstone, glistening stalactites, rugged stalagmites, and the columns that formed where the ceiling and floor decorations met and merged.

Sometimes the columns were so thick that they made an impassable barrier. Then all Joy could do was stand on tiptoe and shine her light longingly through the hand-size openings that remained between formations. Beyond, where only her light could go, she saw more parts of the Maze, hidden parts, openings that could only be reached by destroying the cave.

She marked the barrier on her map and set off in another direction.

Sometimes the stalactites growing from the uneven ceiling had no stalagmites beneath them. When that happened, the formations hung down like a extraordinary, delicately colored fringe. In other places the stalactites were no larger than soda straws and far more delicate.

Once they had discovered an opening with a ceiling of flawless white gypsum "chandeliers" that all but filled the small room. Light had spun back to them in every possible shade of white and silver, light dancing, light alive far below the reach of any sun.

There was so much beauty to explore. So little time.

"Gabe, look," Joy said, wonder in her voice. "Be very careful," she added, stepping backward, easing around his body in the narrow gap between two slender columns. "You'll never see anything more fragile, more beautiful."

He felt the sweet, changing pressures of Joy sliding by him and wanted to cry out at the stolen pleasure of the moment. Silently telling himself that nothing he would see could be half so beautiful as she was, he walked carefully toward the grotto that she'd just abandoned.

As his light swept past the last barrier, his breath came in sharply. Within the grotto grew incredibly slender crystals that reflected light in tiny glittering splinters. The formations grew neither up nor down, but had a spiral orientation, as though the laws of gravity had been magically suspended deep within Lost River Cave.

The least current of air, including Gabe's breath, caused hair-fine curves to quiver and sway. He backed up a step, afraid that he would destroy the eldritch beauty shimmering in the circle of his helmet lamp.

Slowly he turned toward Joy. "What are they?" He whispered as if the impossibly fine crystals were alive and would be frightened by the sound of his words threading among the eternal murmuring of the Voices.

Joy felt the same way. "Helictites," she said, her voice as hushed as his.

"How are they formed?" Then, quickly, Gabe added, "Wait. I'm not sure I want to know. I don't want to spoil their mystery." He made an odd sound and shook his head. "Listen to me. I'm the guy who makes a living taking the mystery out of the unknown for others."

Joy's gentle smile made his breath thicken in his throat. It was a smile from his memories, when two lovers had looked at each other and shared something silently yet just as completely as though they had spoken aloud.

"Your writing enhances what you describe." Her hand briefly touched his arm. "Knowledge, real knowledge, always enhances. It's ignorance that destroys."

"Then enhance me."

As she spoke, he memorized the elegant lines of her face and remembered what it had been like to have the right to bend down and taste peppermint from her mouth.

"The latest theory is that helictites are formed by water squeezing through solid stone," she said. "If the water finally reaches an air pocket, the drops that emerge on the interior hollows of the bedrock are so tiny that they aren't affected by gravity. The crystals form without reference to up or down or sideways. They follow their own rules, their own internal logic."

"They do it with extraordinary beauty."

"Yes. But it isn't free or easy," she added, her voice both whimsical and serious. "Those crystals spend a long time suspended within bedrock, waiting for just the right circumstances that allow their beauty to be born."

"I must be part helictite," he said, searching her luminous gray eyes. "I know how they feel. Suspended in bedrock. Waiting."

After a moment she was able to look away from the naked hunger in his eyes. She trained her light on the notebook in her hands. She braced it on her thigh and wrote quickly. It gave her hands something to do besides reach for him, soothe him, want him.

"What are you calling the crystals?" he asked.

"Gabriel's Grotto."

"People will think you mean something biblical."

"Good. Names should have as many levels as caves do."

He laughed softly. "You know, I'd almost forgotten what it's like to be around someone whose mind is as quick, curious, and off the wall as mine."

"As in warped?" she suggested wryly.

"Definitely. Like helictites. Shaped by our own spiral necessities in a world where most people only recognize up or down."

She glanced up and smiled as if it was seven years ago. "It seems like that sometimes, doesn't it? Maybe it comes from exploring caves. Most people only live in two dimensions. Caves live in three."

"Or four."

She waited, her eyes intent, her heart beating oddly. "Four?"

"Time," he said quietly, watching her. "Time changes everything."

Joy didn't know how much time—and how much change—passed before she looked away from Gabe.

"You're right," she said. "Four dimensions."

TWENTY

Working slowly, Joy and Gabe found a new part of the maze poking out from the twisting route that had brought them to the helictites. Joy gently eased herself between columns, under stalactites, and around the fluted bases of stalagmites. Flowstone formed by water seeping over the cave's uneven surfaces began appearing everywhere. Soon it was impossible to go any farther without walking on some type of cave formation.

"Now what?" Gabe asked.

"We go forward. Carefully."

"My feet are bigger than yours."

She smiled. "Don't worry too much. We can't help leaving some marks, some sign of our presence. In time it will all be covered in flowstone, just part of the cave itself."

"With enough time everything heals, is that it?"

She searched his shadowed green eyes. "Yes."

Picking her way with great care, she went deeper into the Maze. When she paused to write down a compass reading, she felt a cool breath slide across her face. With the faint stirring in the air came a very slight increase in the sound of falling water.

She froze, not even daring to breathe.

The cool movement of air came again.

With a quick jerk she pulled off her glove, licked her index finger, and held it upright. The left side of her finger felt cooler than the right.

"Joy." Gabe's voice was urgent, excited. "Can you hear it?"

She spun around. He was turning his head slowly, helmet held in his hands as he sought the direction of the new sounds murmuring among the old Voices. In her headlamp his eyes flashed like green gems.

"Yes, to the left," he said.

He had already pulled off a glove and licked his skin. Like her, he knew that skin was one of the most sensitive organs of the body for detecting slight differences in temperature and pressure.

"There's air moving," he said, turning toward the left. "This way."

She grabbed his arm. **"Wait."**

He stared down at her.

"Mark this point with a light stick," she said. "It may be the only place in the whole Maze where we can really feel a distinct current of air. We've lost so many other leads. I don't want to lose this one."

He reached into his rucksack, took out a slender tube, and twisted it. Pale green light flowed over him. A thin piece of cord and a few knots made a harness for the stick. Gently he looped the light over a small knob on a stalagmite that was as thick as his body.

While he worked, Joy took a compass reading off the other two light sources she could still see and made notes on her crude map. When she looked up again, Gabe was watching her.

"Ready?" He held out his hand to her.

She felt her bare hand resting on the hard warmth of his palm and didn't even remember reaching for him.

"Lead the way," he said, squeezing her hand and releasing it.

Fingers tingling, she followed the vague stir-ring of air through a breathtaking variety of cave formations. There were pools as small as her hand and as big as a banquet table, and the fluid in them was so perfectly clear that it was invisible until water dripped from overhead, leaving rings on the transparent surface of the pools.

Each pool was surrounded by shelfstone grow-ing out over the surface of the water itself, an-chored on the limestone shore. Often the shelf stood alone as a fragile lip jutting over a pool that had shrunk down below the shelf. Sometimes stalactites grew down, only to later be flooded by a rising water level. Where that had happened, shelfstone grew out from the stalactites like a string of fantastic mushrooms. Each jut of shelfstone marked a change in the depth of the pool at some time in the past.

The effect was like being on another planet, where gravity was a matter of opinion and the shelfstone around the pools had voted to float on air or grow underwater.

"I can't stand it any longer," Gabe said when Joy paused to make notes.

Her head snapped up. "What's wrong?"

"The upside-down mushrooms and the rims of stone hanging over air or floating on water. How?"

When she understood what he couldn't stand any longer, she smiled in relief. "I thought you might be tired and want to go back."

"Sweetheart, they're going to have to drag me out of here with a team of mules. I've never seen anything so purely incredible."

"Lucky for you, we can't get even one mule down here."

As they pushed deeper into the Maze, Joy explained what she could about the formations they saw. Her words became farther and farther apart, then fell into mutterings. Only frequent compass readings and the light sticks they had left behind kept her from becoming totally disoriented. The air current she was trying to follow was baffling, coy, and elusive. It breathed out from glittering stalagmite forests and curled among columns of golden stone seven stories high.

When she finally lost the vital breath, Gabe came to stand behind her, listening intently, holding himself with the stillness he'd learned in the wild places of the world.

"There," he murmured. "To the right."

As he spoke, he put his hands on her shoulders and turned her toward the fey breeze. She held herself as still as he was and half closed her eyes, trying to reach into the Maze with primitive senses that were more useful than sight within Lost River Cave's mysteries.

After a moment she sensed a tiny, trembling current of air caressing her face.

"There," she whispered. "So close."

She shivered as she felt Gabe's warmth and strength behind her and sensed the rich mystery beckoning ahead. His hands squeezed her shoulders. She thought she felt the brush of his cheek against her helmet just before he released her.

"Go find it," he said.

Her head tilted back, seeking the vertical dimension of the section of the Maze that they were in.

"Ceiling coming down," she said, her voice oddly taut, almost breathless.

She pressed deeper into the Maze, seeking

pathways through or around crowded formations. When she was blocked, Gabe's helmet light swept the cave alongside hers, probing the darkness from a different angle. The unusual dual illumination made formations leap into high relief.

For the first time Joy noticed that there was a tantalizing hint of pattern to the cave floor in front of her and the stalagmites beyond, as though they were signposts on a loosely curving road cobbled by smaller, younger cave formations.

"It's a piece of Lost River," she said, excited.

"What?"

"Lost River. The one the cave is named after, the river that makes it not quite like any other Guadalupe cave we've found so far. A river flowed through here once, long after the majority of the cave itself was eaten out by hot, dilute acids. The Voices holds parts of the ancient river channel, but I've never been able to trace it this far before."

She looked up and saw from Gabe's face that he didn't understand yet.

"The cave's levels have been dried out and decorated and drowned again and dried out and decorated repeatedly," she said. "During some of that time, a river flowed, dissolving stone. Unlike thermally driven cave formation, a river follows some kind of predictable pattern. As it flows from room to room, cavern to cavern, a river carves out connecting passages. All we have to do is—"

"Find out where Lost River went," he finished, excitement kindling in his green eyes. "But it looks flat here. How can you tell which way is upstream and which is down, or doesn't it matter?"

"It matters."

She dropped to her hands and knees and pushed forward into the narrowing confines of the ancient streambed.

"We know upstream was at a higher cave level, so we want to go downstream, where we haven't been before," she said as she examined the ground. "But there's no problem. All we have to do is follow the channel markers."

"Glad to," he said dryly, crawling along behind her. "Just point them out."

"The scallops." She directed her helmet light to the point where the cave's wall joined the floor. There Lost River's ancient flow had hollowed out a long shallow curve, like the side of a tunnel. Smaller curves overlapped along the wall, making a scalloped pattern that was repeated on the far side of the channel. "They're caused by moving water. In limestone the upstream end is rounded and the downstream end is more pointed."

"The things you learn in school," he said, his tone both teasing and admiring.

She laughed.

The ceiling came down until the overhang was a slit barely three feet high and twenty feet wide. She knew that stream channels such as this one rarely contained pits like Surprise, but rarely was not the same as never.

Especially when pits were a standard feature of Guadalupe mountain caves.

She moved slowly, literally feeling her way, alert for a downward slant in the floor or any pool of shadow in her helmet light that could signal the mouth of a pit.

"Wait," Gabe said.

Joy heard the sound of canvas scraping over rock and knew that he was having trouble with his backpack.

"Stuck?" she asked.

His only answer was a grunt and the sound of air being expelled forcefully.

"Back up, take off your backpack and loop your elbow through a strap," she said. "Or tie the backpack to your ankle. You can try pushing the pack ahead of you, if you can handle both it and your rope sack."

As she talked, she was following her own advice. With careful contortions she managed to secure the rucksack to her ankle.

"Does it get smaller ahead?" he asked.

"Count on it."

As they crawled forward, Gabe's muttering was lost among the increasing volume of the Voices. The breeze hadn't increased. It was still a fine, hardly noticeable exhalation over their faces. Soon Joy could hear little except the many-tongued whisperings of water, the sound of her own clothing rubbing over stone, and the occasional thump of her helmet on an unexpectedly low portion of the ceiling.

The farther she went, the more the passage took on the aspect of a true tunnel rather than simply a long narrow strip gouged out of the Voices' overhanging wall. The floor pitched down slightly. The passage narrowed even more. The ceiling came down.

And the breeze caressed her face, stronger with each yard she crawled forward.

Joy's heart beat faster in sudden exhilaration. There was little doubt now that this channel would lead to another room instead of ending in a wall of debris or the breakdown of the ceiling. That sort of thing happened depressingly often in caves. For every passage that went somewhere, many more dead-ended at a natural, impassable obstacle.

The sound of Gabe's occasional searing curses came above the increased murmuring of the

Voices. The passage twisted like a snake, a streambed tunnel carved through solid stone, complete with bends and deposits of stony debris swept from the huge room behind them.

Very quickly Joy and Gabe were pushing along on their stomach or their side or their back, depending on which way the opening turned. Their progress was limited to strenuous, eel-like motions. Neither of them really noticed the effort. They were gripped by the possibility of a discovery just around the next twist or turn.

From the dark opening ahead came the multiple voices of falling water, a siren song that grew louder with every moment.

Joy's light rarely revealed more than the next few feet of the passage, and as often as not the plugs leading to the battery pack pulled out as she wiggled around the narrow tunnel. Several times she came to a place where the limestone had been more easily dissolved. There the passage widened enough to allow them to rest.

Each time they stopped, she checked her watch. As much as the lure of discovery called, she didn't want them to stay long enough for the chill of the bedrock to seep into their bodies or for them to miss answering Fish's hourly yodel.

Radio contact wasn't possible anymore. Too much solid stone lay between the radios.

"Ready?" she asked after a few minutes.

"After you," he said wryly, giving a sidelong swipe of his arm toward the muddy tunnel that awaited them.

A few minutes farther into the passage, she ran up against a barricade of debris that had been deposited by Lost River. The river was long since gone, but what it had left behind was damp, slick, muddy, as saturated with moisture as the air itself.

After a single hissing word, she saved her energy for digging and avoiding the thought that the debris dam might be too deep, too thick, and too well packed for her to dig through it.

"Problem?"

Gabe's voice came from behind Joy and to her right. Though the ceiling was no more than twenty inches from the floor, the tunnel itself was nearly four feet wide at this point.

"Clastic fill," she said, the words clipped.

"Dirt." This time his voice was nearly beside her.

"Not to a biologist," she said. "No worms."

"For these small things, Lord, we are extremely grateful," he muttered as he wriggled alongside her and began digging.

"Don't like worms?"

He made a throaty sound of disgust. "Give me a nice dry snake any day of the week."

Joy smiled to herself at the discovery that the

great Gabriel Venture, a man who had proved his physical courage many times over, was icked out by worms.

Working together they quickly scraped away silt and water-rounded limestone pebbles. Soon they could push through between ceiling and floor to the wider tunnel beyond.

Joy forged ahead, making encouraging noises to Gabe, who was just behind her heels. The passage closed down, forcing her to work very hard to eel between floor and ceiling. She wondered if he was going to have to turn back. Or worse, if he would get stuck.

Then she realized that she couldn't hear him behind her anymore.

"Gabe?" Her voice was breathless from more than snaking through the narrow opening. "Are you all right?"

The answer was a hot curse and the sound of something ripping. "Just bloody fine, thanks," he said a moment later. "Emphasis on **bloody.**"

She hesitated, then squirmed around until she could bring her wristwatch in line with her helmet light. The face of the watch was muddy. Automatically she rubbed it against her chin. That didn't work because her chin was as muddy as her hands. Her nose proved to be fairly clean. She rubbed and peered at her watch again.

They had been in the passage twenty minutes.

They had thirty-seven minutes before Fish would call out the hour.

"Damn," she said. "Maybe we should head back."

"Not on my account. Blood makes a great lubricant."

"We're running out of time."

"That's not all we're out of."

"What?" she asked.

"Room. I'd have a bitch of a struggle slithering out of this place backward."

"It's not as hard as it sounds. Davy can do Gotcha nearly as fast backward as he can forward."

"Davy's mother must have been a python."

She laughed, relieved that Gabe wasn't frightened at the thought of being so tightly held by limestone that he couldn't even turn around.

"You'd only have to do the first few minutes feetfirst," she said. "After that, you'd come to the wide spot where we rested and you could turn around."

"I'd rather go forward. If you want to."

She didn't hesitate. "Five minutes. Seven at most. All right?"

His response was a low laugh that ruffled her nerves.

"Get moving, beautiful," he said, pushing at her feet. "There's a whole new world waiting to be discovered."

"Beautiful?" She laughed, knowing full well that by now she was as muddy as a swamp puppy. "Turn on your lamp. You're hallucinating in the dark."

He laughed again with an excitement that was contagious.

She attacked the next section of the tunnel with high spirits, feeling like it was seven years ago, when she and Gabe had explored some of Lost River Cave's secrets. It felt good to laugh with him again. For a few precious instants he wasn't the man who had suspended her between yearning and hatred for long, long years.

There was no warning. One instant Joy was snaking forward on her side. The next instant much of her upper body was touching nothing at all. She snatched at her falling rucksack.

"Grab my feet and hang on!"

Strong hands clamp around Joy's ankles.

"Don't let go," she said urgently.

"Not a chance, sweetheart. Not one chance in hell."

TWENTY-ONE

Slowly Joy let out the breath she'd held in order to wedge herself more tightly in the tunnel. She couldn't see anything ahead because the leads to her helmet lamp had come unplugged. She could be in a small expansion of the tunnel or she could be suspended over a drop hundreds of feet deep. Without light there was no way to be sure.

As always in complete darkness, her other senses heightened. She could feel the faintest brush of air moving over her cheeks, or perhaps it was a motion caused by a thousand liquid voices whispering to her. When her heartbeat settled, she separated the sensations pouring into her.

Distance.

Space.

Moisture.

A beautiful rushing sigh.

Somewhere ahead, cloaked in darkness and diamond mist, water was leaping from one level of the cave to another, a river shattering itself on stone and then flowing back together, healing itself, curling down and down into the limitless earth.

"I'm going to try to connect the leads to my lamp," she said, "so things might . . . change."

"No matter what, I've got you."

She smiled in the darkness. "I know."

Cautiously she connected the leads to her lamp. Light flared out into blackness, light that defined darkness and was itself defined in turn.

For an instant Joy saw nothing but the stark opposites. Slowly a world condensed out of the void, a place of fantastic golden shapes, inky shadows, impossible spires and draperies and columns, a vision of flowing stone condensed out of water through time spans so great they could only be numbered, not understood.

"Oh, Gabe," she said, her breath rushing out. "It's the most beautiful thing I've ever seen. I wish you could see it too."

Relief swept through him. Despite whatever danger had made her demand that he hang on to her ankles, she was all right.

After relief came a fierce pleasure that her first reaction had been a desire to share the instant of discovery with him. After that came the more pragmatic concerns of a man who had spent his life in wild places.

"Are you safe?" he asked. "Is it a pit? Should I pull you back?"

"As long as you don't let go, I'm safe," she said absently.

All her concentration was focused on the astonishing room that lay ahead. The certainty that no other human being ever had seen this exotic landscape sent currents of awe through her.

Yet she wished Gabe was beside her, seeing it as she did, sharing it with her. There was too much beauty for one person to hold alone. It overflowed, nearly drowning her.

"It's not exactly a pit," she said in a husky voice. "It's a high entrance to another room. I think water once poured out of here into the cavern below."

He saw in his mind a tunnel in the sheer face of a cliff, an opening suspended between an invisible ceiling above and an equally invisible floor below.

"I'd feel better if I had a rope on you."

Gabe heard his own words and smiled rather grimly. He'd feel better if he had Joy roped and tied to himself permanently. Failing that he'd settle for the usual methods—safety harness, carabiners, and anchor points.

"I'm going to wiggle forward a bit so I can see if there's a way down," she said. "Ready?"

"Joy—" he began.

"It's all right," she interrupted quickly. "If

you don't let go and I keep my center of gravity inside the tunnel, I'll be safe."

Even as he started to object, he remembered that a woman's center of gravity was usually in her hips, whereas a man's was usually about twelve inches higher. Given that, she could get a better, safer look than a man could.

"All right," he said. "But first I'm going to put some half-hitches around your ankles."

While Gabe worked over her feet, Joy surveyed as much as she could of the space ahead. Everywhere her light touched she saw flowing stone formations, stone sculptures both massive and delicate, turrets and naves and walls, columns that tapered in the middle like an elegant woman, flaring above and below into the velvet darkness.

She couldn't tell how big the room was, only that it must be huge. Even when she twisted the focus of her helmet lamp to the narrowest possible beam, darkness absorbed the light before it reached ceiling, floor or walls.

With or without boundaries, the cavern was a place of extraordinary beauty. It sang with water, a chorus murmuring amid fantastic shapes, a three-dimensional poem composed out of confinement and space, limestone and water, darkness and light.

And time. Immense time, eternity dreaming in stone.

"Xanadu," she said, and the word was a sigh.

"What?"

"Like the poem. 'In Xanadu did Kubla Khan/A stately pleasure dome decree . . . '"

Gabe tested the knots on her ankles. "Xanadu, huh? Be careful, sweetheart. I didn't come all this way to go back alone."

"I'll be careful." Her voice was husky. She heard the word **sweetheart** echo in her mind and her blood as it always had in her dreams. "I'm going to stuff my rucksack alongside my body as a wedge, then inch forward. Ready?"

He cinched the rope more tightly around her ankles. "Ready."

She twisted around until the rucksack was alongside her. As she inched forward, the rope holding her resisted, then gave slightly. Very slightly. He was keeping a pressure on her that was just short of painful.

It was also very reassuring.

Her headlamp swept directly over and beneath the lip of stone where she lay. There was nothing at all under her but a velvet darkness that looked heavy enough to walk on.

"Go back down the tunnel at least ten feet," she said quietly.

"Overhang?" he asked in a clipped voice, already backing up.

"Yes." She was grateful that he understood the danger instantly instead of hanging around and waiting for a long explanation. "It feels solid but—"

Her words ended in a startled sound as she found herself being dragged backward down the tunnel whether she wanted it or not. She started to protest, then shut up and helped him retreat.

In Gabe's place she would have done the same thing. If the limestone overhang where she'd rested for a moment had any built-in weakness, the lip could give way at any time. Then she would be dangling by her heels over nothing at all.

"This is far enough," she said.

The tugging on her ankles stopped.

"I'm going forward again," she said.

"Like hell you are."

"Someone has to do it. I'm the lightest one."

A long silence answered her, followed by a single word.

"Shit."

While Gabe chewed over the inevitable, Joy reached into her muddy rucksack and pulled out a slender tube.

"I'll check for cracks as I go," she said.

Grudgingly he played out enough rope to allow her to move forward again.

This time Joy looked carefully at the surface she was crawling over and through rather than at the opening ahead. The stone was chill, smooth, even textured, and didn't have any visible cracks or seams or joints. It stayed like that right up to the brink of the cavern.

"Looks solid all the way," she said.

"Now what?"

"Now I wish we'd found this four hours ago. Why do you always find the most interesting things toward the end of your exploring time?"

Facedown in the mud and stone, hands wrapped around the line holding Joy, Gabe laughed. "Works the same way up top."

"I'm going to spend a light stick."

"Go ahead. I've got three more if you need them."

She twisted a light stick and threw it up and out into the void, counting beneath her breath.

Pale green illumination washed over stone, throwing a nearby fluted drapery into fantastic relief. The light arced down and down, glowing like a comet across unknown skies before it struck a thick column and ricocheted. Still the light slid down and down and down, pulling darkness after it like a cloak.

Finally the light stopped falling and became a motionless green glow calling to Joy. She ached to answer it, to explore every bit of the mystery opening before her, but she couldn't.

Not yet.

She eased backward as Gabriel pulled in the rope behind her.

"How far down?" he asked, retreating down the tunnel as he spoke.

"Roughly—very roughly—ninety feet straight down. I couldn't see, but I assume there's some sort of breakdown before you get to the floor of the room. If this was once a waterfall, the bottom of the wall would have been undercut, leaving a pile of fallen stone where the floor meets the wall."

They came to a widening of the tunnel. Joy looked at her watch and calculated quickly.

"Want to take a look?" she asked.

"What do you think," he retorted, the electric excitement of discovery in his voice.

She laughed. "Then make like a snake and slither on by."

As she spoke, she put her arms above her head and rolled onto her side with her back to the tunnel wall, giving him all the space she could. He didn't wait for a second invitation. Facing her, arms above his head, his body turned partway on his side, he began his snake act.

There was barely enough room. He was squeezed between stone and the much more forgiving surface of Joy's body. Even through layers of muddy clothes, he felt the flexibility and the softness of her. He even felt the laughter rippling through her.

And then he sensed the sudden, hot instant

when she went utterly still, feeling him pressed against her from her forehead to her toes.

"Joy," he whispered.

Trapped between the chill of the stone and the warmth of his body, she couldn't move as his mouth closed over hers. And even if she could have moved, she wouldn't have. As his tongue teased her lips, fire exploded through her so hotly she thought she must be radiating like a light stick twisted in his hands.

The knowledge that she could still respond to a man was as overwhelming to Joy as the instant when she'd found herself half dangling over darkness with nothing but Gabe's hands to anchor her. She made a sound that could have been his name as he teased open her lips, asking for further exploration, a deeper intimacy.

She didn't deny him or herself. The heat and taste of him swept over her senses. She forgot where she was, forgot that he was the man who had left her behind while he chased the lure of discovery throughout the world. She forgot everything but the sweet, hot presence of him inside her mouth.

With an incoherent sound she pressed against him, giving herself to the kiss, regretting only that she couldn't put her arms around him and hold him as completely as she had in her dreams.

After the first few moments of mutual exploration, Gabe felt his own control burning out of his grasp. He wanted to do so much, feel so much, share so much, and he couldn't even put his arms around her. His mouth bit into hers, straining to be closer to her warmth. When she made a soft, eager sound in the back of her throat, it felt like the stone caught fire around him.

He called her name, demand and apology at once. He hadn't meant to come to her like this, half wild, control slipping away with each small movement of her tongue over his, his mind reeling and his body shaking, starved for her. Slowly, sinuously, his whole body caressed her while he searched every texture of her mouth with his tongue.

She felt the strength and urgency of his passion in every movement of his powerful body. She made a sound of frustration and hunger, wanting to be able to touch him, to hold the heat and arousal of him. She needed to feel his skin sliding against hers, all of it, hot and sleek and utterly naked. It was the only way to reassure herself that this wasn't a dream, that she was awake and wholly alive for the first time in seven years.

With a low moan she moved against him, returning the twisting caresses of his body, not holding back any her response. She'd never been able to deny him or herself, even in her deepest dreams.

His teeth delicately ravaged her lips. He whispered her name again and again in a litany of joy while he licked her mouth with tiny, hot strokes, savoring and caressing her.

"I used to wake up shaking after I'd dreamed of you," he said. "I'm shaking now but I'm not dreaming. Tell me I'm not dreaming."

Dreaming. Yes.

Her dream.

His.

But this wasn't a dream.

Reality broke over Joy in a cold wave. She shuddered convulsively. She would have pulled away but there was nowhere for her to go. There was rock pressing against her and there was Gabe. That was all.

Dream and nightmare combined.

"Joy?" he asked, sensing her withdrawal even though she couldn't move anywhere but closer to him.

"I . . ." Her voice came apart on another shudder.

He kissed her mouth with ravishing tenderness, sipping at her lips and tongue as he wanted to sip at the tips of her breasts. And then his tongue filled her mouth her mouth the way he wanted to fill her body, stroking her slowly, deeply.

Rings of pleasure expanded through her, shimmered, threatened to burst. She'd been wrong, so very wrong. She was capable of responding sensually to a man—as long as that man was Gabriel Venture.

Somehow she managed to turn her head aside.

"Don't," she said, her voice shaking. Her breath caught when his body moved over hers again and rings of pleasure burst into shimmering light within her. "Ahhh, Gabe . . . stop. You don't know what you're doing to me."

"I hope it's half of what you're doing to me." His voice was ragged, husky, rich with the extraordinary pleasure of touching Joy again. His hips moved sinuously, hotly, caressing her.

"Please," she said wildly. "**Don't**. Stop teasing me. I haven't been with a man since you left me!"

He froze, unable to believe what he was hearing. He'd never touched, ever, a woman half so sensual, so responsive as Joy. It was unbelievable that she'd denied herself the physical pleasure she so clearly hungered for.

"Why?" he asked, his voice hoarse.

She wondered how she could tell him that a man's touch, any man's touch, hadn't moved her, even when she'd been determined to go out and get pregnant with the sibling Kati so desperately wanted.

"I tried, God how I tried, but I couldn't respond," Joy said. "When a man touched me, I'd miss you even more. It was like rope whipping through my hands, out of control, burning me. Finally I just—gave up."

Emotion speared through Gabe, light through darkness, defining him even as it changed him. He remembered the times he'd taken a woman in the hope of filling the emptiness expanding inside him, a hollowness where nothing existed. And each time the nothingness had been worse, the void deeper, wider, more complete, growing until he sensed it would devour him and he would live forever in the dark emptiness.

That was when he'd stopped seeking women at all.

Now, finally, he understood why. When he'd joined his body with Joy's the first time, he'd wanted to equal her generous sensuality, to melt her to her bones so that she'd never be touched by anyone without remembering him.

It had been just like that. Hot. Perfect. Enduring.

And it had worked both ways.

Never again had he touched another woman without remembering Joy, remembering as her loss ate deeper into his soul, emptiness growing.

"I'm sorry," he whispered, brushing her lips with his breath, his tongue. And then, in a ragged rush, "No, I'm not sorry. I should be, but I'm not. I've missed you in ways you'll never

know, in ways I'm only just discovering. Whatever I did to you I did to myself too. I just didn't
know it, didn't understand."

Joy could no more speak than she could pull
back from him. She was suspended between the
passionate present and the bleak pain of past betrayal. **She was falling, falling, falling** . . . and
the regret in Gabe's anguished voice was a safety
rope burning against her body as she fell.

She didn't know if he could hold the rope, stop
her fall. Or if she wanted him to. If she wanted
her life held within his hands again.

Her watch alarm cheeped urgently, startling
both of them.

Gabe drew a deep breath, pinning her intimately between his aroused body and the stone
wall of the tunnel.

"Time to go home?" he asked, trying and failing to make his voice calm.

"There's still time for you to have a look at the
new cavern," she said, controlling her breathing
with an effort. "A very fast look."

"How much time?"

"A minute. Maybe mo—"

She didn't have a chance to finish. Gabe tilted
his head and found her mouth again, blending
their bodies together in the only way he could
right now.

The kiss was different from those he'd given

her before. There was flaring passion, yes, but there was something more, something both tender and enduring, apologies and promises spoken in silence, a warmth that went beyond the cold stone passage wrapped around both of them.

After more than a minute he slowly, reluctantly, ended the kiss.

In stunned silence Joy felt him slide past her, moving back toward the Voices, moving **away** from the newly discovered room. Automatically she followed him, working backward by reflex and experience, for her mind was still spinning around a fact more incredible to her than the discovery of her own renewed capacity for passion.

Gabe had stayed in the tunnel to kiss her rather than going on to see the undiscovered territory just beyond the stone overhang. He never would have done that seven years ago.

She could barely believe he'd done it now.

TWENTY-TWO

A few hours later, arms loaded with gritty caving gear, Joy and Gabe wearily climbed the steps up to her screened porch. Behind them the desert's hot, brilliant sunlight filled the air to bursting. Around them Cottonwood Wells was completely silent. Everyone else had stayed at the cave to grab a few more precious hours.

Joy would have stayed, but she had too much paperwork to do up on the surface. Closing down the exploration required more forms than beginning it had.

Gabe held open the screen door and followed her inside, letting the door swing shut behind him. She looked at her watch, then at him.

"Sure you don't want to change your mind?" she asked. "I could belay you down and you could help the others look for a shorter way to Small Favors. In fact—"

"Small Favors," he said, laughing and shaking his head.

"The new tunnel," she explained.

"As in thank the Lord, no worms?" He watched her with luminous jade eyes. His smile was as wide and warm as the sun itself.

"That's the one."

"Small Favors leading to Joy's Castle."

"I still don't—"

"Nope," he interrupted. "Too late. Fish, Davy, Maggie, and I all agreed that even though you found it, you'd never name it for yourself, so we would. It should be named for you. Joy."

She started to object again, then shrugged, accepting the name. She dropped her equipment and stretched, enjoying the freedom and dryness of the desert day as much as she would enjoy the mysterious darkness and damp of Lost River Cave when she returned.

"Okay," she said. "Joy's Castle it is. People will think it refers to the emotion, anyway."

"To tell the truth, I'm having a hell of a time separating them myself."

She gave him a startled look.

"You have the most beautiful smile I've ever seen," he said simply, tracing her lips with his eyes. "That hasn't changed. Not in all the years, all the memories, all the dreams. I didn't know it then, but I used to measure how empty I was by remembering your smile."

Joy's lashes dropped over her transparent gray eyes, concealing them for an instant.

"Gabriel," she said, her voice tight, strung between the past and the present.

"Yeah, I know. I promised you that I wouldn't talk about the past."

And now his editor was calling every evening, asking about progress, hinting that two weeks was more than enough to spend on this article. Something big was in the works that Gabe should clear the decks for. Something only he could do.

Something.

No, I can't tell you what or where or when, Gabe. But it could come at any moment and it will be the chance of a lifetime, the kind of career rocket for you that the Orinoco article was. You have to be ready.

Gabe wasn't.

Period.

Sighing, he put down his equipment and dirty clothes, then ran silt-stained fingers through his hair. He remembered the flash of hatred he'd seen more than once in Joy's eyes during their first few days together. Yet he no longer believed she hated him.

She felt fury, yes. A hot desire for revenge, probably. But hatred?

No.

When he touched her, currents of hunger ran through her like a river seething through darkness. She couldn't hate him and still respond like that, no matter how long it was since she'd been with a man.

"But it's damned hard not to talk about the past," he said, watching Joy, wanting her, wanting much more than a few weeks. Wanting it all. But that couldn't happen until they talked, really talked, to each other. "There are things we have to settle."

"There's nothing to settle."

"That's not true and you know it."

She turned away and put her helmet on the shelf. Automatically she pulled the batteries out of the pack and plugged them into the recharger.

"What I know is the simple truth," she said finally. "The past is gone. Out of reach. Nothing can affect it in any way."

"And the future?"

For an instant her body stiffened. Then she continued caring for her equipment.

"The same," she said, her voice bleak. "Out of reach. Forever."

"I'm Kati's father. That began in the past and will go on forever. How's that for a simple truth?"

She spun toward him. "While you're passing out simple truths, try this one on for size. Whether or not I tell Kati who her father is, when this assignment is over you'll go on to the next one, leaving your daughter behind, rejecting her all over again, crushing her heart. Have you thought about that, Mr. World Explorer?"

Anger flashed through Gabe, a need to hurt as he himself was being hurt. After the intimacy of the cave he hadn't expected her to attack him. "What do you want me to do? Stay here in New Mexico with Kati while you get your revenge playing international globe-trotter?"

"Didn't we already have this conversation? We know all the answers. They haven't changed."

"And just what are those answers?"

The very softness of his voice should have warned Joy. It didn't. She was in the grip of a searing rage that was every bit as deep as her passionate response to him had been.

It was the same for him, passion and rage mingling hotly.

"The answers all boil down to the same thing," she said. "Nothing means as much to you as your career. You don't know how to love. Haven't you learned that about yourself yet?"

He was too stunned to respond, but it didn't matter. Joy was still talking, shredding his fragile, unspoken hopes for the future with every razor word.

"That's why I'm not going to tell Kati who her father is until she's eighteen, when she'll be old enough to handle it. Tell her sooner and you'll destroy her. You won't mean to, but you'll do it just as surely as you almost destroyed me."

Emotions ripped through Gabe, anger and something more, something deeper, a twisting anguish that he couldn't express. But he could give words to anger. That was easy. He'd had a lifetime of practice at that.

"Are you saying that **you** know how to love?" he asked savagely.

"Yes."

"Gee, that's odd. I always heard that forgiveness was the hallmark of love."

Joy went pale beneath the streaks of rich silt smeared across her cheeks. "Is that why you were so **forgiving** when you thought I'd had an abortion? Did your **love** just overflow with the understanding that you'd put me in the position of having to choose between an abortion and my own sanity?"

His eyelids flinched in a pain greater than any anger. Talking about the past wasn't helping. It was making it worse. "Joy—"

"But you didn't think of that, did you?" she said relentlessly, talking over him. "You just thought that—"

"I thought that you'd lied when you said you loved me," he broke in. "**I was wrong.** You loved me. If I'd known that seven years ago, I'd have—"

He stopped because he didn't know what he would have done. If he'd stayed seven years ago, it would have meant turning his back on his brother and mother and career. It would have meant marrying a girl and having no way to support her. He would have been trapped as she'd been trapped, no way out but to keep going forward because going backward wasn't possible.

Maybe they would have done better together. Maybe they simply would have come apart.

Seven years ago, they both had been too young.

"You would have left me just the same." Joy's voice was flat and unflinching as she finished Gabe's sentence.

"I don't know. All I know is that I came back."

"But you didn't come back here for my love or even my forgiveness, did you?" she asked, her voice low, trembling. "You didn't even know I was here. You came back because the Lost River Cave article was one of the best pieces you'd ever written and your editor wanted another one like it. Work, Gabe. You came back here because of your damned career. Forgiveness and love had nothing to do with it."

"Do you really believe that?"

"Don't you?"

"I might have, once. But I haven't known what to believe since I watched my life peeling away with each strand of rope."

She flinched. No matter how furious she was, the thought of him dying was a knife turning in her soul.

"That's the real reason I came back here. I

spent a long time in that filthy hospital thinking about life. My life. I thought about all the mountains I'd climbed and the ones I hadn't, the wild places I'd known and the places I'd never know. And through it all Lost River Cave was like a candle burning in an overwhelming darkness, calling to me in ways that I still don't understand. It . . ."

He hesitated, understanding part of himself for the first time. The discovery was bittersweet, because it brought with it a knowledge of his own past limitations.

"It frightened me," he said simply. "I ran. Everywhere. Mountains, oceans, jungles. A year. I ran until I was too exhausted to fight my obsession with Lost River Cave any longer. So I came back here. And I saw you. Joy."

She looked at his eyes, startled by the hesitations and emotions resonating within his voice. He was a man who had always known what he wanted, what he thought, what was or was not worthy of his time and consideration. Self-confident. Sensual.

Joy closed her eyes suddenly. That, at least, hadn't changed. He was still as sensual as her memories and dreams. More sensual. Less confident.

And, oddly, much more intriguing.

When she was twenty, Gabe's lack of philosophical questions about himself and the world had excited her. Now she realized that a man without questions wasn't exciting to anyone but a girl.

She was a woman now.

Yet Gabe still appealed to her, for in many ways he was more of a man than ever before. His searching, aching, questioning intelligence was much more intriguing than his untested self-confidence had been.

He was different now. Stronger. His mind had grown, breaking out of old certainties, flexing against the intimate unknown that was himself. He'd begun an internal exploration that equaled in danger and fascination any that he could have found in the external world.

Joy knew what such explorations were like, the danger and the excitement, the risk and the reward and the despair. She knew how necessary it was to explore and accept yourself, your limitations and strengths, your fears and hopes, your ability to love.

And to hate.

If she hadn't begun to know herself, she wouldn't have survived the loss of Gabe and her parents. She wouldn't have survived raising a fatherless child. Survival had meant no longer asking old questions. Survival had meant beginning a search for new answers.

It had been the same for Gabe. New questions. New answers. It was all there in his eyes as he watched her, waiting for her decision.

"I don't understand what brought you back to Lost River Cave," Joy said finally. "I don't understand why you left. I do know that each of us has to do what is necessary, what we can live with. Hatred isn't one of those things, Gabe. I can't live with it."

He touched her cheek gently. Just that. No more. "Neither can I."

She took a shaky breath. "As for forgiveness—you're right. It's a part of love. And love—" Her voice broke. "Love like that just isn't a part of me anymore. So if you came to Lost River Cave to be forgiven, you came to the wrong place. I've never forgiven myself for being such an innocent fool. How can I possibly forgive the man who took the innocence and left only the fool?"

"Joy," he whispered. His voice fragmented into silence. He swallowed against the emotions burning in his throat. "You weren't a fool. Your love was the most beautiful thing I'd ever known. I was the fool. I left you."

She smiled sadly, trying to keep her tears from falling. "No, Gabriel. I was the only fool. I loved the wrong man. But it was a long time ago. Please—**oh God, please**—can't we just let go of it?"

He looked at her tear-filled eyes and knew with great certainty that if he let go of the past now, he would lose the future as well. Somehow he had to convince her of that.

Words weren't enough.

"I can't let go." He bent over to kiss Joy's long, honey-colored lashes, wet with tears. "Only a fool would let go of love. I'm not a fool anymore."

Her breath broke as his lips both soothed and incited hers. His tongue was a hot moist flame licking over her. She leaned toward him yearningly.

"It will be good, sweetheart," he promised in a low, husky voice. "It will be unbearably good."

TWENTY-THREE

Suspended between passion and fear, Joy trembled in Gabe's hands, remembering too many things.

It will be unbearably good.

She wanted him until she shook with it. Yet he'd offered nothing beyond the satisfaction of the hunger that raged through her. And through him.

What did I expect—a promise to spend the future with me, happy ever after, world without end amen? she asked herself wildly. **He's being honest with me.**

This time.

No. That isn't fair. He was honest before. He never promised a damn thing. Why should it be different this time?

And then an idea came, a thought both sweet and savagely triumphant.

Yes, why shouldn't it be the same? Why shouldn't he make love to me while he's here and then leave me the way he did before?

Pregnant.

Why shouldn't I give him the passion that's all he wants and take from him all I want— passion and another child?

There was no answer but the liquid heat of desire uncurling between her thighs. With a moan Joy gave herself over to Gabe's touch, saying nothing, asking nothing of him beyond the hot, sensual glide of his flesh over hers.

As her response swept through him, his hands tightened almost painfully on her shoulders. She felt him try and fail to control the urgency driving him, felt his kiss go in a single instant from tender to devouring.

Triumph flashed through her. It had been like this the first time they made love. When he would have gone slow, might have drawn back, she'd come to him like fire, burning away the real world.

And he hadn't pulled back.

The barely leashed strength of Gabe's arms should have been painful, but Joy was straining against him just as harshly, her body on fire with demands now as it had been the first time. When he lifted his mouth from hers, she protested with a hungry, throaty sound.

He laughed shakily and watched her with burning green eyes.

"If I don't slow down, I'm afraid I'll hurt you. I'd never forgive myself for that. It's been so long for you. And—" His breath broke as discovery raced through him, illuminating part of his inner maze that he'd never known existed. As he bent to kiss her with an aching hunger that was new, he shared his discovery with her. "In all the ways that matter, it's been just as long for me."

She arched into his kiss, not wanting to talk, afraid that he would pull back and ask her questions whose answers would turn hunger into hurt and anger. She didn't want that. All she wanted was the endless, passionate present she'd found only with him.

Eagerly her fingers moved over the mesh of the body-covering underwear he wore. No matter how she probed, she couldn't feel the smooth heat of his naked skin or the rough silk of the hair that she knew curled across his chest. She'd loved playing with that hair, had teased and tantalized him mercilessly, using the tip of her tongue to comb through the dense mat to the tiny nipples hiding beneath.

She wanted to do that again, to know again every texture of him, every taste, **everything**.

"Are you going to take off that damned underwear," she asked huskily, "or am I going to get out my pocketknife?"

"I was just thinking of making you the same offer."

His eyes were black except for the brilliant rim

of green circling the enlarged pupil. The clean line of his lips beckoned her.

"What are you waiting for?" she whispered.

She stood on tiptoe and traced his mouth with the moist tip of her tongue. His fingers kneaded hungrily down her back and hips, pressing her against his body, letting her feel the hard length of his arousal.

It was like falling into fire.

Her hips made repeated twisting movements against him, telling him of a need that equaled his. His breath came out in a groan.

"I want to kiss you like this," she said, tracing his lips again, nibbling. **"Everywhere."**

He threaded one hand into her short, silky hair and pulled her head back until she was arched like a bow, her thighs taut against his. She smiled and slowly rubbed against him, glorying in the sexual need that made his face tight, dark, exciting.

His hand ran urgently down her body the instant before his mouth closed over hers, stifling her gasp of pleasure as he found and caressed the soft heat between her legs. His tongue thrust into her mouth until she had no room even for breath.

And still she strained to be closer, closer, **now**.

With tiny, teasing nips, his teeth tormented her soft mouth while his palm rubbed her intimately, hungrily, knowingly. She moaned, shivered, and gave him a taste of the sultry pleasures that waited inside her.

His whole body went taut. It was like his memories, but better. This time she knew what she wanted. So did he. He had an overwhelming need to sink into Joy, transforming her, loving her so perfectly that she would never look toward another man. But this time he also knew he would never look to another woman.

It was like being set free.

With an effort of will that left him aching, he stepped back from Joy.

"Gabe? Don't you want—"

"God, yes," he cut in. "But all these damned—"

Instead of finishing, he started stripping off her clothes. Yet even when she was naked he simply looked at her, almost afraid.

He hadn't known he could want anything as much as he wanted Joy.

"Gabriel?" she asked, her voice like his eyes, almost afraid.

He was trembling as he looked at her.

"Get in the shower," he said, his lips thinned with the effort of controlling himself. When she took a breath that sent her breasts swaying, he closed his eyes. It was that or take her right here, right now.

"But—" she began.

"**Go.** Or I'll take you right here, right now, on the floor, because I've never wanted anything so much as I want you now, even my own life when it was hanging by a thread." His eyes opened hot and green. "Do you understand?"

He saw the wild blaze of response in her, felt her hands seeking him, shaping his hot, rigid flesh in a caress that made the air hiss out between his clenched teeth.

"Joy, **I mean it.**"

"Good." Her voice was shaking as badly as her hands. She tugged at the mesh underwear separating her from him, pulling it off his powerful body. "I want it like that. I want to watch you take me and know that you've never wanted anything more than you want me now."

He stripped off the last of his clothing with careless strength, ripping the tough mesh and taking her down to the floor in the same continuous motion. She moved eagerly beneath him, opening herself to him, watching him want her.

He tried to stop, to ask her if this was what she really wanted, but her sultry need pulsed out to meet him, licking over his aroused flesh, searing him with a promise of pleasure so great it stopped his breath. With a groan he pushed into her even as she reached up to take him. And then he cried out with the sweet agony of being alive within Joy again.

The liquid heat of her body enclosed him tightly, completely, and the tiny cries she made as she felt him inside her again were like crystals glittering in darkness. He felt the instant, deep ripples of her release tug at him and knew that she'd wanted him as unbearably as he'd wanted her.

The discovery exploded through him, bringing a searing, pulsing release so great he could only arch against her sweet, clinging body and pour himself into her as she cried out his name in passion and triumph.

After that, there was no sound but ragged breathing. Spent, Gabe laid his cheek next to hers while the world slowly took shape around him again.

It was then he realized that he hadn't protected her.

Again.

He swore painfully, savagely.

"What's wrong?" she asked, her gray eyes searching his.

"I didn't protect you. It's the past all over again. I get close to you and nothing else is real, especially tomorrow."

She smiled crookedly. "Don't worry." She kissed him lightly. "This time I know the risk of sleeping with you."

"What's that supposed to mean?"

He rolled aside so that he could see her face

clearly. What he saw first was the unspoken protest that tightened her lips when he left her body.

And then he saw the smooth mask of Dr. Anderson descend, veiling the vivid sensuality of Joy.

"It means I'm not young anymore." She stood gracefully and walked into the kitchen. "This time around I'm an adult. I know that love between a man and a woman is a figment of human imagination rather than a fact of human relations. This time around I'm not trapped in my innocence. And neither are you."

"But—" he began.

"But nothing. If I'd wanted protection, I would have demanded it."

"Next time I'll—"

She interrupted him again. "If you come to me wearing a condom, I won't have you."

With that she disappeared inside the house.

TWENTY-FOUR

For a moment Gabe simply stared at the empty doorway. Then he surged to his feet and followed Joy, determined to talk to her. Now, at least, she couldn't pretend that she didn't want anything to do with him. He knew better. He had felt the proof of it flowing hotly over him.

Like Kati, that part of the past was very much alive.

And it was good.

The sound of the shower told him where Joy was. When he got to the bathroom, steam was already rising from the tall showerhead that loomed over the old-fashioned bathtub.

She looked over her shoulder and held out her hand to him. "Want to share the shower?"

He took her slender fingers. They moved over his palm as though tasting him. The thought of that kind of pleasure hazed his brain.

"We have to talk," he managed.

"In the shower. I'll explain. Okay?"

He stepped into the bathtub with her and pulled the curtain in place, shutting out the world.

"If you're pregnant—" he began, only to be cut off.

"It's not your problem, so don't worry about it," she said calmly, stepping under the warm spray.

Almost warily he took the soap from her hands and began making a rich lather, which he smoothed over her body. He was uncertain, every instinct alert to danger. He felt like he was climbing a cliff and had suddenly sensed it quivering on the brink of landslide.

"You can't believe that," he said slowly, washing and caressing Joy at the same time.

The feel of his hands made her breath catch and her eyes widen in surprise. A few minutes ago orgasm had exploded hotly through her. Surely that couldn't be new arousal she felt prowling through her blood, her body.

Yet even as she denied the possibility of new desire, she felt tension gathering in her breasts, in the pit of her stomach, between her thighs, heat coiling tightly, hungry for release.

Then she saw Gabe's eyes watching the sudden, hard rise of her nipples, saw his slanting smile, saw the renewed heat of his blood in the male flesh stirring against her thigh.

"Listen to me," she said huskily, taking the soap from his hands and bathing him in rich lather. "When you have what you need for your article, you'll leave. I accept that, Gabriel. That's the only truth that matters. No injured innocence, no responsibilities to anyone but yourself. It will be the same for me, I promise you. No past for us, no future. Just the hot, endless **now**."

"That's not what I—"

His voice broke as her fingers slicked through the hair on his chest and teased his sensitive nipples. A shudder ripped through him, tightening his whole body. He couldn't think when her small hands followed his body hair down and down. His breath came out in a ragged groan when she cupped her palm between his thighs, weighing and enjoying his very different flesh.

"I love your body," she said as she caressed him. "So different from mine. So wonderfully different."

He tried to say her name, but all that came out was a thick sound. Only in his dreams had she taken the lead in sensual exploration. The sight of her pale fingers caressing him, defining him, loosened his knees. He told himself that this was real, that he wouldn't wake up shaking, sweating, alone, filled to bursting with hot dreams.

Her hands shifted upward slowly until she captured the blunt statement of his desire. She felt a fierce pleasure when he became even harder in response to her sensual exploration. She had touched him like this only in her dreams, when she wanted to drive him wild with need.

"This time there are no ties, no traps, no hidden expectations," she said.

As she spoke, she stepped aside. Hot water flowed over him, chasing dissolving sheets of lather down to the drain.

"That's the past," she said, flicking the spent lather with her toe. "There is no future." Her mouth brushed over his chest, searching through dark hair until she found the tiny, hard thrust of his nipple. "There is only now."

Her teeth raked lightly over him. She felt his instant response in the leap of his aroused flesh between her hands.

"Let's make it last forever, Gabe."

Her husky whisper was like her tongue— maddening, searching, caressing every bit of him as she slid down his body and the hot water beat against his back. He saw the flash of her smile against his dark hair, felt the sweet sting of her teeth testing the flexed muscles of his thighs.

"I didn't do this before," she said. "I didn't even know I wanted to. I know it now. I want this."

"Joy, sweetheart, we have to talk."

"I am. You're just not listening."

Then her soft, hungry mouth closed over him and he couldn't think at all.

A shock wave of desire slammed through him. All the heat and power of his blood rushed into the flesh she was caressing so intimately. His body tensed until he could have been carved of stone. He endured the sweet agony for as long as he could, and then longer still, until finally he called to her.

She didn't hear. She was lost to everything but the wild pleasure of loving him, the taste and heat of him burning through her.

With a hoarse sound Gabe pulled Joy up his body and wrapped her tightly in his arms. If this was the only communication she allowed, he would make it more binding than words.

"Turn off the shower," he said.

While she fumbled with the faucets, he bent over her and caught her erect nipple between his teeth. Sensation shot through her, arching her into his mouth. Her hands slid away from metal and back to her lover's slick, exciting body.

Water kept beating down on his head.

"To hell with it," he muttered. He turned off the faucets himself, yanked aside the shower curtain, and lifted her out. "The only thing I want to drown in is you."

It was just a few steps to Joy's bedroom. He set her on the narrow bed and looked at her.

Simply looked at her.

Her body was smooth and creamy against the textured mauve of the bedspread. Desire flushed her skin, darkened her eyes, pulsed through her softness.

He saw it, all of it, and he wanted even more.

"Do you remember the first time we made love?" he asked, running his fingertips from her lips to the peak of her breasts.

"Yes," she said tightly, twisting against him.

Neither one of them knew whether she'd answered his question or had asked for a more satisfying caress than his fingertips teasing her nipples into aching life.

"I remember it," he said. "Awake. Asleep. Dying. It doesn't matter. **I remember.** Do you know what that kind of remembering does to a man?" His voice was soft, hot, like his tongue tracing her lips.

"N-no," she said raggedly, watching him with eyes that were almost black.

"I'll show you. So when I'm shaking with memories I'll know that you'll be shaking, too. You'll remember me, Joy. Always."

She saw the certainty in his eyes and would have been afraid, but her body was already reaching for him, hunger stabbing through her with each speeding heartbeat.

He came down on the bed beside her, not

touching her, memorizing her with a hungry glance that went from her honey-colored hair to the trim nails of her feet. She trembled as though he had stroked her.

Then his shoulders blocked out the room as he bent over her, kissing her temples, tongue tracing the spiral of her ear, thrusting languidly into the sensitive opening. Against the chill of the water drying on her skin, his textured heat was exquisite.

She turned toward him, wanting him, needing to feel the hard evidence of his desire between her hands, in her body.

He laughed and evaded her by lifting her in his arms.

"No, sweet Joy," he said, turning her and placing her on her stomach, smiling down at her. "That's no way to make it last forever."

"Gabe—**I want you.**"

"And I want you. Now it's your turn to listen to me."

He ran the ball of his thumb all the way down her spine in a slow caress that didn't end until he had curved down the shadowed cleft to find the incredible softness concealed inside her. He listened to the ragged intake of her breath and smiled again, a smile as slow and sensual as his thumb tracing her hidden flesh.

"I'm going to explore you," he said as he kissed

her shoulder, her spine, the delicate inward curve of her waist. "I'm going to know each texture, each creamy curve, each beautiful peak and hidden valley."

As he spoke, his hand moved slowly between her legs, spreading a sweet fire that made Joy want to roll onto her back and pull him into her arms, into her body. But when she tried, he just laughed deep in his throat and moved smoothly over her, covering her, pinning her in place with her arms stretched above her head and his fingers interlaced with hers. The roughness of his hair caressed her back and the heat of him lay snugly between the shadow crease of her legs.

"Gabe," she said. "I . . ."

Her body writhed as she moved helplessly against his exciting weight, wanting him desperately yet not able to touch him.

Nor was he touching her. Not really. Not the way she wanted to be touched. Her breasts ached for his hands, his mouth. She cried out her need to be filled by him.

He bit her nape with exquisite care.

"It's like being caught in Small Favors again, isn't it?" he asked huskily, biting her repeatedly, delicately. "You can't touch me the way you want to, yet we're close." His hips rocked against her, dragging his erection over her sultry flesh. "So **close.**"

"No," she said raggedly. "This is worse than Small Favors. At least in the tunnel I could feel you against my breasts, my—"

Her words were lost in a gasp as he swiftly turned her over. Then he pinned her again in exactly the same way, settling over her.

"Better?" he asked, rubbing his body over hers, letting her feel him, feeling her softness in return.

The long caress of his body swept through her, making her tremble. She felt the heat raging through her own flesh and wondered if he could feel it too.

"I ache," she said. "For you."

He smiled darkly and rubbed over her again, teasing her with every look, every breath, the hot length of his penis pressed between their bodies.

Her eyes half closed and she moved helplessly beneath him, wanting him, his name coming as a moan from her flushed lips.

He laughed and teased both of them some more.

She shifted suddenly beneath him, opening her legs, trying to force more than the exquisite torment of being so close and yet so far away from the release that burned to be free.

He caught her legs between his thighs, denying and inciting her with the same hot movements.

"Remember Small Favors?" he asked.

She was suspended in a fierce, sensual grip that withheld the release she craved and instead drove her higher, burning her until she wanted to scream. Her body twisted and she panted as if she was trying to force her way through a tight passage in Lost River Cave's velvet darkness.

"This is much worse," she said raggedly.

"Are you sure? In Small Favors, I couldn't do this."

His mouth took her breast in a fierce and tender suckling. Wild pleasure poured through her, a river hidden within her that had no beginning, no end, only the powerful, rushing present. She cried out Gabe's name and her need and felt the answering shudder of his body.

He shifted slightly, rewarding her sensual struggle with enough freedom to move her legs. Instantly they wrapped tightly around his hips.

"Better?" he asked again.

Her only answer was a ragged sound and the seeking thrust of her hips.

He stretched her arms above her head until her nipples were tight and quivering beneath his skillful tongue. The hard, sensual tugging of his mouth made her cry out in the same rhythms as his caress. She moved convulsively, using every bit of her strength to capture his hard flesh within her body.

"Not yet, sweet Joy," he said. "Not yet. You only think you want me."

"Gabe," she said brokenly, straining against him. "I'm going crazy. It's like my dreams, my nightmares, when I could do everything but feel you alive inside me."

His body trembled. "You dreamed, too?"

"**Yes**. Awake, asleep—"

"Dying," he said against her lips. His tongue licked into her mouth in a rhythm that turned her bones to searing currents of desire.

"Ah, God," she said. "You're destroying me."

"No," he said, sliding down her body, his mouth hot and wet and hungry. "I'm exploring you. There's a difference. All the difference in the world."

She felt his weight shift over her body while his mouth tugged at her. Tiny, husky cries rippled out of her. Slowly he explored the soft skin of her belly and the creamy smoothness of her inner thighs. Her heart stopped, then beat wildly as his explorations became unbearably intimate.

Unbearable, yet she wouldn't have ended the moment to save her life.

"A warm world opening for me." He nuzzled against her unbelievable softness, tasting her, loving her as he'd never loved another woman. "How did I ever leave you?"

She didn't answer. She couldn't. She could only

twist slowly against his hot, hungry mouth. Giving herself wholly to Gabe's consuming sensuality, she forgot the past and the future and even the present. The fierce pleasure gathered, coiling deep inside her like a river caught within dissolving stone, pushing for release.

Tension wracked her. "Now, Gabe, **now**."

He smiled against her straining flesh. "Yes, now."

His teeth closed exquisitely, capturing her for the hot suckling that would drive her over the edge. She arched against him, crying and shaking as the world came apart around her.

"Gabe," she said raggedly, her fingers kneading through his hair to the hot scalp beneath. "I tried to wait."

"Neither of us wanted that. Not really."

He bit her tenderly, caressed her, stroked her, cherished her with exquisitely gentle teeth and tongue, each touch consuming her, creating her, discovering new levels of passion to be explored.

"Oh, God, Gabe. Stop. I can't bear it."

"Yes, you can." His voice was husky and deep, words brushed against her violently sensitive flesh. "You wanted it to last forever, sweetheart. It will."

He held her in loving torment until she was wild again and crying his name with every broken breath, writhing hungrily against him while her nails raked his taut shoulders. Only then did he give her what she demanded, sinking into her until there was no more to give or take, for they were fused hotly one to the other. Tight, deep movements drove her higher, and then higher still. He burned her with dark words and darker caresses until her body squeezed him like a velvet fist.

Then she would have screamed his name and her own unbearable ecstasy, but his mouth was as deeply joined with hers as his body. The first waves of her wild climax washed over both of them, and his hoarse cry of discovery mingled with hers as they shared a long, pulsing release that kept every promise he had made.

It was unbearably good and it lasted forever.

For both of them.

TWENTY-FIVE

Gabe and Joy arrived at the Childer Ranch late, but they had called ahead so that no one worried. Joy knew the rough roads with hair-raising accuracy, and drove them the same way. Hair-raising. Dust, too. It boiled around them like a pack of eager dogs.

"I'm going to be spitting grit for a week," he said.

"Your fault. I was willing to stop at one, but somebody talked me into a regular . . . um . . ."

"Marathon?" he asked, deadpan.

She tried not to laugh or blush. She didn't succeed.

Laura Childer and Kati bolted from the ranch house and ran toward the Jeep where dust still swirled.

"Did you really find a new cave?" Kati asked. "Is it bigger than the old one? Can I see it?"

Her high young voice bubbled over with an eagerness that made Gabe smile. He'd felt the same way when he was young and the whole world was one constantly unfolding miracle for him to explore. He didn't know when that had changed for him, when he'd become weary rather than excited, driven rather than lured. He **did** know the exact instant when he'd once more felt a blinding, incredible excitement at just being alive.

It was a few hours ago, when for the first time in seven years he'd felt Joy soften and run like sun-warmed honey in his hands.

"I want to see the new cave too!"

This time the excited young voice belong to Laura, who was impatiently dancing in place near the Jeep.

Susan Childer laughed and ruffled her daughter's dark hair. "The last time you talked Joyce into a cave expedition, you got twelve steps down below the entrance and decided to have a picnic up top with me instead."

"That was a long time ago," Laura said solemnly. "I'm much older now."

"Mmm," Susan said, nodding wisely. "A whole five months."

Joy spoke quickly, heading off the objections she saw clouding Laura's face. "No one has really been in the new room. We just found it. And it looks like it will be kind of a rough trip getting there."

"Does that mean I can't go?" Kati asked.

Joy hesitated. "Probably not, button. So far, the only way we've found into the room is to rappel down a rope for at least ninety feet. That's like nine cottages stacked on top of one another, taller than the tallest cottonwood in the yard. The most you've ever rappelled is twenty-seven feet, and you hated climbing back up the rope to get out."

Kati looked stubborn. "Gravy-bear would carry me."

"We've talked about this before. If you can't do it yourself, you can't do it, period. It just isn't safe. What would you do if Davy hurt himself and couldn't get you out?"

Frowning, Kati drew patterns in the dust with her toe. "So this is worse than going into the old cave?"

"Uh-huh," Joy said. "Lots."

A deep sigh, then, "Okay. But I still think I could do it. I mean, I got born without any help," she said with a child's odd logic, "so I've got to be good enough to climb down and up a silly old rope."

Susan laughed again and ruffled Kati's flaming hair with the same easy affection she had given her daughter. "That's it, Kati-me-girl. You tell 'em."

"Born without help?" Gabe asked, puzzled.

Joy started to cut off that line of conversation,

but it was too late. Susan was already talking, telling one of her favorite stories.

"You mean you've known Kati for more than ten minutes and she hasn't told you?" Susan asked in mock horror.

"Not a word." He smiled at her with the easy charm of a man who has made his living meeting new people and drawing information from them. "Guess you're the only one who can help me, huh?"

"We'd better get going," Joy said quickly. "We should be at the cave by—"

It didn't work. Susan just kept talking.

"Kati is a real pioneer kid, just like in the old days," Susan said, putting her arm around the girl's shoulder and giving her a hug. "She was born in the desert a few miles from here. Literally."

Joy saw the color leave Gabe's face and stifled a groan. She really didn't want him to know how stupid she'd been six years ago. She hadn't meant to have Kati on the side of a deserted road.

It had just turned out that way.

"What?" Gabe asked softly, his lips barely moving.

"Yeah." The older woman smiled wryly. "That was Fish's reaction. He came driving up here like a madman with Joyce and a squalling little scrap of life in the front seat. Poor man was white as salt—and him a field medic in the army."

Gabe opened his mouth. Nothing came out but a hoarse sound.

"All Fish's kids had been born in a hospital," Susan explained with a chuckle. "I still tease him about it. Just because there was blood here and there, he thought he was going to lose both of them. He didn't know that childbirth isn't Mother Nature's tidiest moment." Smiling, she shook her head at Fish's naïveté. "I knew better. All my kids were born right here, with my husband at my side."

Kati smiled proudly up at Gabe. "Mommy and me are a team."

"Yeah." Susan slanted Joy a laughing glance. "Your mom does the work and you take the credit."

Gabe knew he should smile politely or say something, anything. He couldn't. He was as off balance as he'd been when his feet slipped on the water-smoothed pitch leading down into Gotcha. Only this time there wasn't a safety rope belaying him, nothing to catch him when he lost his balance and fell.

And he was falling.

The idea of Joy giving birth to his child in the desert horrified him. He wanted to know what had happened, why she hadn't been in the hospital with doctors and nurses at hand if something went wrong.

"How in hell—" he began.

Then he saw Joy's embarrassment and stopped. Questioning her right now wasn't a good idea. Not only was she uncomfortable, he didn't trust himself not to reveal just how intimately the answers about her past concerned him.

He'd given Joy his word that he wouldn't tell Kati he was her father. He would keep his word if it killed him.

And he was beginning to think it might.

"Amazing," he said to Joy. "You'll have to tell me about it sometime. The whole story."

Her weak smile said she wasn't in any hurry for that conversation.

Kati grinned and started climbing into the Jeep

"Hold it," Susan said. "I promised you and Laura some cookies. Run and get them, kids."

With small squeals of anticipation, the two girls pelted back up the porch and into the weathered ranch house. As soon as the door slammed behind them, Susan turned to Joy.

"I know you miss Kati when she isn't with you," Susan said quickly, "but Laura and I would very much like to have Kati stay with us."

"For the weekend?"

"For as long as you'd let her." Susan's mouth turned down at the corners and she smiled sadly. "Laura knows Kati will be leaving in a few weeks. So do I. We'd like to spend as much time with her as we can before you go."

Joy bit her lip and looked unhappy.

Gabe bit his tongue to keep from demanding that he have as much time as possible to get to know his daughter before the closing of the cave forced Joy to carry out whatever her plans for the future were.

He had a few of his own.

He might have a real uphill struggle convincing Joy that he was worth keeping around, but Kati was an easy sell. She loved sitting in his lap and having him read books to her while Joy worked at the kitchen table, frowning and shifting papers from one pile to another.

Then there was the simple, immovable fact that he was damned if he would let the past repeat itself—Joy alone, having a baby in the desert.

"And I know how hard it is for you to juggle Kati and all the underground work and paperwork that has to be done before Lost River is closed," Susan said. "I thought maybe you wouldn't mind if we sort of kidnapped her for a while after school is out."

Hand in hand the two girls burst from the house and leaped down to the dusty yard.

"Think about it," Susan said quietly. She turned to greet both girls with open arms and a big smile. "Who brought one for me?"

Kati and Laura each handed over a cookie to Susan.

"What about Gabe and Joyce?" Susan asked.

Two more cookies changed hands.

Gabe managed a smile at Kati as he took the cookie, but it was one of the most difficult things he'd had to do in his life. He kept thinking about Joy and the desert and all the things that could go wrong during childbirth.

I should have been with her.

Is she pregnant even now? If she is, where will she be when she gives birth?

Where will I be?

The questions came at Gabe like rocks careening down the face of a Peruvian cliff. And like the cliff, there was no cover for him, nowhere to hide, no way to turn aside the battering tide.

Has she learned to protect herself?

Has she simply cut the possibility of pregnancy from her life?

Does she think that now is a safe time for her, that she can be my lover for a few days and not get pregnant?

Or did she want me so much that she took the risk without thinking?

The most logical answer—that for whatever reason Joy couldn't get pregnant right now—was probably also the correct one. But he couldn't be certain.

The Joy of today was not the Joy of seven years ago. She gave her body to him, yes, perfectly. But the rest of her was like Lost River Cave, moments of glittering illumination against a back-drop of mystery as deep as time.

It wasn't so much that Joy hid.

It was that she didn't reveal.

Despite their time together, he wasn't much closer to truly knowing Joy than he'd been in Peru.

She trusts me enough to be my lover. That's progress, isn't it?

But becoming his lover today didn't require the same level of trust for her that it had seven years ago.

Not once in all the shattering intimacy of their recent hours together had Joy cried out her love for him. Not once had she even hinted that she wanted a future that included him.

Not once.

This time there are no ties, no traps, no hidden expectations.

There is no future.

There is only now.

Seven years ago he might have accepted the passionate moment and asked for nothing more.

It was too soon for you to love seven years ago—and now it's too late for me.

Gabe told himself that Joy was wrong, that it wasn't too late. Then he told himself again. And again.

He couldn't lose her before he even knew what he had found.

TWENTY-SIX

As Joy drove the Jeep back toward Cottonwood Wells, she sensed Gabe watching her with shadowed eyes. The only conversation in the Jeep was Kati's chatter, bright and overflowing with fun. Joy answered her daughter's questions with part of her mind, which left plenty of time for her to wonder what Gabe was thinking that had put such darkness in his eyes.

She was afraid that it was the circumstances surrounding Kati's birth. He'd been visibly shocked. Well, that wasn't surprising. She'd been shocked herself when she realized what was going to happen. And then she didn't have any time or energy or emotion left over for anything but giving birth to her impatient daughter.

Joy knew that he would question her about the birth as soon as they were alone. She was grateful that he was waiting to satisfy his curiosity. Seven years ago he wouldn't have let anything get in the way of his questions. He'd been almost ruthless then. He still could be now.

But so could she.

She understood now what she hadn't understood seven years ago: some ruthlessness was necessary in order to survive.

"Can Laura stay this weekend?" Kati asked eagerly. "You can pick us up after school and you can take us to the bus on Monday. Then I can go home with her for the last week of school."

Joy made an all-purpose mothering sound that said she was listening but not promising anything.

Quickly, earnestly, Kati kept talking, words spilling out one after the other. This was just one of many skirmishes in the two girls' continuing effort to persuade both mothers that they should have two daughters at a time or none.

"Then you won't have to get me to the bus stop all the time, and you'll have lots and lots of time to go caving, too. 'Specially since I can't go with you anyway," Kati finished triumphantly. She turned to Gabe with a bright smile. "Don't you think that's a great idea?"

"I think you're asking the wrong person," Joy said.

"But—"

"Your mother's right," he said. "It's not fair for you to try to get someone else to say yes for her."

Kati gave him a very disappointed look out of big gray eyes. "You're no fun."

He smiled and shook his head slowly at her.

"Won't work, button," he said, tapping the golden freckles on her nose with a gentle fingertip. "I was a kid once. I know all the ways to wheedle a yes out of parents."

In flat disbelief Kati looked up at the man beside her. "You were a kid?"

"Sure was."

"Really? Did you have a mother and father and everything?"

Gabe managed not to wince or look at Joy. "Yes. And a brother, too."

"Did you get to live with him all the time?"

"Whether we liked it or not." He smiled crookedly, remembering the times when he and his brother had fought. Then the smile slipped. Their most recent fight had been by radiophone, when Gabe had reamed Dan for saying that Joy had had an abortion. Dan hadn't been pleased.

Hey, don't yell at me, little brother. She told me to go to hell and she would do what was best for her. What was I supposed to think? In my shoes, what would you have thought?

"Gee, were you ever lucky," Kati said.

"Yeah," Gabe said, meaning it. He might want to kick his older brother's ass around the block a few times, but he couldn't imagine life without him.

"I want a sister but Mommy says they don't grow on trees."

His smile was almost sad. "You sure about that?"

Kati rolled her eyes at his teasing and leaned closer to him. "I used to think they did. Every morning I'd get up and run out and look at the cottonwoods near the cottages." She sighed hugely. "Just leaves or twigs and branches. Lots and lots and lots of them. Even on Christmas morning."

"Tell you what, button." Joy's smile was tight, aching. She heard her own endless longing for a sister or a brother in her daughter's voice. "I'll call Susan and we'll work something out about Laura. Okay?"

"Okay! When? Could we have a cookout when Laura comes over? Will Fish bring his guitar and Gravy-bear sing?" Kati fairly bounced with excitement as she turned to Gabe. "Do you sing?"

"Not for a long time."

"Oh." Kati's face fell.

"For you, I'll sing."

"Oh, goody!" Kati's face lit up with a smile that was very like her mother's. "It'll be so fun! We'll have a fire and marshmallows and ketchup and—"

"Ketchup?" Gabe asked warily.

"Yeah. You know, for the hot dogs."

"Oh. Well, that's a relief."

"What is?" Kati asked.

"That you don't put ketchup on the marshmallows."

"Eeeeewww. Gross. Who'd do a yucky thing like that?"

"Someone really, really hungry?" he asked, deadpan.

Joy snickered.

Kati rolled her eyes again. Adults could be so silly. "When we're done eating we stay up late and sing and watch the Glitter River. That's my favorite part."

After the ketchup and marshmallow mix-up, Gabe was almost afraid to ask. Curiosity got the better of him. "Glitter River?"

"Yeah. That's the, uh, the—I forget the name. Mommy?"

"Milky Way."

"Milky Way," Kati repeated seriously and turned back to Gabe. "It's not made of milk, you know."

"Really?"

"How would that many cows get up there?"

"Um, good point."

"It's stars. Lots and lots of stars. They must be easier to move up there than cows. Mommy showed me a book with lots of pictures. I want to go there when I grow up."

Gabe pulled his mind back from visualizing a cosmic herd of Holsteins. "Go where? The stars?"

"Sure!"

Emotion closed around his throat in a vise, squeezing words into silence as he heard echoes of his own childhood dreams in his daughter's eager voice. When he'd been Kati's age, he'd wanted to go to the stars. That hadn't been possible, so he'd done the next best thing. He'd explored as much of the earth as he could.

And it had been there for his taking, for his exploring, for his unending delight. He drank the wonder of earth's beauty and variety until he overflowed. Then he shared what he could in words.

For a time it was enough.

But no matter how diverse, how extraordinary, how mysterious, the wonders of the world could no longer fill the emptiness he'd sensed growing inside himself. Yet the unknown would always call to him. He could no more imagine a life without exploration and discovery than he could imagine being dead.

"Glitter River," he said. "And each possibility is a separate bit of shining beauty."

Kati laughed and held out her hands as though to grab it all.

Smiling, he touched the flyaway softness of her hair and wondered how a child could have summed up his own feelings toward life and living so well. His smile faded when he realized that this bright and beautiful child might slowly, unknowingly, become as empty as he had, an emptiness he was only now beginning to measure as it was filled by Joy.

He didn't want emptiness for his daughter. He wanted life to be one magnificent Glitter River, possibilities cascading endlessly into her outstretched hands. He felt for his daughter the same helpless love that had made Joy pray Kati would find life more gentle with her dreams than her mother had.

But there was no guarantee that life would be kind to Kati Anderson.

The realization sent a shaft of agony through him. He couldn't live Kati's life for her, couldn't choose for her from among the men who would come to taste her sweetness. He could only pray silently that she chose a better man than her father.

His prayer was no more comforting than Joy's had been.

TWENTY-SEVEN

As the Jeep pulled up to the cottages, Davy came out to greet everyone with a triumphant smile. "Fish's wife is on the way out with supplies. Said she'd play War with Kati while we go caving."

"I'll cook dinner tonight," Gabe and Joy said at the same time.

They looked at each other and laughed.

"Enlightened self-interest at work," Gabe said in a low voice.

She gave him a smile and a sideways look that made him catch his breath. It reminded him of how rarely she smiled now compared to seven years ago. The thought that he might have taken her laughter as well as her innocence was as painful to him as the knowledge that he couldn't save his daughter from life's unpleasant surprises. He could only watch and pray and love.

"I'll clean up," Davy said quickly. "I hate cooking," he added to no one in particular.

"Really?" Gabe's dark eyebrows lifted. "I

thought it was just that everything you touched turned to"—he looked hastily at Kati—"mutt mulch."

"Oh, but Kati loves my cooking, don't you?" Davy asked, lifting the little girl out of the Jeep and tossing her gently toward the sky.

"You cook just like a Gravy-bear," she said, laughing and tugging at Davy's blond hair.

"I think that child has a career as a diplomat," Gabe said.

"Stabbed!" Davy spread one hand over his heart and settled Kati in the crook of his other arm. "By my own sweet little girl, too."

"Where's the blood? Show me!" Kati giggled and pulled at the top of Davy's T-shirt until she could peer inside. "Eeeeew! Hair! Gravy-bear is hairy, Gravy-bear is hairy," she singsonged while he carried her up the porch and into the house.

Gabe laughed softly as he and Joy climbed out of the Jeep. He was amazed by Kati's unending energy and laughing acceptance of life. He looked over at Joy when they started up the path to the cottage.

"That's a fine little girl you've raised," he said. "She's so open. So alive."

Unable to speak, Joy simply stood and watched him with transparent gray eyes. She couldn't prevent the fine, sudden shimmer of tears as his words sank into her, dissolving away years of hidden fear, secret doubt. There had been so many days when she wondered if she was doing the right thing in raising Kati alone, and so many nights when she'd been too tired or too busy to give her daughter all the time she deserved.

"Thank you," Joy whispered. "There are times when I feel I've done everything wrong as a parent."

He looked into her eyes and saw the hesitations, the doubts, the relentless pressures of raising a child alone. He framed Joy's face with his hands and bent low, brushing his lips over her damp eyelashes.

"You've always loved her," he said. "No child can ask more than that of a parent."

Her tears felt hot on his lips. He sensed the tremor that went through her. When she turned her face up to him, he kissed her very gently, felt her breath sighing into his mouth as her hands opened against his chest.

"Dr. Joyce, I think we should try—" The front door of the cottage slammed and Davy's voice stopped at the same instant.

Gabe nestled Joy against his body and turned her face into his chest, concealing her tears.

Davy stared, shocked.

"We don't always fight," Gabe said. "Sometimes we make up."

Davy looked from the hard-faced older man to the woman he held so protectively against his chest. "Uh, right. Looks like this is one of those make-up times." He ran his hand through his thick thatch of blond hair and sighed. "Guess I better get lost."

"No problem," Gabe said. "Just wanted you to know the way things are." With barely a pause he added, "I'll bet Maggie could use some help getting lunch ready."

"Maggie," Davy said.

"Yes. Maggie. If you're interested. If not, that's okay." Gabe shrugged. "She's a lot of woman and nobody's fool. She'll find someone else."

Davy met Gabe's hard green glance for another moment before he smiled crookedly. "Funny. In the two years I've known her, she never mentioned your name."

Both men knew that Davy wasn't talking about Maggie.

Gabe didn't answer. He simply continued to hold Joy against his chest, caressing her hair gently with his hand, shielding her from any eyes but his own.

Davy hesitated, then shrugged. "Looks like a good time to make sandwiches." He smiled suddenly. "If you see Dr. Joyce, would you ask her if we're going to take on Joy's Castle after I eat?"

"Yes," Joy said.

Her voice was muffled against Gabe's chest. She shook her head and started laughing helplessly.

"God," she muttered, meeting Gabe's amused, gentle glance, "I feel like a teenager caught on the front porch swing with her date."

Davy smiled slightly. "You look like one, too. Didn't know you could blush. Or is that sunburn on the back of your neck?" he teased.

She groaned and buried her face against Gabe's chest again. She didn't lift her head until the sound of Davy's laughter faded behind the noise of Maggie's creaky cabin door opening and closing.

Sighing, Joy put her arms around Gabe and absorbed the sweetness of being held by him beneath the brilliant desert sun. She didn't care that Kati or Fish or Maggie might appear at any moment. She needed Gabe right now, needed his strength and his concern, his gentle, supportive hug.

It had been so long since anyone had held her, simply held her, giving to her rather than asking something of her.

Silently Gabe bent his head until he could rest his cheek against Joy's sun-streaked hair. He inhaled deeply, feeling like he was breathing her into his soul and she was a light filling him. He couldn't remember the last time he'd held a woman with no expectation of immediately making love to her.

Then he realized that he'd never held a woman

like this, ever, absorbing her like she was life it-self.

"Mommy," Kati said, coming out onto the porch, "when are you going to call Susan?"

Reluctantly Gabe loosened his arms to let Joy turn and face their daughter. Instead of stepping away, Joy put her arms over his and leaned against him.

"Soon, button," Joy said.

Kati looked curiously from her mother to the tall man who held her. "Why were you hugging Gabe?"

Joy had never ducked Kati's questions in the past, no matter how difficult they were to an-swer. She wouldn't duck them now. "Because I like him."

"Don't you like Gravy-bear and Fish?"

"Of course I do. Very much."

"But you don't hug them."

"They aren't Gabe," Joy said simply.

Kati thought that over for a moment, her gray eyes as serious as her mother's. Then the little girl nodded, accepting both the explanation and the emotional logic beneath it. "I'm hungry."

Joy let out a soundless breath of relief. "On to the really important things in life," she said so softly that only Gabe could hear.

"Like food?" he asked equally softly.

"Like food." She smiled at her daughter.

"Maggie's fixing sandwiches right now to take down in the cave."

"Oh boy! Suppose she's finished yet?"

"Suppose you could help her?" Joy countered.

Kati sighed. Fixing tacos was fun. Fixing sandwiches was work. On the other hand, she was really hungry. "I'll ask."

She started toward Maggie's cottage with about one-third her normal speed and enthusiasm.

Together Gabe and Joy walked through the cottage to the backyard, where a long clothesline was hung with freshly washed caving gear. She could have used the electric dryer, but preferred the sun-fresh smell of clothes dried on the line. It took some of the load off the generators, too.

While Joy took down the warm, clean clothes, he watched her as if seeing her for the first time.

"Tell me about Kati's birth," he said.

Joy's hands hesitated over a piece of mesh underwear. Then she lifted the clothespins. "It was a classic case of too much, too soon and then too little, too late."

He stood with his arms out while she added a piece of clothing to the growing pile he carried.

"I was living with the Childers," she said.

"Were they friends of your parents?"

"No. Susan had advertised for live-in help, and after my parents died I needed a place to live. The job was perfect for me. Room and board, enough time to study, and enough pocket money to pay for gas to get to school."

He'd known Joy's parents weren't wealthy, but he hadn't thought that she'd been left without any money at all. "Didn't your parents leave you something? Insurance money or . . . anything?"

"They left me memories." She unclipped another piece of clothing and handed it to him. "Good memories. And the Jeep."

He was stunned. The check he'd left for her hadn't been nearly enough for her to live on. He'd meant it only to tide her over until he got back from the Orinoco.

Yet when he'd finally come back to civilization, he'd discovered that she didn't need or want him anymore. At least he thought that was what her words to Dan meant.

She told me to go to hell and she would do what was best for her.

Both men had been wrong, but it was Joy who paid.

"How did you manage?" he asked, his voice husky with emotion.

"I used your check to help pay for the pregnancy and delivery."

"But what about your day-to-day expenses?"

She shrugged and handed him more clothes. "I did what everyone else does who needs money. I worked two jobs. Susan was my live-in job. The other job was as a research assistant to several professors in the geology department."

"Was the pregnancy . . . difficult?"

"The doctor called me her prize patient. Young, strong, healthy, and flexible. Cave crawling keeps you in good shape. Physically I was fine."

Gabe didn't ask about her mental health. He didn't need to. He could imagine how difficult it had been for her to go through with her pregnancy in the face of her parents' death, his own total absence, and the necessity of holding down two jobs while still going to school.

"What happened?" he asked finally. "Why was Kati born in the desert?"

Joy piled more dry clothes in his arms. And didn't say anything.

"Sweetheart?"

"I had false labor on and off for several days. I'd get halfway to town and the contractions would stop. Then I'd turn around and drive back to the Childer ranch." She smiled wryly. "Repeat as necessary."

"Why didn't your doctor do something?"

"Like what? At the end of term, false labor is just a part of giving birth, especially for first-time mothers. Perfectly natural."

"But why didn't you check into the hospital just to be safe?"

"I'd budgeted enough money for a one-day stay."

His fingers clenched around the clothes, but he bit off his hissing curse before she heard it. "So you drove back to the Childer ranch. Then what?"

"I did the back-and-forth thing three times. The fourth time the contractions came, I just ignored them and kept working. I didn't have any more time to waste on false alarms. All the men were out in the field. A tractor had broken down or something, and Susan was already overdue with Laura, so she wasn't feeling very lively."

"Go on."

Joy pulled the last of the clothes off the line and folded them over her own arms. The grim look on his face told her what he was feeling.

"There was a lot to do around the ranch for everyone," she said, "and I just kept doing it until I couldn't. Then I got in the Jeep and headed for town. By the time I realized my body wasn't fooling, it was too late. I was only halfway to town and I wasn't going to make it. Kati was impatient to be born."

"**God**. What did you do?"

"The only thing I could. I pulled the Jeep over to the side of the road, dragged a bedroll out of the back, and . . ." She shrugged and tried not to remember how frightened she'd been.

How horribly alone.

"You must have been terrified," he said in a raw voice. "A scared twenty-year-old giving birth alone in the desert."

"I was pretty scared at first. Later on there wasn't any time for fear." She smiled wryly. "Birth isn't exactly a voluntary process on the mother's part. Toward the end I was pretty much along for the ride."

At first he couldn't force out the words. Yet he had to know. **"You were alone the whole time?"**

Joy glanced up. The pain and regret in his eyes made her wish the subject of Kati's birth had never come up.

"No," she said quickly, touching his arm. "Fish came along after a while. It was all right after that. He'd had some emergency medical training, and he was very kind, very gentle with me. He knew how to help. Kati wasn't hurt at all. That's what really had terrified me—that something would go wrong and I wouldn't know what to do for the baby."

"When . . ." Gabe swallowed and tried again. "When did Fish get there?"

"I don't know. One moment I was alone and hurting and scared to death, and the next moment he was there, reassuring me. It was easier after that. Kati was born very quickly."

The clenched strength of Gabe's muscles beneath Joy's fingers was frightening. He looked like a man who had never smiled and never would.

"Gabriel," she said in a low voice, "don't. **It wasn't your fault.**"

As the words left her lips, she realized how true they were. For a long time she had blamed Gabe for leaving her to bear a child alone. But it hadn't been all his fault. Not really. She'd wanted his lovemaking, had demanded it, and hadn't thought beyond the moment when he would move inside her.

Yet she hadn't been stupid or ignorant of the mechanics of conception and contraception. She simply hadn't cared. Childishly she'd assumed that it would turn out all right, that all she had to do was love Gabe and everything would work out in the end.

It had.

Just not the way she'd expected.

That wasn't Gabe's fault. She couldn't blame him any longer for her own willful naïveté and the fact that her parents had died so soon after he left her.

Yet he was blaming himself. It was there in the bleakness of his eyes and in the brackets of pain around his mouth. At one time the sight of his suffering would have given her a vindictive plea-sure, but she didn't feel that way anymore.

His pain was also hers.

And it was destructive.

"Gabriel, listen to me," she said urgently. "I don't blame you anymore. I was smart enough to know better, but I didn't want to know anything except you. I wanted you. I did everything I could to make sure you wouldn't think of anything but making love to me. I didn't have a thought beyond that." She laughed. "For a certifiably bright girl, I was really stupid."

"Don't," he said hoarsely. "Don't blame yourself. I'm the one who should have known better. I never should have taken a virgin."

"You didn't **take** anything," she interrupted fiercely. "I gave myself as freely and—and as passionately as any woman ever has!"

"Oh, God, yes." He closed his eyes, remembering. "There was never anyone like you. Ever. You haunted me to the ragged ends of the earth."

The words went through her like a flood, sweeping up the shattered debris of the past and carrying it away, opening new possibilities where before there had been only old barricades.

"That's only fair," she said. "You called to me in every one of the Voices."

"You hated me."

She started to deny it, but couldn't. "Yes. For a time. I hated myself, too. I hated **life**. But

I'm growing up. Finally. Don't hate yourself, Gabriel. It's not worth it. Nothing is."

Unable to meet her eyes, he tilted back his head and let the sun's savage light wash over him.

How can I not hate myself for what I did to her?

"How did you manage not to hate me?" he asked finally.

"It's called growing up. It's knowing yourself, warts and all, and not hating yourself."

He took a deep breath and looked again into Joy's luminous eyes. After a long silence he said, "You told me if I came to Lost River Cave to find forgiveness, I came to the wrong place. Yet you're trying very hard to forgive me."

Her breath came in sharply. He was right.

Seeing and learning about the Gabe of today had made her understand much better the Gabe of seven years ago—and herself. She had participated in the passionate recklessness.

She had paid.

So had he.

"Are you forgiving yourself, too?" he asked softly. "Do you still believe you were a fool to give yourself to love? To me?"

"I—I don't know. It's too soon. I just found out that I don't blame you anymore."

"Joy," he whispered, bending to her, arms full of sun-drenched clothes. "Kiss me. Please. I want to know what forgiveness tastes like. Then maybe, just maybe, I'll be able to forgive myself too."

Her arms as full of clothes as his, she stood on tiptoe, touching his lips with her own. When his tongue teased the curves of her smile, she sighed and opened her mouth. For a long moment she leaned against him, knowing only the sweetness of his kiss.

"Well?" she asked finally, nuzzling against his lips, teasing and at the same time very serious. "What does forgiveness taste like?"

"Sunlight. Peace. And peppermint."

Her laughter rippled through the afternoon.

He watched her transformation, the pleasure so clearly revealed in her smile, her eyes as radiant as his deepest dreams. This was one memory that hadn't been a lie.

There was nothing on earth as beautiful as Joy laughing.

TWENTY-EIGHT

As Gabe hammered a piton deep into limestone, the sound of steel ringing against steel echoed painfully within Small Favors. He drove in a second steel spike, and then a third, carefully selecting his angles to ensure maximum holding power.

The stone was dense. It took the pitons cleanly, with no visible fracturing.

Two pitons would have been enough for safety. He knew it. He also knew that Joy would be the first one dangling over the void. That was why he drove in a third metal spike. A backup for the backup.

Steel carabiners snapped securely into place, anchoring the rope Joy would use to rappel down into the unexplored room that bore her name. But not just yet. He wasn't quite satisfied with her safety.

He wrapped the climbing rope around his body, braced his feet against the side of the tunnel and heaved back again and again, grunting with effort as he tried to break loose one of the pitons.

Nothing gave. Nothing shifted. Nothing felt the least bit loose.

Gabe kept on throwing his full weight back against the rope. He didn't stop until he was as certain as possible that the pitons and rope would hold.

"I still wish you'd wear a safety rope," he said.

"On rappel," Joy said patiently, "a safety rope is more trouble than it's worth. The two ropes tangle all the time, which leaves me—"

"—knotted and dangling like a fly in a spiderweb, not able to go up, down or sideways," he finished. "I know, I know. I'd do the same if I was the one going down. I just don't like it when you're the one going without a safety rope."

He yanked at the line again before he went to the lip of the overhang and began feeding the rope out over the edge a few feet at a time. The climbing rope was one hundred and twenty feet long. If it didn't find bottom, he'd switch to the two-hundred-foot rope Davy had carried into the cave.

Perhaps fifteen feet of rope was left when he felt the weight taken from his hands. In the darkness below, the free end of the rope was resting on something. Bottom, he hoped, rather than a ledge jutting out over another drop.

"Want the two-hundred-foot rope?" he asked.

She shook her head. "Not until we're sure we need it. If I come up short, I'll climb out and try again."

He looked out into Joy's Castle. The green glow from the light stick that Joy had thrown still gave an eerie illumination to a huge flowstone palette that was fringed with a beautifully fluted drapery. The bottom of the formation wasn't visible. Nor was the light stick itself. There wasn't any way to tell whether the light lay on the floor of the cave itself or was caught within one of the many intricate formations.

Invisible in the darkness, water danced and sang. Ghostly conversations rose on the air currents caused by Lost River's undiscovered waterfall. Joy's Castle was an extraordinary place, as enthralling as any Gabe had ever stood on the brink of exploring.

And he was stalling rather than send Joy alone into the unknown territory.

So quit spinning on your thumb, he told himself. **She's exploring with the same extremely sane safety measures you would have used. She's doing it just the way you're going to do it when it's your turn. As she pointed out, what's sauce for the gander is sauce for everything else in sight.**

But the thought of losing her to an exploring accident made him realize how hollow life would be without her—and how full it had become when he was close enough to feel her laughing within his arms.

When he found himself seriously considering driving in a fourth and absolutely unnecessary piton, he didn't know whether to laugh or swear. Instead, he eeled backward to the wide spot in the tunnel where Joy and the other cavers waited.

"Ready," he said to her. In a tone that admitted no argument he added, "I cut a very short section of my own rope and tied it to a third piton. Put the rope on and keep it on until you're out of the tunnel and in position to rappel. When you're on your stomach, the climbing rope is on the left and the safety rope is on your right. Got it?"

Davy and Fish exchanged a quick look and waited for Dr. Joyce to tear a strip from Gabe Venture's overbearing hide. Not that the two men didn't agree that the safety rope was a good idea. They did, because they knew that the most dangerous part of this kind of descent came during the scramble off the overhang.

But their boss had never taken kindly to people who told her how to do things. Suggestions, sometimes.

Orders, never.

Joy's head snapped up. She opened her mouth to tell Gabe that she'd crawled a hell of a lot more caves than he had and had survived to tell the tale. Then she saw the tension drawing his face into hard lines and knew that he was worried about her safety, not her ability. He'd explored enough wild country to know that luck was sometimes more important than skill.

"All right," she said, letting out the angry breath she had drawn. "Thank you, Gabriel."

Davy swore softly. "Damn, Fish. I owe you five bucks."

"What for?" Maggie asked.

"Fish bet that Dr. Joyce would let Gabe belay her into the cave and drive the pitons to hold the rope. Fish was right both times," Davy explained.

"So Gabe's climbed a lot of rocks and knows more about pitons than we do," Maggie said, not understanding. "So what?"

Davy made a disgusted sound. "So Fish has crawled a lot of caves, too, but Dr. Joyce doesn't let him set anchor slings or cable ladders or . . ." he shrugged. "You get the picture."

Joy heard. She hadn't thought about it before now, but it was true: she never trusted her life to anyone else if there was any way out of it at all. She routinely belayed other people and then climbed down alone. When that arrangement wasn't possible, she let Fish belay her and then she searched until she found a route where she wouldn't need help from anyone.

There hadn't been any conscious thought behind her actions. It was just the way she'd been since Gabe left and her parents died.

"Fish," she said quietly over her shoulder, pitching her voice so that Maggie and Davy couldn't hear, "it's not that I don't trust—"

"I know," Fish said softly, cutting her off. "Hell, if some bastard had left me helpless by the side of the road, I wouldn't trust a soul, neither, less there weren't no damn choice. Hard lessons stay learnt the longest."

Gabe heard each blunt word. He crouched against the tunnel wall, feeling as cold as the stone itself, wishing he could crawl out of his own skin, disowning himself and a past that he'd never meant to be.

But the past had happened whether he liked it or not. The past couldn't be changed. It couldn't be forgotten.

And it couldn't be forgiven.

Not by him.

Joy felt the tension in Gabe's body and knew that he was hating himself. **The bastard who had left her by the side of the road.**

She also knew that it hadn't been anything like that. He hadn't set out to seduce her and then abandon her to have his baby alone in the desert. If he'd known it would turn out like that, he would have prevented it somehow, no matter what it cost him.

She knew that as certainly as she knew that she was alive.

But did he know?

She started to tell him, then stopped. She couldn't say anything to comfort him without giving away to Fish who Kati's father was. But she could reach Gabe in another way.

"I'm going to test our lights," she said.

With no more warning than that, she unplugged the leads from her helmet and Gabe's, concealing their bodies within Lost River Cave's velvet night. She took his hand and peeled away the glove until her mouth could find his palm.

He stiffened, trying to pull his hand away, refusing the comfort she was offering.

She hung on, cradling his hand against her cheek and lips, murmuring softly, just one voice among the many whispering through the tunnel.

Abruptly he stopped trying to withdraw. With a fierce, inarticulate sound he pulled Joy against him. When his lips met hers she tasted the scalding heat of a man's tears.

"Gabriel," she whispered raggedly. **"Don't."**

His only answer was a kiss that was both hard and gentle. Then he eased her away from his body, turned his back to the people behind him, and plugged in the leads to her helmet.

She saw the tears glittering in the corners of his eyes and felt like she was being cut in two.

"Get going," he whispered huskily. "If you

need me, this time I'll be within reach. **I promise you.**"

Blindly she pulled off her glove and touched his lips.

He kissed her fingertips.

"It's all right," he whispered. "Go explore your new world. I'll be right behind you."

For a moment she savored the warmth of his breath on her fingers. Then she pulled on her glove and began to wiggle feet first into the final narrow stretch of Small Favors. Almost immediately she heard the scuffle and scrape of Gabe following her.

A few minutes later her boots connected with the thick metal eyelets of the pitons he'd driven into stone to hold her climbing rope. She turned on her side and inched down the tunnel between the pitons until her hands found the climbing rope. She attached it to the figure eight descender she'd already snapped on her Swiss seat. The friction of the rope passing through the figure eight would act as a brake, slowing the speed of her descent. There were fancier ways of doing it, but none she trusted more.

After the rope was properly attached, she quietly cursed and squirmed until the climbing rope passed between her legs from the front, over her right hip, diagonally across her chest, and then back over her left shoulder. Only when the rope was in position for rappelling did she attach the short safety rope to the Swiss seat with a locking carabiner.

It wasn't the easiest or neatest arrangement she had ever used, especially in the narrow tunnel. But the short rope did ensure that if she lost her balance during the tricky transfer from the overhang to a safe rappelling position, the fall would be frightening, bruising—but very brief.

She inched closer to the lip, feeding the climbing rope through the figure eight with steady pulls. As soon as she was rappelling, her own weight would pull the rope through the descender. Until then she had to do it the hard way.

Suddenly her feet dangled over nothing at all. She kept going by using her arms to push herself. At the mouth of the tunnel, she tried to pull her legs back under her body, crouch, and walk slowly backward over the lip in the normal manner of a climber beginning a rappel.

There wasn't enough room.

"Well, hell," she muttered.

There was no help for it. She would have to take a few scrapes as the price of admission to her castle.

Whispering words as dark as the unlit cave, she bumped over the edge of the overhang like a lumpy snake until she dangled from the climbing rope. Gabe had cut the safety rope short enough that there was little chance of a tangle unless she was out of control and spinning like an badly thrown yo-yo.

She wasn't out of control. She let herself down by inches until she was beneath the overhang and tapping gently against the cave wall. By then just enough slack remained in the safety rope for her to release the carabiner's locking mechanism.

"Nicely calculated on the safety rope," she said. "Thank you."

"Anytime."

Joy positioned herself against the wall, feet spread as wide as her shoulders, climbing rope wrapped snugly in position for rappel. A sweep of her headlamp downward showed only a clean wall.

"Up safety rope," she called.

"Rope coming up," Gabe answered.

The rope went very slowly up the overhang until he was sure that the attached carabiner was well beyond Joy's face. Then he pulled swiftly.

"Rappelling." As she spoke, she kicked outward and released the tension on the rope with her right hand.

If Gabe had been belaying her, he would have answered in the normal manner. But he wasn't, so he didn't.

"Give 'em hell, sweetheart!"

After his husky encouragement there was an instant of silence, then Joy's pleased laughter floated up. The sound was surprising, exultant, vital, like the woman kicking out over unknown territory, confident of her own skills and those of the man who had anchored her climbing rope to stone.

She rappelled smoothly, controlling her descent with small pressures of her right hand. At the end of each outward and downward swing she met the wall feetfirst, absorbed the small jolt on flexed knees, and then kicked out again, feeding rope as her controlled fall continued.

When she checked for obstacles coming up to meet her, the headlight played over a fantastic subterranean landscape far below. Nothing was in her way. It was a clean fall right to the floor.

Soon she stood on the edge of what had once been a pool below a thundering waterfall. Now the basin was quiet, swirled with ancient watermarks, and held a pool that had been there for unknowable years. Golden shelfstone grew out over the pool, slowly engulfing it. The water that glistened in her reflected helmet light looked no deeper than her hand.

She knew better. Long experience in judging the depth of Lost River Cave's incredibly clear waters told her that this pool was at least eight feet deep, perhaps more. The giveaway was the water's luminous shade of green in some of the deepest curves and hollows of the pool. There was no color like it—except for Gabe's eyes when he became a part of her, wanting her with an intensity that made her shiver to remember.

Beautiful. Exhilarating. Wild.

Laughing softly she tilted her head back, wanting to lift her arms and embrace the cave itself.

The overhang where Gabe waited was lost in a night that her light alone couldn't penetrate. Yet she knew he was up there, waiting for her signal. And she was down here, laughing like a giddy girl amid the murmurous sounds of water dripping, falling, sliding, water infusing and creating Joy's Castle even as she stood there.

Working quickly she pulled rope through her figure eight descender. At first the rope was taut, eager, bouncing back from being stretched by her weight. When the rope went slack she unsnapped herself and stepped clear.

"Off rappel," she called up to the darkness.

"Yo!"

She glanced around quickly, looking for a place where she could safely wait while Gabe rappelled down. The shelfstone around the pool looked fragile but wasn't. Even so, she was careful as she picked her way along the edge of water that was haunted by tints and tones and shades of green.

When she was well away from the area where Gabe would descend, she turned and called, "Clear!"

Almost instantly he warned that he was rappelling down.

Joy stood transfixed, head tilted back, absorbing the sight of Gabe descending to her in a series of powerful, utterly controlled arcs. If he had any fear of being on a rope after the accident in Peru, he'd conquered it.

She respected and admired that. The nerve to climb **before** you had an accident was taken for granted. The plain courage it took to trust your life to a rope **after** a climbing accident was never taken for granted. As Fish had laconically pointed out, hard lessons stayed learned the longest. To take that kind of brutal lesson and use it to find out about life and yourself required not only physical courage, but courage of the mind and spirit as well.

Instinctively Gabe had known that. He'd responded to the challenge with determination: **As soon as I physically could, I went back. That mountain took a lot from me. I didn't want it to take my self-respect too.**

Standing there in a vast darkness illuminated only by a single cone of light, she understood that he had taken his accident and used its terrifying lessons to expand rather than shrink the possibilities of his own life. Watching the smooth arcs of his descent, she wondered if she'd used the brutal lessons of her own past as well as he had, if those lessons had expanded or reduced the boundaries of her life.

But most of all she wondered if she would have had the sheer guts to dangle on a rope again as he was doing, knowing full well that any moment her life could peel away again strand by strand.

A grave two thousand feet deep.

That kind of courage was humbling.

Gabe had learned to trust a rope again. Except for Kati, Joy hadn't learned to trust people and life enough to love again. She was still frozen within the moment of terror when her emotional world had given way beneath her feet and she fell endlessly, screaming deep inside herself because there was no one else to hear her.

She hadn't learned anything subtle or profound from the harsh lessons of seven years ago. She had survived. Period. It had been enough, all and more than anyone could have expected of her.

But now, for the first time, she questioned if mere survival was enough, if a mother's love for her child was all that she expected for and **from** herself for the rest of her life.

In a seething silence Joy watched Gabriel flying down toward her like his namesake archangel, power wrapped in darkness and light. He came to her where she stood surrounded by mystery, wrapped in a thousand nameless Voices whispering questions that had no answers but the taste of a man's tears on her lips.

TWENTY-NINE

"Off rappel," Gabe called. then, more softly, "Joy? Are you all right? You didn't slip?"

"I'm fine," she said, her voice husky. "The shelfstone seems solid, but watch the pool. It's deep enough to drown in."

"That little handful of water?"

"I'm little," she said as she watched him find his way quickly over stone to her.

"Yes." He bent and kissed her. "And you're deep enough to drown in, too. But what a sweet drowning."

She hugged him suddenly, fiercely. "Have I told you that I'm glad you're here?"

He closed his eyes, letting her words sink into him, unable even to respond except to hold her close.

Maggie's voice came from the darkness above. "On rappel."

"Clear," Gabe called.

His voice was almost rough as it rose above the

compelling murmur of water flowing, water dissolving away the old, creating the new, changing everything. He searched Joy's eyes, seeing and accepting the clarity and the shadows.

She was a woman now, a fascinating mixture of light and darkness. Unique.

He wanted her even more for her shadowed depths than he had for her innocent clarity. She could share so much more of life now, understand so much more, hold so much more.

Deep enough to drown in.

He wondered if she knew that he was drowning. Then he wondered if she would even care, if she could see that he too was deeper than he'd been, able to hold more, understand more.

Want more.

Maggie hit the floor with a thump, staggered slightly, and began feeding rope through her descender until there was slack. She unclipped, called up to Fish and came over to where Joy and Gabe waited.

"What a gorgeous green," she said, looking into the depths of the pool. "Just like Gabe's eyes."

He almost laughed out loud. The comment was like everything else about Maggie—matter-of-fact rather than flirtatious. He rapped his knuckles lightly against her helmet.

"Keep it up," he said, "and I'll have to buy a

new helmet when my head gets too big for the old."

"You should anyway," she said. "I get chills just looking at the dents. Was Davy right? Did you really wear that through a landslide and over a cliff?"

"Yeah. One of life's little surprises."

Maggie grimaced. "I don't know how you can be so casual about it."

"I survived. That's all anyone can ask."

"Is it?" Joy asked suddenly, looking up at him. "Is that all you ask of yourself and life?"

His green eyes searched her face. "No. I'm asking a hell of a lot more now. I don't deserve it, but I'm asking for it just the same."

She wanted to ask what he meant, but didn't because they weren't alone. So she simply returned his unflinching glance and the pressure of his hand holding hers.

Fish's light seesawed gracefully through the darkness as he rappelled down the wall. Then Davy lowered all the equipment they would need. Finally he rappelled down himself. They divided up the equipment and split into two groups.

Gabe and Joy took the west wall. Maggie, Fish, and Davy took the east. Normally they would have stayed in a single group to explore virgin territory, but there was nothing normal about this trip. They had to explore as much as possible of the room, as quickly as possible.

"Remember," Joy said, "this is a fast reconnoiter only. Davy, don't be a perfectionist with your map. Don't even be good. Just mark down the rough positions of possible passages, pits, and chimneys. Don't explore them. We'll do the same. Stay in sight of us when you can, and be damn sure you're within yelling or radio distance at all times. Questions?"

There weren't any.

Joy twisted a light stick, left it a few feet from the climbing rope, and the two groups took off in opposite directions. Using Gabe's compass, he and Joy stayed as close as they could to the right-hand perimeter of the Castle.

It was hard to move quickly, both because of the uneven surface and the constant siren call of velvet shadows, exquisitely decorated grottoes, colorful columns and draperies, pools shimmering like silent laughter; and through it all, the glisten and shine of water sighing, sliding, falling, dripping, the liquid sheen of a living cave.

She had expected the sound of the hidden waterfall to get louder as they went farther into the room. Instead the muttering thunder faded.

"We're losing the waterfall," he said as he wrote compass directions in his notebook.

"I know."

"Want to go back and try another direction?"

"No point. This room is like the Voices—it whispers about Lost River, but the river isn't here."

"You sound more wistful than disappointed."

Joy laughed and swept her headlight in a slow arc across the vast, unexplored room. "How could I be disappointed with this?"

Everywhere they went, there were signs of water. Sounds both mysterious and musical filled the air, as if somewhere just beyond the range of light the cave dreamed, and in dreaming, sang.

Gabe turned his head slowly from side to side, trying to pinpoint the rushing, singing sounds.

"Waterfall?" he asked.

"Maybe a small one. Not the source of the Voices. They come from a good-sized waterfall that's either way off or nearby but muffled by stone."

"Lord, but it's beautiful."

Water gleamed in runnels among tiny stone channels, pooled transparently in hollows, and glittered as rivulets met and braided into swift, miniature streams. Sometimes the tiny streams ran musically among golden stalagmites and columns. Sometimes the braids came unraveled and vanished through cracks in the floor, sinking down and down in a network of channels far too small for human exploration.

Yet still there was water everywhere, water gleaming from stone surfaces, water shining from the hems of draperies both stately and elegant. Formations grew out from the wall in a series of graceful curves that resembled the palettes used by artists. From the edges of the palettes hung fine, banded draperies, shapes so elegant and fluid it seemed impossible they were made of stone. When brushed by light, small pools winked back from darkness. Each time a drop of water fell, a pool shivered as if alive.

And through it all came the murmur of water, the lifeblood of Lost River Cave flowing through hidden arteries and veins, rushing through darkness, singing over stone.

Joy's fingers closed over Gabe's wrist. "Look."

The white cone of her light showed what looked like round bird eggs lying within a stone nest as big as a dinner plate.

The sound of surprise and wonder he made joined the other murmurings of the Castle. He crouched down as she did, careful not to disturb anything. Patiently he waited while she took readings on nearby landmarks, fixing the position of the rare formation as best she could on her rough map.

"What are they?" he asked as soon as she paused in her note making.

"Oolites."

"That's a textbook word. What do you call them?"

"Cave pearls."

He laughed. "Scratch a caver and find a romantic every time."

She looked up at him, smiled, and said, "Now I suppose you want me to tell you all the theories about how they're formed."

"Romantics?" he asked innocently.

"Oolites."

"Do I have a choice?"

"Nope," she said cheerfully. "None of the theories satisfy me, so I'm not going to tell you a single one of them."

"How do **you** explain cave pearls, then?"

"They're fantastic, utterly miraculous seeds," she said, her voice serious and her lips tilted in a smile. "Like the ones that Jack of Beanstalk fame grew. Only my magic seeds grow **down**, not up. They're tomorrow's caves in embryo, waiting to be born. Someday the shells will split and new caves will develop out of the old, branching and spreading, alive with water, beauty growing through darkness, waiting only for the first touch of light to be revealed."

She leaned closer and whispered against Gabe's mouth, "But if you tell my colleagues what cave pearls really are, I'll be out of a job."

He kissed her swiftly. "My lips are sealed."

"I noticed," she retorted.

He kissed her again. Slowly. Thoroughly. Deeply. Then he lifted his mouth just enough to ask, "Was that better?"

"Much." She caught his lower lip delicately in her teeth, then reluctantly released him. "But not enough."

"I know what you mean." He stood and pulled her to her feet. "If we don't get moving, I'm going to do the kind of exploring that doesn't require ropes, safety lines, and layers of clothing. Especially the clothes."

His face was taut, dark with desire. Just looking at him made Joy ache. She forced herself to turn her thoughts back to exploring the cave rather than the man.

It wasn't easy. She knew the time she had for both man and cave was very short.

And she knew it wouldn't be enough. Not nearly enough. A lifetime wouldn't be enough to discover all of Lost River—or Gabe.

She'd been given only a few weeks.

Greedy little girl. You want it all, don't you?

She didn't have to wait for an answer. She already knew it. She wanted Gabe with an intensity that she hadn't ever expected to feel for any man again. The realization frightened her, making her heart race and her mouth dry and her palms damp. She wondered if he'd felt like this when he went back to the mountain that had nearly killed him.

Terrified.

She turned to ask him, and as she turned her light swept along the wall of the room.

The wall returned her light in glorious bursts and ripples. The surface was alive with water, a fantasy of banded flowstone veiled in liquid silver and gold. Water seeped from cracks and tiny channels high in the limestone wall. Water fell in fluid braids and golden veils, clothing the stone in grace.

The massive flowstone formation suggested a seated woman with her skirts swirling around her and her head thrown back to a limitless sky. Her long, unbound hair was transparent silver strands of water, and her dreams were the thousand pure voices of water singing. At her feet lay curve after curve of multilevel rimstone pools, a fantastic lotus of silver and gold and jade unfolding, revealing the woman seated amid a beauty that could be equaled only by the singing of her dreams.

Water slipped from pool to pool, each movement a separate voice, a separate song, a separate dream dancing through darkness and sudden light.

Slowly Joy realized that another light was moving with hers over the face of the Dreamer, doubling the area of illumination. Gabe's arms were around her, holding her, sharing the moment of discovery; and his name was one of the Dreamer's songs.

When she heard him say her name, she turned to him, answering him.

Wrapped again in velvet darkness, the Dreamer whispered around them, adding two more names of love to its endless song.

THIRTY

Gabe held the radiophone in his hand like a poisonous snake. He didn't want to take one of the nightly—and, since ten days ago, twice nightly—calls from Gerald Towne. Lost River Cave would close in seven days; his editor didn't understand why Gabe hadn't finished up what should have been a simple assignment weeks ago.

"Like I told you when you called an hour ago," Gabe began.

"You'll be telling me again in another hour if you don't goddamn listen to me!"

"The government frowns on swearing over the air."

"The government can get hosed. The Chinese have offered this magazine—and you—the chance of a lifetime, but instead of leaping at it you're being cute and crawling around on your hands and knees in the dark like some crap-for-brains shitkicker that can't understand what the Tibet assignment means. What the hell is wrong with you!"

It wasn't a question, which was good. Gabe didn't think his editor would like the answer.

Joy doesn't love me.

I'm a selfish bastard, but not selfish enough to ask Joy to share her life with a man she doesn't love, but might marry so that her daughter can call someone Daddy.

Maybe that will change in the next week. Maybe in the next seven days Joy will realize she wants more from me than sex.

God knows I want more than sex from her.

"I'm sorry," Gabe said evenly, "but I can't leave yet. There's too much left to be done. Only seven more days before—"

"Chrissake, man, the goddamn cave's been there forever. Hell, the magazine has enough pull to get it opened again for whatever odds and ends need wrapping up for your article. All I ask is that—"

"It's turning into a book," Gabe cut in. "You'll get first North American serial rights. And I appreciate the offer about getting the cave opened again. I'll take you up on it if—"

Gabe never got to finish. Gerald Towne was yelling the kind of words into the phone that would mean big fines if the feds ever caught up with him.

From the living room, over the sound of his editor's outburst, Gabe could clearly hear Kati. He could see her and Joy in the living room, where Joy had dragged her makeshift desk after the interruptions from Gabe's editor had proved too distracting.

"Mommy, is Gabe on the phone again?"

Without looking up from the piled paperwork, Joy made an absent sound. She knew her daughter could see very well that Gabe was in the kitchen talking on the radiophone.

"Mommy," Kati said sharply.

Joy forced herself to confront her daughter. "Yes. Gabe is on the phone. If you turn your head three inches to the right you can see him for yourself."

"Why does that man keep bothering Gabe?"

"Why do you think?" Joy's voice was brisk. She and Kati had covered this particular ground many times in the past week.

Kati's mouth flattened. "He's going away."

It was an accusation.

In spite of Joy's determination not to show any emotion, her mouth turned down unhappily. "We're all going away from Cottonwood Wells, remember?"

Hope leaped in Kati's transparent gray eyes. "Together?"

Pain twisted through Joy. She looked down at the papers stacked in front of her, forms and more forms, epitaph for a dead government grant.

"Just you and me, button."

"Can't they all come with us? Why can't they? Why not?"

Joy fought not to show her impatience and pain at Kati's insistence that everyone could just find another cave to explore and go on living together forever.

"Why do you think, Kati?" Joy asked evenly.

The little girl's mouth thinned into a stubborn line that was very like Gabe's. She knew the answer and she didn't like it. Her chin jutted out. "Don't want to leave."

"No one **wants** the cave to close," Joy said, her tone as neutral as she could make it. "But that doesn't change what will happen next week. The cave will close. Maggie and Fish and Davy all have work to do in New Mexico. Our work here is done. That's why you and I have to find another place to live."

"Don't want to."

"I know."

"What about Gabe?" Kati persisted. "He likes me. Can't he stay with us? He'd be a **won**-der-ful daddy."

Joy winced and ran her hand through her hair. She didn't want to think of Gabe leaving, of the pain his leaving would cause.

And the worst of it was the certainty that she wasn't pregnant. Her period had just ended.

Soon the cave would close. She and Gabe would go in different directions. She didn't fool herself that now she would find other men sexually appealing. If anything, it was the opposite. When Gabe left, he would take with him any hope of a sibling to ease Kati's lonely-only life. All that remained would be memories. Memories and dreams.

A lifetime of them defining the lonely present.

"Isn't that a good idea, Mommy? Having Gabe for my daddy?" Kati leaned forward now, her young voice challenging, rising into anger.

Joy knew her daughter was spoiling for a fight. Right now, Joy was trying to avoid one because her own temper was uncertain. Like her emotions. Raw.

"Mommy's busy right now, button. Laura and Susan are in Maggie's cabin. Weren't you going to help them fix cookies for the barbecue tonight?"

"Don't want to."

Joy didn't respond. Kati's voice and eyes said more than her words. Her daughter didn't want to do anything now except fight, blow up, release the pressures that came from the growing, unwanted certainty that the cave would close and they would move and nothing would ever be the same again.

"Don't want to!"

"That's enough," Joy said in a clipped voice. "Gabe can't hear the man on the phone if you're shouting."

"Don't care!" Kati retorted, her voice rising higher. Her face was flushed and her eyes were narrowed. **"He's leaving and I don't care!"**

Gabe hung up the radiophone, cutting his editor off. He crossed the kitchen quickly, silently, not stopping until he saw Joy's face. The anger and the underlying pain in Kati's voice were reflected in her mother's expression. The pale exhaustion of Joy's features told him more than he wanted to know.

He'd said little to her about his editor's frequent and increasingly irate calls. Gerald Towne wanted to know more than the arrival date of a cave article. He wanted to know why Gabe hadn't left Cottonwood Wells ten days ago, when the Chinese had come through with their incredible, totally unexpected offer of allowing him unfettered access to Tibet and its people.

The Chinese could change their minds in the next hour! Don't be a fucking idiot! Grab that story or you're finished!

"I think it's time for you to pack your clean clothes," Joy said. "Susan will want to leave right after dinner, and—"

"Don't want to! Don't—"

"Kati," he interrupted firmly, "your mother has work to do. I'll help you pack."

The little girl gave him a look that was pure mutiny.

"Hey, button," he said in a gentle voice, "even if you bug your mom so that she can't get any work done, Lost River Cave will still close right on time. There's nothing you can do about it except help make it easier for your mom—and for yourself—by being as cheerful as you can."

It was the truth, and that only made it harder to take.

Kati had finally found the excuse she was looking for. **"I hate you! I'm glad you're leaving! I'm glad you aren't my daddy!"**

She turned and bolted to her bedroom before either adult could stop her. The door slammed behind her. Hard.

Joy came to her feet and started for Kati's room.

Gabe intercepted her. Despite his grim expression, his voice was quiet. "I don't want her punished for being honest."

"That wasn't honesty," she said, her eyes dark with anger. "That was plain old-fashioned revenge."

"For what?"

"What do you think?" she asked angrily as her own temper slipped out of control. "Because Kati loves you and you're leaving, and she wants you to be her daddy very much." She took a harsh breath and leashed her temper. "I'm sorry. I didn't mean that the way it sounded."

"How do you think it sounded?"

"Like a cage door shutting." She turned away and sat down at the table again. "I'll give her ten minutes to get a handle on her redheaded temper, and then I'm going in after her."

By then I might even have a better handle on my own temper, Joy added to herself sardonically.

"She's hurting," Gabe said.

"That's no excuse for lashing out at you like that. You've been more of a father to her in the last five weeks than some kids get in years of living with a full-time dad."

Gabe just shook his head.

Joy threw down her pen. "You've played War and Go Fish with her, talked with her about mountain peaks and coral reefs and jungle butterflies, and walked with her while she showed you lizards and coyote tracks and cactus. You've washed her clothes, fed her peanut butter sandwiches, and tucked her into bed at night with a story and a hug."

"It's not enough. Not nearly enough."

Joy blew out a fierce breath. "It's never enough with children. Welcome to the wonderful world of parenting."

He sat heavily on the couch and closed his eyes.

She looked at the lines on his face and remembered all the smiles and laughter he'd shared with Kati. **He's given her so many beautiful** memories—and what does she do? She throws it in his face.

Because she wanted it all.

Like me.

Greedy little girl.

When Gabe opened his eyes again, Joy was hard at work on the endless, frustrating government forms. Each hour, each minute, each second that she spent on paperwork meant less time between now and the moment Lost River Cave would close. He knew how much that must be gnawing at her. He'd shared the magic of exploration with her, the overwhelming instants of beauty and discovery.

Yet instead of being out exploring right now, she was stuck inside filling out forms in quintuplicate, hearing seconds tick away in her head. No wonder she was ready to scream.

Like Kati.

Like him.

He wanted to go to Joy, to ease the knots in her shoulder muscles that came from tension, to feel her warmth flowing up through his hands and to hear her groan of thanks when she relaxed beneath his touch. He wanted to help her, to take some of the load that she was carrying, to share all of it, the good and the bad and everything in between.

And all he could hear was the clock ticking,

telling him that he'd lost more than time. He'd lost a woman's love.

The only time he heard Joy say **I love you** was in his memories and dreams. The words that she'd given to him so freely seven years ago didn't exist on her lips now.

Without those words he couldn't believe she'd forgiven him.

It was too soon for you to love seven years ago—and now it's too late for me.

Yet he hungered for her love. He needed it as deeply as he needed her. He ached to know that she wanted more than the physical ecstasy he could give her.

Most of all he needed time to win her again.

There wasn't enough time.

He was looking at seven years ago all over again, but this time he knew **all** that was at stake. Like the Orinoco River expedition, the Chinese offer was literally a once-in-a-lifetime thing. Not only had he never been to Tibet, but he'd be the first Westerner in two generations to have the freedom of the land. All of it. No boundaries, no political hassle, nothing but a glittering undiscovered landscape stretching across the top of the world.

Turning down the Tibet offer would be the end of his relationship with the magazine and the editor who had been the backbone of his career.

And for what?

For a woman who doesn't love me.

That was the new twist in an old tangle. He loved.

She didn't.

There were other differences. She wasn't pregnant. She wasn't twenty. She wasn't interested in a life with him. He was free to go to Tibet right now. The Lost River Cave story had been wrapped up weeks ago, in the bag, everything ready to go.

Except me. I've been stalling. I'm still stalling.

Like Kati, I want it all.

Like Kati, I'm afraid I've already lost it.

Through his circling thoughts he heard the bedroom door opening and light footsteps coming across the bare wood floor. He expected the footsteps to stop at Joy's chair while Kati apologized for her tantrum and reassured herself that her mother still loved her even when she wasn't acting lovable.

The footsteps didn't stop. They came straight across the room to where he sat with his head resting against the back of the sagging couch and his eyes closed.

He opened them.

Kati was watching him, her little face wan.

He held out his arms and she ran into them,

clinging to him as he lifted her into his lap. Suddenly she was sobbing against his chest like she had a lifetime of tears and only a few seconds to cry.

With a gentle hand Gabe stroked his daughter's fiery hair and shaking body. Between her broken apologies he gave her reassuring words. He was still her friend. Friends didn't stop being friends just because they got angry sometimes.

After a while the emotional storm passed, leaving Kati spent and silent but for an occasional ragged breath. When even that stopped, she lay quietly against him, watching his face.

"Okay now, button?" he asked softly.

"Okay."

Without warning she wrapped her arms around his neck, kissed his cheek hard, and said, "I love you better than anyone but Mommy."

Before he could respond, Kati was off his lap and dancing away across the living room. The front screen door slammed behind her.

"Susan!" Kati called across the yard, her voice bubbling with life again. "Is it time to make cookies yet?"

Gabe looked up and saw tears glittering in Joy's eyes.

Instantly she looked back down at the paperwork, concealing her face from him.

He wanted to go to her, to comfort her and

himself, to hold her and be held while reassurances flowed like tears between them. He wanted to wipe out the past, to make time a closed loop surrounding him, Joy in his arms and he in hers. No Orinoco seven years ago. No time running out tomorrow.

Nothing but the two of them.

And love.

But time doesn't go backward or in circles, Gabe told himself painfully. **One way only. Straight ahead. I'm stuck going with it no matter what.**

Don't want to! said part of his mind, echoing Kati's angry yell.

Then stay.

With a woman who doesn't love me and no job at all?

How do you know she doesn't love you?

I betrayed her. How could she love a man who betrayed her?

She forgave you.

Did she? Did she really? Then why doesn't she talk to me about the future? About love. Because she doesn't love me and there's no future, that's why.

Fool. Why do you think she's sleeping with you?

Passion. With her I'm one hell of a lover.

And without her you're one hell of a fool.

In silence and darkness his internal argument raged without pause, like the undiscovered Lost River itself, pounding and grinding against existing channels and tunnels and troughs, trying to find new solutions to old questions of how to get there from here.

He had until tomorrow morning to find one. Then Towne would demand an answer.

Don't want to! wouldn't get it done.

THIRTY-ONE

Gabe refused to spoil the barbecue that Kati had looked forward to like it was Christmas come early. He put away his bleak thoughts and sat outside with his daughter on his lap and the woman he loved curled against his shoulder while they sang all the old camp songs. With every note, he tried not to think that this might be his last chance to look up with Kati at the Glitter River and try to count the timeless, cascading possibilities of life.

When the last phrase of the last song faded into the deep silence of desert night, he carried his sleeping daughter to Susan's car. The old station wagon had been made up as a bed. Gently he put Kati in the back next to her sleepy chum, kissed Kati's soft hair, fastened both seatbelts, and tucked a blanket around the girls.

When he looked up he saw Fish watching him with speculation in his shrewd eyes.

Gabe turned away and went to Joy's darkened

cottage to wait for her. Through the window he saw Susan's car drive out into the desert, leaving the cottages behind. Beneath the full moon Joy crossed the dusty yard toward the cottage. Her hair shifted and shimmered with subdued light, making her look unreal, ethereal, as impossible as the Dreamer singing among transparent pools.

The sight of Joy coming to him through the moon-silvered darkness made him ache with emotions he couldn't name, except one. Passion. He'd always felt that with Joy.

As the screen door snapped shut behind her, he pulled her into his arms. His voice was husky when he spoke, and his caresses had a lifetime of hunger burning in them. Tonight he wanted to seduce more from her than physical hunger. He wanted the words that he heard in his dreams and memories.

I love you, Gabe.

Then he could ask to share her life. Then he would know that she wanted **him** as well as a father for her daughter.

He bent and kissed Joy hotly, sweetly.

"I miss Kati when she's gone," he said, "but I sure as hell don't miss sleeping alone."

Joy smiled and pulled him closer.

"I love falling asleep with you curled in my arms," he said, "and waking up to feel your breath on my skin. I love looking at you, talking to you, exploring with you. Ah, God," he said huskily, lowering his mouth to her neck, "how I love exploring **you**. You're different each time. Like the Voices and the Dreamer singing in my blood, in my soul."

She felt the passion beating in Gabe's veins, an urgency that made his hands tremble when he began to undress her. She sensed there was something more than simple desire driving him. This was deeper, wilder.

Then she understood that he was feeling time rushing toward them, the future coming down on them like eternity, bringing the end of passion and the beginning of haunted dreams. It was all she could do not to cry out her protest aloud. She'd believed she was giving Gabe no more than her body and her professional knowledge.

Now she wasn't sure.

Don't be stupid, she told herself savagely. **Sex and a caving partner is all I can afford. It's all I'll get. It's all I** want.

She couldn't go through what she had seven years ago. She simply wouldn't. Memories of Gabe were all she could afford emotionally. Not love.

So she would see that the memories were as perfect as the Dreamer veiled in water, singing within stone.

With a sigh that was Gabriel's name, Joy

threaded her fingers into his thick, soft hair and held his mouth against the pulse racing at the base of her throat. His lips moved down, retracing the path of his fingers as he brushed aside her clothes, baring her to the silver moonlight.

The tip of her breast was another shade of velvet darkness crowning soft, luminous flesh. When his tongue touched her, she tightened into a shining peak that tempted his tongue again and again.

"You're so beautiful," he whispered, and his breath caressed the taut, hungry nipples he'd called from her softness.

She watched the dark planes of his face and the glistening tip of his tongue caressing her. "No, you're the beautiful one."

Smiling, he shook his head, and with every movement his lips sipped at her breasts.

Her finger traced his dark eyebrows, his lean cheeks, his sensual lips, and finally the hot and teasing tongue that was making her shiver with anticipation.

"You touch me so perfectly," she said.

"Do I?" His teeth closed with exquisite care over one nipple.

Heat uncurled low in her body, a pulsing rush of longing that was echoed in her low moan. **"Yes."**

She gasped as his hand slipped inside her unfastened jeans to discover her hot, layered softness.

"I want you inside me," she said urgently. "Don't tease me anymore. I want—"

Her words scattered in a burst of sensation as he caressed her intimately, deeply, melting even her bones. Dizzy, her breath ragged, she clung to him and moved her hips against him, telling him without words how much she wanted him to be a part of her.

She'd done the same thing seven years ago.

He'd responded in the same way then as he did now, a groan of discovery and need.

Her hips moved intimately, knowingly, promising both a welcome and a release for the hunger stretching rigidly beneath his jeans. Her hand slid inside the fly, found the hard rise of his need, traced it, and rubbed over it with a hot, searching intent that equaled his exploration of her softness.

He saw the passion tightening her face, making her eyes a midnight darkness, flushing her lips and her breasts with heat. With a rough sound of need he took her mouth, holding her straining hips against him with one hand and with the other caressing her until her response pulsed over him, a hot promise of the deeper union to come.

With a shudder, he forced himself to step back from Joy.

"Gabe?"

"If I touch you now, I'll take you now," he said

hoarsely. "It's always been like that. You fill me to overflowing and yet I can't get enough of you."

She swayed toward him and whispered against his lips, "It's like that for me. Never enough. Take me. Let me take you. Fill me to overflowing and then hold me, hold me hard. Give me enough memories for a lifetime."

A chill went through him. **She doesn't want me in any lasting way. She just wants sex and memories.**

Yet he was helpless to do anything except give them to her in the hope that this time, **this time,** she would recognize his love.

And return it.

"Yes," he said thickly.

His arms closed around Joy, lifting her. He carried her to her single bed and lowered her into the shaft of silver light that gleamed on the cover. With slow, caressing motions they undressed each other. When they both wore only moonlight, when she lay open and hungry for him, he simply looked at her.

She started to speak but the sight of his tight, almost tormented expression froze the words in her throat. He'd looked at her like that seven years ago, just before they made love for the first time.

Is this the last time? Is that why he looks like a man being torn apart?

"Gabriel, what—"

She abandoned words as he took the invitation of her body and pressed deep inside her. The sensation of fullness was so exquisite that she shivered and made tiny sounds at the back of her throat.

It was the same for him, tightly sheathed in her sleek body, able only to make a deep sound of pleasure. He wanted to burst with the hot perfection of their joining, but he knew that even more levels of ecstasy waited to be explored.

He moved slowly, powerfully, and she was with him, moving as he did. He saw the first level of pleasure break over her, felt the ripples hot and sweet around him, and arched hard against her, increasing the intensity of her climax even as he withheld his own.

When Joy no longer cried out and clung to him fiercely, Gabe moved again, deeply, calling to her with words as well as the potent sensual pressure of his body deep in hers. Her eyes were half opened, dazed with the aftershocks of ecstasy still coursing through her. At each sliding caress of his potent flesh, desire shot hotly through her, tightening her around him.

He took her mouth as completely as he had taken the rest of her sultry softness. He incited her with teeth and tongue, movements and words that made her arch wildly against him.

Then her hand slid down the gleaming muscles of his back and buttocks, seeking the tight male flesh, caressing him until he could go no higher.

"No," he said hoarsely, biting her lips, burying himself deeply in her straining softness. "Don't let me leave you behind. Come with me, sweetheart. **Come with me.**"

The words and caresses burst within her even as he did—and she was with him, ecstasy racing wildly through their joined bodies until nothing existed, neither memories nor dreams nor even time itself. Moonlight lay softly over them, making their joined bodies shimmer like the Dreamer bathed in silver water.

Gabe kissed Joy's forehead and cheeks, her lips and the curve of her throat, her sweet-smelling hair and the quivering lashes veiling her eyes. And he waited to hear the words she'd once given him.

He heard murmurs of pleasure and contentment.

"Joy, sweetheart, I—"

"You're leaving," she cut in swiftly, eyes still closed. "Yes. I know. I've always known."

"That's not—"

She opened her eyes and kept talking. "I'll make it right with Kati. You trust me to do that, don't you?"

He looked into her eyes; they were desperate

and wary at once. "I love Kati. She'll hear it from both of us."

"She already knows."

A corner of his mouth turned down in a sad smile. "Feminine intuition, huh?"

Joy made a choked sound that could have been agreement. "When are you leaving?"

"Sweetheart—"

"When."

"I'm supposed to leave tomorrow but I'm trying to stay until the cave closes."

His words poured over Joy like cold, black water, drowning out everything else.

"I'll come back to you as soon as I can. Give me a chance, Joy. I want to be part of your life, not just your memories."

Tomorrow.

She felt like she had seven years ago, when she'd pleaded with him to stay for just another day, an hour, a minute, **anything**. For a wild instant she thought that she was pleading still, that time had turned around on itself, making a full circle of anguish and regret, destroying her.

No. Not this time. This time he won't destroy me. This time I don't love him.

I can't.

Fear froze her, driving every bit of heat out of her body. She looked desperately for a place to hide, a place to pull darkness around her, a place where she would never again know the threat of light. It was the past repeating itself, time eating itself, eating her.

Seven years ago all over again. Only this time she wasn't pregnant, and she desperately wanted to be.

Tomorrow.

It wasn't quite the past after all.

It was worse.

Gently Gabe turned Joy's face toward him. "Did you hear me, sweetheart?"

His words ended in a hoarse sound as he saw her face. There was nothing of joy there, no light, no laughter, no hope.

"I won't be gone long," he said quickly. "It won't be the Orinoco all over again. I swear it."

She heard nothing beyond the fact of his leaving and her own echoing emptiness. She gave herself to tears as passionately as she had given herself to him and blurted, **"But I'm not pregnant."**

The words ran together, almost strangled by her sobs as anger and despair overwhelmed her.

For an instant Gabe was frozen, watching Joy shudder with her wild grief—and then elation shook him. **She was pregnant!** He pulled her fiercely against his body. **She didn't protect herself after all. She gave herself to me as completely this time as she did seven years ago.**

She must love me, even though she won't admit it.

"Sweetheart, that's wonderful." He buried his face in the curve of her neck. "It's all right, love," he said fiercely. "I'll stay with you, hold you, care for you. I love you so much. Our baby will be born into my hands, not some stranger's. I won't leave you alone again."

A few of Gabe's words penetrated Joy's sobs, enough so that she knew he'd misunderstood her words. She lifted her head and spoke as clearly as she could between broken breaths.

"I'm **not** pregnant and I want to be. I don't want Kati to be a lonely-only all her life and having your b-baby was the perfect solution, just the kind of relationship for you. No strings, total freedom to go wherever you want whenever the chance came. But it came too soon. You're leaving and I'm not pregnant."

The words went into his soul like a steel piton into stone, anchoring him forever to pain and betrayal. "That's why you slept with me? To get another baby? You didn't forgive me after all, did you—much less love me. **Christ, what a fool I've been**. I loved you. I would have given up everything to stay with you, and all you wanted was a ready source of sperm."

Joy couldn't hear anything except the sound of her own crying, but even through her tears she could see betrayal set its bleak stamp on Gabe's features.

He rolled out of bed with a swift, powerful

movement and began dressing in a silence that seethed with fury. Like his mind. Seething.

She used me like a goddamned stud.

Fully dressed, he turned at the bedroom door and raked her naked body with a stranger's glance. "If you've made a mistake and you're pregnant, give my brother a call. You two can talk about old times. Then you can talk with my lawyer about financial support and visitation rights for **both** my children."

Seconds later the front door slammed.

Gabe went to his cabin just long enough to throw his notes and a change of clothes into his suitcase. The rest could be forwarded to wherever he went next—Tibet or Timbuktu, it was all the same.

He dumped everything in the Explorer and scattered sand and gravel in a wild rooster tail as he accelerated out of Cottonwood Wells. The engine sounds rose in a series of screams while he slammed through the gears as though his life depended on outrunning the past, the present, the future.

Himself.

But he couldn't go fast enough. Wherever the road turned he was already there, waiting for himself.

Fool.

THIRTY-TWO

Long after the sound of Gabe's vehicle faded into deep silence, Joy lay motionless in the bed. She felt like she was sinking endlessly, helplessly through time, layers of loss and regret closing over her until she couldn't breathe.

She hadn't felt like this in years—used up, spent, unable even to cry. Yet at the same time her body seethed to be free, to move, to do something besides lie here waiting for the sound of a car coming back over the desert toward her, Gabe's beloved arms closing around her, his voice telling her that he would never leave her again.

But he would.

He had.

As she'd done years ago, she dragged herself out of bed and stood beneath the stinging needles of a cold shower. She dressed mechanically, pulling on layer after layer of caving gear, turning to the only comfort she knew, Lost River Cave's unearthly beauty.

Silently she closed the back door of the cottage behind her.

"Going caving?" Fish asked, his voice casual, his eyes penetrating.

Joy was too intent on her own needs even to be startled by Fish's unexpected appearance.

"Yes," she said.

It was a stranger's voice, remote and lifeless. She didn't care enough to change the tone. The stranger was also herself, a self she thought had died seven years ago.

"Was that Gabe tearing out of camp?" Fish asked.

"Yes."

With a swift movement he plucked the Jeep keys from her hand. His shrill whistle split the night.

"Yo, Davy! Shag your butt out here. We're going caving."

Davy appeared in the door of his cabin, his face flushed. Maggie was right behind him, looking breathless. "Dr. Joyce said we weren't—"

"Now," Fish snarled.

"Well, **shit**. Gimme a minute." The door slammed.

"No, it's not necessary for—" Joy began.

"I'll meet you right here in five minutes," Fish cut in. He hoisted her into the Jeep. "Now you just sit there before you fall on your face."

With that he headed for the cabin where he stored his caving gear. The Jeep keys left with him.

She sat and tried not to think. It was a trick she'd perfected seven years ago. Or thought she had. Gabe's angry, hurting face haunted her. Even with her eyes closed she still saw him.

Davy and Fish arrived at Jeep at the same time.

"All right, I'm here," Davy said. "Now what's the flaming . . ." His words died as he saw Joy's face. He looked at Fish.

Fish shook his head and jerked a thumb toward the backseat.

Davy wasn't entirely dense. He looked at Fish's grim face and Joy's pallor and decided that shutting his mouth was a really good idea right now.

In silence the three of them drove over the rough road to the parking place. Fish led the way to the entrance of Lost River Cave. Joy came second. Davy brought up the rear and wondered—silently—what the hell was going on.

"I'm belaying you tonight, Dr. Anderson," Fish said, settling into the anchor sling.

She didn't argue. She simply snapped herself to the rope and let herself down into the cave's seamless, welcoming embrace. She went quickly, automatically through the routine of rappelling. Or almost all of it. Once she got to the bottom, she set off into the cave without waiting for a partner to join her.

"Off rope."

Her words were so faint they almost didn't reach the top. Davy heard and reached for the slack rope.

"Nope," Fish said as he released himself from anchor position. "I'm going down. You're staying up here to belay Gabe."

"Huh? When is he getting here?"

"Maybe never," Fish said, "but it'd be a damn shame to lose him to an accident if he came back to her. Never met two more headstrong, stubborn, proud sons of bitches in my life."

"All right, what the hell is going on?" Davy asked as he settled in to belay Fish. "Why should I wait around for Gabe if you don't even know if he's coming in the first place? And why does Dr. Joyce look like death warmed over?"

"Gabe left her again."

"Again?"

"He's Kati's father."

With that Fish dropped swiftly into the cave. He knew Joy wouldn't be waiting around at the bottom for anyone. He would have to move fast to catch up with her.

Even though he hurried, Joy retreated in front of him in a ghostly aura of light, pausing only to be belayed down the steep slide leading to

Gotcha. Neither of them said a word as they went deeper and deeper into the cave.

The Voices condensed around them.

Joy managed to shut out the silky murmurings all the way through the Maze, hearing only her own heartbeat until she emerged from Small Favors and rappelled into the fantastic castle that bore her name. She walked quickly through the glistening formations, giving them barely a glance. She had room in herself for only one thing—the knowledge that Gabe was gone.

But it's all right. I'll be all right because this time I don't love him.

I can't love him.

Fish followed at a cautious distance. He watched her stand without moving in front of the stone she called the Dreamer. The very stillness of her body told him that she'd found whatever she was looking for within the cave's dark mystery. She wouldn't be going anywhere for a while.

Silently he retreated to the rope dangling from the mouth of Small Favors. Sitting on his heels, he waited for whatever came next.

A distant part of Joy's mind registered that Fish was gone. She was alone. Finally she could let go of the agonizing control she'd been holding over her body and her mind.

As she'd done seven years ago, she opened herself to the healing darkness.

The Voices rippled through the veils of her fear and anger and grief, speaking directly to her core, whispering words that shook her to her soul.

I love him.

I never stopped loving him.

I never will.

He's within me as deeply as water is within Lost River Cave, water dreaming through stone. Whether I'm here or not, whether I see it or not, the cave goes on living, changing, becoming more beautiful with every glistening drop, every instant of time.

Like love.

Growing whether I will it or not, spreading through me, destroying and creating me at the same sweet and terrifying time.

I love him.

Slowly Joy sank to the floor, her posture echoing the Dreamer as she let the thousand Voices sing through her. After a long time she removed her helmet and gloves and shut off her light, watching with more than her eyes, giving herself to the dreams that lived in every movement of water gliding over stone, creating beauty where once there had been only emptiness.

Somehow I'll find you again, Gabriel. If it takes another seven years, so be it. Our love will be within you the whole time, growing like the Dreamer within stone, singing to us with a

thousand voices. Even if you leave me again and again, our love will still be growing, singing in darkness, waiting to be discovered. Our love.

Because you love me, too, Gabriel.

Your love was written in the fury and despair on your face when you left me tonight. You felt betrayed, as I once did. To feel betrayed like that, my bittersweet lover, first you must give yourself to love.

And lose.

Eyes closed, her mind deep within the Dreamer, Joy heard nothing around her but the hushed music of creation. The sound of footsteps winding through the room toward her were consumed by the sweet rushing whispers of water.

The cone of light that swept over her was intangible, unnoticed, quickly extinguished.

After one glance Gabe turned off the light. He would never forget the sight of Joy seated in front of the Dreamer, her face washed in tears, glistening even as the Dreamer did.

Slowly he pulled off his helmet and sank down next to her in velvet darkness. With motions that were both gentle and determined, he removed his gloves and took her hands in his.

"I'm not going to be a fool twice," he said quietly.

His husky voice slid among the Dreamer's songs, sinking deeply into Joy. Invisible, she turned toward one voice, one song.

"Without you I might as well be in a cage, because wherever I am I'll be looking for you through the bars of my loneliness." He cradled her hand against his cheek, kissed her palm swiftly. "I'll give you that baby you want so bad, but first you'll have to marry me, live with me, let me care for you and Kati as I should have cared for you the first time."

Joy's hand stirred beneath Gabe's palm, warmed by his flesh. She laced her fingers through his slowly, completely.

He began to breathe again.

"What about Tibet?" she asked softly.

She felt the shrug of his shoulder against hers.

"There will be other articles," he said, "other books. There's only one Joy, one Kati."

"But—"

"Sometimes being an adult boils down to facing and making choices," he continued gently, relentlessly. "I didn't understand that seven years ago. I do now. I choose you, Joy. You and Kati. I'll take different assignments now, places where you and Kati can come with me if you want. I want you to come with me. I know you don't want to hear it," he added huskily, rubbing his lips blindly along her palm, "but I love you. It took me too long to discover that loving you was the answer to so many of my questions, but I know now. I love you even though you don't love me. I can't help loving you. It simply is."

Joy's throat closed as she felt the heat of his tears flowing between her fingers. She reached for him and held him with aching strength.

And once again he heard the words that had haunted his memories and dreams, the hidden answer to so many questions.

"I love you," she murmured, kissing him, not knowing whose tears were on her lips. "We'll go with you wherever you want, stay behind whenever we must. But—" She hesitated, then said in a rush, "Kati and I would love to see Tibet with you. She's as hungry for a piece of the Glitter River as her parents are. If not this time, then maybe the next, or the next. You're so good at what you do, Gabriel. I don't want you to give it up. Just come home to us, to love. We both love you so much."

"Do you mean that?" he asked, holding her like he was afraid she would run between his fingers into Lost River Cave's limestone floor and vanish forever. "Would you and Kati really travel with me?"

"Anywhere."

He buried his head in the curve of Joy's neck and felt possibilities pouring through him in a glittering rush.

"We can have it all, can't we?" he said, his voice

rough with emotion. "Love and children and the whole world to explore."

"We can try. But it won't be easy."

"Have we ever done things the easy way?" he asked ruefully.

"No." She laughed softly against his ear. "We never have."

Their laughter and words of love mingled with the sounds of Joy's Castle, becoming part of the Dreamer's thousand songs . . . love murmuring through stone, creating a world that would always be new, always changing, as unexpected and enduring as Lost River Cave itself.

THIRTY-THREE

In the thin, cold air, the ancient city was a sculpture of cream and white stone, rust and pearly gray, luminous with its own timeless dreams. The highlands around the holy city of Lhasa were a favorite campsite of the nomads who now were free to pursue their ancient and demanding way of life. Bright against the nomads' dark tents, prayer flags fluttered from posts and lines; and each individual movement was a separate prayer to Tibetan gods. Flags both faded and fresh hung from every shrub and stunted bush, proclaiming the devotion of the people.

The colorful, wind-tossed flags fascinated Kati, but she was careful not to touch them, remembering what her father had told her. **They're prayers, button. The world needs all the prayers it can get.**

Behind her came excited cries as her newfound friends chased each other in a mad game of tag between the tents. Tag was the first game she'd taught the kids. And she'd to work hard to keep up with them. Despite all the bulky clothes they wore to stay warm, the kids were quick. While they played, they taught her their words and she taught them hers and they got into whatever mischief they could when they weren't learning how to write or helping their parents with the herds.

The time she'd spent with the nomads was almost as much fun as having her own brothers and sisters. But now it was time to go to another place, another camp, another city for her daddy to write about. She was sad to leave new friends—and eager to race on to new experiences.

"Kati?"

She turned toward her father's voice. "Here!"

Hand in hand, Joy and Gabe came toward their daughter. Kati grinned to herself and then laughed aloud. She loved having a daddy. He was so much fun to tease, and Mommy wasn't nearly as tired as she'd been before Gabe came back to stay forever. She laughed more too. She was as much fun to tease as Daddy.

"Did you say goodbye to everyone?" Joy asked.

Kati nodded energetically, making her red hair fly. It was her hair that helped her make friends in every camp. The color was like a magnet to the people of Tibet.

"I gave them some of your peppermints and they gave me something I can't pronounce yet that tasted yucky, but I'll bet they thought your peppermints were yucky too."

Gabe laughed and lifted Kati into his arms. She wound her legs around his waist and burrowed in.

"We've got some great news, button."

"Sisters and brothers?" she asked instantly.

"Not quite," Joy said with a smile. "Remember, I told you it takes time to grow quality babies like you."

"Then what?"

"Your daddy's article on Lost River Cave drew enough attention that we're going to be able to reopen the cave for five more years. It will take time to get everything lined up, but—"

"Fish? Maggie? Gravy-bear? Them too?" Kati interrupted, bouncing up and down against Gabe in excitement.

"Fish and Maggie for sure," Joy said. "Davy has some maps to finish for his boss before he can come back. That will take him a year and we're opening the cave in six months, right after we leave Tibet."

"Davy won't be far behind Maggie," Gabe said, kissing Kati's forehead. "They're engaged, so I don't think he'll let her get away from him for long."

"Engaged? Does that mean they're making babies?"

Gabe and Joy tried very hard not to look at each other.

"Probably not for a while, button," Joy said, fighting a smile.

Carrying Kati, he turned and started toward the battered Land Rover that was their transportation—and their overnight quarters, if it came to that.

"Wait," Kati said. "I gotta do something first."

As soon as Gabe put her down, she was off and running toward a line of prayer flags that had been strung between two lean, angular poles. She stood on tiptoe and carefully tied her own prayer to an open space on the line.

When she let go, wind breathed life into the bright cloth, lifting it, sending her special prayer into the sky with every movement of air and cloth. Smiling, she watched the bright flag flutter for a few moments before she turned and ran back to her parents.

She was certain now that it wouldn't be long before she had sisters and brothers of her own.

And she was right.